DEAD MAN'S GAME

A DCI GARRICK THRILLER - BOOK 4

M.G. COLE

TANGLEBOX
BOOKS

DEAD MAN'S GAME

A DCI Garrick mystery - Book 4

Copyright © 2021 by Max Cole (M.G.Cole)

Cover art: Shutterstock

READ THE FREE PREQUEL...

SNOWBLIND

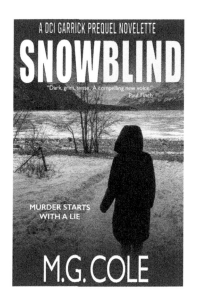

Start the puzzle here...
... and get inside DCI David Garrick's head.

DEAD MAN'S GAME

1

She thumped the keyboard in frustration. An irrational act, but one that gave a little sense of satisfaction knowing it was attached to the rest of the computer. And it seemed to do the trick as her email finally loaded up again. The system had been acting sluggish for days, no matter which workstation she sat at. In the small office everybody had to hot desk, taking whatever computer was available on the day, so the problem must be with her email program.

As her messages loaded, she glanced at her Apple Watch, which told her it was 17:26. A raft of emails came through. Eighty per cent spam, but amongst them some emails she had been anxiously waiting for. One stood out with the striking name of WHISTLE-BLOWER. She'd checked it out only to discover it was a free Yahoo email address that anybody could have created, but the information contained within was gold dust.

She double clicked it. With intolerable slowness, the message opened. Just a few short lines, but it was everything she had been hoping. Finally, they were meeting. It ended with an ominous, *be careful.*

For days, she had the growing sense that she was being followed and watched. The erratic computer compounded to her growing paranoia. She hurriedly logged off the system and crammed her phone and a few printed research papers into her Louis Vuitton bag. Her hands were shaking. She had little time to make the rendezvous; one that would change *everything.*

Calm down, she warned herself. Focus was the key to the evening. The day had ticked by with agonising slowness as she went through the motions of work.

She took off the glasses she wore for reading, but often kept on to lend a more sophisticated, intelligence edge to her persona, and rubbed her tired eyes. Holding the breath for a slow count of three, she slowly exhaled.

"You can do this," she said aloud to the empty office.

Another glance at her watch, and her mind began planning. It would take about fifty-minutes to get home, and then...

Taking the stairs to the ground floor, she gave quick goodbyes to everybody she passed, but didn't linger for a reply. Hurrying from the building and through the busy street, she didn't register the usual noise of the town, or the knots of chatting people heading home or out to eat. If she was being watched, then there was plenty of cover for them to hide. A group of noisy school kids was the only detail she processed as she reached the multistorey carpark. She passed the elevator, which she never took on principle, but this evening the stench of stale piss coming from it made her walk even faster to the staircase.

She bounded up two at a time. Her car was on the

fourth level, but she had only reached level two when she heard the door below squeak open as somebody stepped through.

Her heart hammered from a surge of anxiety. It was still daylight and at a busy time of day, in a popular town centre car park – she told herself that she had nothing to be nervous about.

The soft shuffle of footsteps below indicated somebody was trotting up the steps. It was foolish to think it was anybody who harboured any malicious intentions towards her...

And yet...

She rushed up the steps again, this time keeping her weight on her toes to minimise the noise. She felt foolish, as if acting like a child, but she was too much on edge to take any chances. Fishing the key fob from her coat pocket, she kept a steady pace, aided by her weekly jogging routine. It ensured that she wasn't out of breath by the time she reached the door leading to level four. She yanked it open, wincing as the squeals from the worn hinges amplified through the narrow concrete stairwell. If the person below wasn't aware of her, they certainly were now.

Was it her imagination, or did the footsteps suddenly pick up pace? It was difficult to ascertain, and now her mind was screaming at her to run. Just as it was when she'd arrived, the car park was full, yet there was nobody around. No sound of engines starting up, or people eagerly heading home. Even the noise of traffic outside didn't seem able to penetrate through the open spaces, allowing light to flood in. She ran towards her white Volkswagen Beetle, which she'd deliberately parked facing out the bay to facilitate a quick exit. Her plan was thwarted because the car next to her had parked so close there was no way she could open the driver's side door and get in.

"Bastard!"

The word tumbled around the car park. She darted around to the passenger side, just as she heard the whine of the door opening as somebody joined her on the fourth level. Thumbing the unlock button on the fob, she winced as the vehicle's indicator lights flashed and the doors clicked open. She didn't waste any time in climbing in. She clambered over the gear selector, banging her head against the mirror in her haste, and was in the driver's seat before realising that she hadn't locked the doors. A shaking finger stabbed the central locking button – but nothing happened.

A glance across revealed that, in her haste, she hadn't closed the passenger door.

Blood pounded in her ears, deafening her to the sound of anybody approaching. She lunged across the passenger seat. Her fingers felt thick and numb and failed to make contact with the door.

It was the chance her attacker needed.

But he didn't come.

Pushing herself inches closer, she hooked the door handle and slammed it shut. She slumped back into her seat and hit the central locking button again. This time there was a satisfyingly heavy thump as the doors locked.

Still shaking, she pressed the start button and the hybrid engine purred to life. Both hands gripped the wheel as she expected somebody to step out in front of her car.

Seconds passed... but nobody came.

Paranoia had laid its grubby hands on her imagination since she had first become aware of what was happening. It was sickening, cruel, and the world had to be told.

She slipped the car into drive and pulled out of the parking bay. Scanning the mirrors, she couldn't see her phantom pursuer. She let out her pent-up breath. The irony of *her* acting paranoid wasn't lost on her. God knows how her whistle-blower was feeling. She imagined the pressures on him or her were ten times worse. If she felt this bad now, how was she possibly going to get through the next few hours?

She knew she had to get a grip in case things turned bad.

She just didn't know how bad her life was about to become.

2

———————

"Tea?"

The cup struck the table a little too hard, spilling some of the liquid over the lip and onto the table. DCI David Garrick's eyes fixed on the brown droplets. They held their shape, slightly elevated from the wooden surface. Two slowly rolled together to form one large bead. Despite the rusty brown colour, he couldn't shake the image of blood droplets crawling along the surface.

"David?"

He looked up, wondering how much of the conversation he'd missed. Superintendent Margery Drury took the seat opposite him and cradled her head in both hands. She was tired after an exhausting twenty-four-hour work marathon, and at just past eight in the evening, caffeine was no longer having any effect on her. If anything, it was tiring her out.

"This is going to get difficult."

Garrick gave a low, ironic chuckle. It was nothing more than an effort to give some sort of reply, since his words continued to fail him. Drury sipped her coffee and savoured the warmth, if not the taste.

"What I mean is, there will be no right steps forward, no matter what we do," she clarified. "My options are limited."

"Mine too," said Garrick as he placed both hands around the cup of matcha tea. Ever since arriving at the police station, he'd been unable to get warm. A grim chill seeped through to his bones, with icy tendrils surging through his veins. It was his body reacting to the stress, but why it thought freezing him to death was a benefit, he couldn't imagine. He'd endured questions, refused a solicitor, and spent a sleepless night in a cell. The rest of the day had been spent in the very interview room he found himself in now. He shivered again, partly from the cold, but mostly from the gruesome image that had confronted him in his own home.

His career had made him accustomed to death. Almost insensitive. The barbarity that one person could inflict upon another had become nothing more than a regular day at work for him. A case only got under his skin when he got to know the victim. When he discovered more about their life and their personality. That was the moment a corpse, a victim, transformed into a fully rounded human being with hopes, dreams, and ambitions.

Except in this case, it went beyond that.

He knew the victim.

And he was, in a second-hand way, a victim too. One of the easily forgotten victims who had to live with the consequences of a murder. The seismic repercussions of losing a loved one were incalculable, echoing down to even those with just a casual association.

There were thousands of questions vying for attention, but there were only a few he could ask Drury, and he knew she was in no position to give any answers. Even if she knew them. He was sitting on the wrong side of the table.

He was the prime suspect.

Throughout questioning, he'd only managed short, almost monosyllabic replies. As a detective, he always found that those were the most infuriating and often the most damning. However, his mind had been in a fog, so he wasn't even sure if he was answering consistently, or accidentally contradicting himself. He knew from experience that even the most coherent witnesses were prone to mistakes, incongruities, and even forming false memories. It was basic human nature when in shock.

Matters were compounded by his own doubts. Of course, he was innocent... but...

The growth in his head. The pressure on his brain. The hallucinations and blurred lines of reality he'd been experiencing had made him question his own innocence while he tossed and turned on the hard mattress in the bleak prison cell; all the while trying to tune out the drunk in the cell next to him who had screamed more obesities than he could recall.

It was impossible that he could have committed such a horrific act. Completely implausible.

So why did he have a gnawing doubt that he was somehow responsible? A faint whispering that hinted at implied guilt. On second thoughts, he cautioned himself that hearing voices, whispering or any other kind, was a sure step towards the pit of insanity he feared he was teetering over.

"David?"

The sound of Drury's voice brought him back to the moment. She looked up from her phone and her eyebrow fluttered inquisitively.

"You didn't hear a word I said, did you?" Garrick shook his head. She indicated her phone. "He's on his way."

The words had the effect of a pair of hands laying pressure on Garrick's shoulders. The next few minutes would dictate which way his future lay. From his point of view, both were shrouded in shadow and stretched beyond the event horizon of acceptable reality.

Drury sipped her coffee and gave a little cough to lubricate her dry throat. "Doing the right thing may sometimes seem to be the most callous." Garrick knew she was covering herself as best as possible for what lay ahead. "But I have your back, David. Even if you think I don't. That's what friends do."

That he and Drury were friends was certainly news to Garrick.

The door to the interview room squeaked open on its dry hinge. Garrick had always prevented maintenance from oiling it. He thought the drawn-out metal groan as the door closed slowly was ominous enough to put his suspects off-balance. Now it was having the same effect on him as DCI Oliver Kane entered.

His greying beard seemed longer and more unkempt than when Garrick had last seen him, and his naturally craggy face showed a lack of sleep. The last time he'd been in the room, his arms were laden with printouts and folders related to the murder in Garrick's home. This time he carried nothing as he sat down next to Drury and idly scratched the side of his salt-and-pepper hair. Drury reached over to start the digital recorder, but Kane held up a hand.

"If it's all the same to you, perhaps we can do that in a second."

Drury moved away and sat back in her seat, linking her

fingers together as she rested her hands on the table. Garrick forced himself to look the London Met officer directly in the eyes. He didn't like the man. He was too full of secrets and, right now, he was playing the role of Garrick's judge and jury.

"The initial autopsy results came in, along with some forensic data," he said in a low voice.

Garrick wasn't sure he wanted to hear the details, but he had little choice.

"The victim was abducted from her vehicle. We found it in a ditch. There were signs of a struggle. Defensive marks on her arms and bruising on her throat as she was gripped as her head slammed against the rear driver's side window. Hard enough to fracture the glass and cause a hairline fracture in her skull. Then she was drugged. Kept unconscious with *flunitrapam*."

Garrick stirred in his seat and looked away. He really didn't want to know more. He knew the drug under its more commonly used name: *Rohypnol*. The infamous date-rape drug.

Kane pressed on. "There is no sign of any sexual assault. From the quantity found in her blood, she was just coming around by the time the first knife wound struck her chest. And that would have been on the landing in your house."

Kane paused as Garrick's brow knitted together. Tears were forming in the corners of his eyes, but with a sharp intake of breath through his nose, he cleared the initial impulse to cry.

"She was carved up there. The coroner thinks the wounds were deliberately designed for a slow death. This wasn't a savage attack. It was calculated. The writing on the wall," Garrick grimaced as he recalled the crudely written words, *Miss Me?* "was her blood. Looks like the culprit wore latex gloves. There are no prints *anywhere*."

Garrick rubbed his temples as his migraine danced merrily on his patience. The Met officer finally took the hint that he didn't want to know the details.

Kane tapped the table with his right hand. His nails clicked against the wooden top.

"Lividity suggests an estimated time of death at about 9:00 pm." Garrick's gaze locked on his. "Which of course places you *here*," Kane gestured around, "with your team." He smiled, although Garrick wasn't sure if it was forced or not. "Which obviously eliminates you as a suspect."

If Kane had been expecting a gasp of relief from him, then he was bang out of luck.

"It was John Howard," Garrick stated with certainty.

"You know he's dead, David," Drury said with an unhindered tone of relief. "You were there."

Garrick leaned across the table, his expression hardening. "I was unconscious in the snow at that point."

"They found his body in the remains of his house—"

"A badly burned corpse," Garrick corrected her.

"He was identified through dental records."

Garrick leaned back in his chair as any further argument escaped him.

Kane spoke up. "Everything points to an *accomplice* of Howard's. Somebody enacting revenge on you, for...?" He left the sentence hanging.

"You tell me," Garrick snapped. "My sister's voice over the phone, the empty envelope sealed by her, the fucking brand-new Range Rover bought in my name and turning up at my house. This is some seriously twisted thinking. Which is exactly why I think it's him."

"I agree, it's odd. Which is why it's confusing that you don't know, don't even an inkling of who would hate you so much to go to such extreme lengths to taunt you."

Garrick remained silent. He'd repeatedly turned the question over in his mind, but had come no closer to any conclusion.

Kane continued. "She had an ex. They were engaged, but split when he cheated on her, so we're looking into him. Her family is taking this hard, and so far, they appear to be a close, loving unit. Family Services are with them now."

"I think considering how extreme this all is, I have to put you on leave," Drury said with a sigh.

"No, ma'am–"

She held up her finger as she continued. "And place you under protective custody."

"No." Garrick firmly shook his head. "I won't accept that."

"David, it's for your own safety. And it was hardly an offer."

"I won't hide. If some maniac wants a piece of me, then they can come right up to my face and look me in the eye and collect it." And then I will kill him myself, he added in venomous silence. Some things were best left unspoken, particularly amongst police officers. "And taking me off service is a waste of my skills, and it will drive me insane. And that's probably exactly what the killer wants."

"What do you suggest I do?" Drury said with a tinge of desperation.

"I was going to ask for reassignment."

"To where?" Before Drury had finished the sentence, she caught his gaze flick towards DCI Kane. "To him?"

"I want to be involved with uncovering what else John Howard did." The man who was once his close friend. The man who may have killed not only his ex-police partner but also his sister. A man of extreme secrets.

"That would've been tough enough because of your involvement with his death," said Kane. "But after this," he waved his hand hopelessly, "there's just no way you can be seconded to my team. Frankly, I really could do with you on it. But it's not up to the Super here," he indicated Drury, "And nobody cares what I think. It's a Met case. The Kent Constabulary are merely assisting."

The image of a pawn sliding across the chequered surface of a chessboard came unbidden to Garrick's mind. The one useful move he could have made in the case had been blocked.

"Our own rules are working against us," Garrick pointed out. "He knows this. He knows how we operated. He always has!" His voice raised for the first time.

"David, sounding hysterical will not help your case," Drury warned.

Kane shook his head. "And if we break our rules, then all the evidence we have will be called into question, especially because of your personal involvement with John Howard, the death of your sister, and now her. It'd no longer be an impartial inquiry. It would be seen a vendetta, backed by the police force. Can you imagine how that would play to the public? To Parliament? We all know you're innocent of *any* wrongdoing. But the optics are all wrong. The game is tilted against you."

A wave of fatigue suddenly came crashing down on Garrick. His limbs felt heavy, and he could no longer hold back a deep yawn. It was as if he really needed to hear Kane's declaration of his innocence, for his own sake.

"I'm going to get you to a hotel," Drury said. "And I *will* be putting protection in place while you're there." She raised her hand to stop his pending complaint. "And I don't give a shit what you think about that. I have a protocol to follow. Don't talk to the press. I must be on Molly Meyers' speed dial, the number of times she called yesterday. I think she's got the message now, though."

Garrick liked to think Molly was one of the journalists on the Force's side, especially as her career, from local paper to BBC TV journalist, had been supercharged with Garrick's help. She had her uses, Garrick thought. A great journalist was a great tool to have in his back pocket, and one he was more than happy to deploy in this instance.

"What about my team?"

Drury and Kane swapped a look. She gave a slight nod for Kane to speak up.

"They have been seconded to my investigation." Garrick sighed heavily, but Kane pressed on. "The murder at your home is obviously tied in with the ongoing Howard investigation. Under you, they can't work on either case. So, maybe it's bending the rules rather than fracturing them. They now work for me. They'll have valuable insights into the case. And into you."

Under the layers of fatigue, Garrick still felt chilled and unsettled. He'd never really shared what had happened to his sister Emelie with the rest of the team. Even the most cursory investigation would reveal it all. Their lifelong animosity. How she tried to extend an olive branch after their parent's death, but he was too stubborn to fully accept it. How she had been on a road trip in America with her fiancé, Sam McKinzie, where they'd both been brutally killed on a remote ranch in Illinois, along with several other victims. Sam's body had been recovered, but not all the others. And that included Emelie's. Since then, he'd been plagued by reminders about her. Somebody was playing games with his sanity…

And now his team would know all about it. They would have an omnipotent eye into his personal life. Something that he had taken pains to keep firmly separate from them. His relationship with John Howard, with his sister, his love life, medical reports, and Dr Harmon's psychological evaluation.

He suddenly felt completely emasculated.

"I don't want them involved," he said firmly.

"That's not up to you," Drury said. "Take a leave of absence until we crack this."

Garrick stared long and hard at his superior. He was through with the veneer of respect the job demanded. He'd been pushed over the edge and was now free falling in a world of confusion. Fortunately, he was too tired to unleash a tirade that would make him sound like a spoiled teenage brat.

Drury took his silence as acceptance. She reached over and started the audio recorder. Garrick tuned out when she stated the time, date, and who was in the room. He didn't care, and he no longer wanted to be trapped within the bland walls.

His mind drifted back to the murder scene in his own home, and the pale face of the victim as she stared open-eyed at him. A face he had found so sweet and adorable… now rendered heartbreakingly lifeless.

It was an image he wanted to forget, but knew he never would.

3

No expense had been made when Drury assigned Garrick to his temporary accommodation at the Maidstone Travel Inn. He'd stayed in one many years ago in London when he'd been strapped for cash and in need of a roof over his head. Garrick still recalled entering the bathroom and finding the sink had been stolen – and, more importantly, the theft had gone completely unnoticed by the cleaning staff. He vowed it would be his first and last time he'd stay in the bargain hotel chain. It had taken a brutal murder to make him enter again.

He sat on the edge of the hard bed and stared at the television. He'd switched it on as soon as he'd entered, not because he needed company to take him out of his brooding thoughts, but because the silence had been overbearing, allowing a whispering accusative voicing to seep into his head. Not a single word from the TV show had sunk in, yet he must have remained motionless for twenty minutes before his phone rang. He silenced it without looking at who the caller was.

No matter how much he tried to divert his wondering thoughts, they always strayed back to the gruesome scene in his home. The fresh blood pooling on the carpet and dripping in a thin rivulet down the staircase. The body slumped upright against the wall, framed by a halo of blood spatter and the words *Miss me?* written in blood just above her head.

And that face. One he had found so pretty, was now pale and lifeless. Glassy eyes staring accusingly at him. Her red-framed glasses had slipped from her nose and laid against her blood-sodden blouse.

Dr Amy Harman had been his psychological counsellor, assigned to him after his sister's murder. Despite his initial resistance to the idea, and compounded by the fact Drury had made it clear that an ongoing psychological assessment was essential for him returning to work, his sessions with Dr Harman had fast become the highlight of his week.

On a base, single-white male level, he had found her intoxicatingly attractive, with shoulder-length, wavy blonde hair, a dimpled smile, and wide blue eyes behind her glasses. She was far smarter than him, and her simple way with words was designed to put him at ease. She enjoyed mangling phrases and over-drawn analogies, but they always made him pause, think, and reassess his own point of view.

When she'd cleared him as psychologically competent and ended their sessions together, he'd briefly experienced a sense of loss because he wouldn't see her again. But that had been replaced by his new – and real – relationship with Wendy Sinclair.

His phone buzzed on silent mode. He turned the screen and saw it was Wendy calling for the third time. He hadn't spoken to her for a couple of days, and there was no way she could've known about the situation he was in. She was so understanding. Too understanding. She accepted his sudden disappearances for days on end when he was on a case, but he knew he couldn't avoid her indefinitely. He should talk to her. Instead, he let the call ring out once again and turned his thoughts on the investigation unfolding around him, and now without him.

With DCI Kane now leading the charge, Garrick was aware of the futility of trying to get involved. His relationship with Harman was well documented; after all, the police department had paid her bills. But it was also secretive. He'd told nobody about his counselling sessions, and other than Drury, there was nobody in the police building who would've knowledge of his private sessions. The HR department would've known. After all, they were paying the bills. They were based in a separate building near Ebbsfleet in North Kent. So why had she been targeted?

The fact the murderer had chosen his psychologist sent a powerful message to him. *Nobody* was beyond their reach. *They were in his head.*

He'd called DS Chibarameze Okon when he'd found the body and begged her to check in on his girlfriend, Wendy. Ever practical, Chib had done so without alerting her and left an officer watching over her house in Lenham.

What sent chills down Garrick's spine was the knowledge the safest person in the whole situation... was himself. The killer was targeting him by making those around him suffer. Drawing him deeper into a game in which he didn't know the rules.

And one in which *anybody* could be the next victim.

For two days, Garrick stayed in his lousy hotel room and kept Wendy at bay with texts claiming he was tied up with work on a time critical case. As usual, she understood, which made him feel all the worse for lying about what was really going on. The news had broken about the murder– it was almost impossible to hide the forensic tents and fleet of police vehicles in suburbia - but the precise details about the victim and Garrick himself had so far not been leaked by the press. Drury was keeping a muzzle on the media for as long as she could. He expected Molly Meyers hounding him for a lead, but since her promotion to regional BBC reporting, he suspected she had her eye on the nationals and much bigger stories than this.

Alone in his room, he was feeling isolated. None of the investigation team had been back in touch with him to chase up loose ends. While he was under no obligation to stay inside, he felt it was the right thing to do. Or was that his own inner demons feeding his fear and making him a prisoner?

By late afternoon on the third day, Garrick lay on the uncomfortable bed while tedious antique shows played ad nauseam on BBC One. Even he could smell the air was ripe with his own body odour, and the pot noodles he'd been eating - as they were the only thing that he could make in a room with just a kettle. Empty MacDonald's cartons were crammed into the bin, a treat when he'd succumbed to ordering from Deliveroo.

He snatched the remote from the folds of the bedsheet and rattled through a dozen Freeview channels before falling onto a rerun of the first series of Broadhaven. For a second, he glared at the leading man, Will Sadler, chewing up the scene, and wondered why the channel hadn't yet pulled the sex pest off their screens. His patience snapped, and he turned the TV off.

He groped for his phone, that was charging on the bedside table, and called Wendy. Just hearing her voice would be a tonic. The pupils in the school where she was a teaching assistant would've gone home by now, and she was probably caught up in the tedious admin work the staff had to process each day.

He'd invite her out for dinner somewhere nice. He fancied some posh fish, maybe sea bass, which his palette would thank him for after the stream of junk food. He thumbed through his recent calls and his finger was hovering over her number when his phone rang. Drury's name appeared, and he quickly tapped it.

"David, it's Drury."

His pulse quickened in anticipation of some dreadful news, but the use of his first name and her usual acerbic tone warned him that this was something else.

"Ma'am."

"Get down here immediately. Something has come up."

He knew better than to question her, but a rebellious sliver bridled at that fact she blew hot and cold when it came to his work, demanding he take gardening leave one moment, then insisting he come in the next.

"What's happened?"

The brief pause on the line was acknowledgement enough that she was surprised he hadn't already hung up and trotted down.

"There's a case that you're needed on."

The request – or rather demand – took him by surprise. He couldn't stop the follow-up question.

"What's so urgent? I thought I was on leave?"

"A kidnapping. Now shut the hell up and move. The clock's ticking."

She hung up, leaving Garrick with even more questions. But as he darted to retrieve his trousers from over the blue armchair in the corner, he put calling Wendy on the back-burner as he wondered why Drury specifically needed him.

The police station was only a twelve-minute walk from his hotel. The air was so mild that he didn't wear the new dark green Barbour jacket Wendy had bought him as a gift, so folded it over his arm as he quickened his pace through Maidstone town centre. It was that twilight period when school kids still combed the screens, as the adults fled from their offices and jammed up the surrounding roads in a bid to get home.

He hadn't expected Drury to be waiting for him as he entered the building. Her mere presence warned him that something exceptional had occurred. She quick-marched down the corridor, forcing Garrick to almost jog to keep up.

"What exactly is going on?"

Drury was pissed off as she threw him a glance. "We have a developing kidnapping, and I need you back in the fray."

"I'm happy with that."

From the thunderous look on her face, Drury clearly wasn't. "You need to be focused on this like a laser, Garrick."

"Of course."

"I mean it. John Howard, Harman, all that needs to be put to one side. We have a life on the line." She reached to pull open the fire door ahead of them, but stopped with her hand still on the handle. "And I really mean it. Kane is solely dealing with that now. You cannot get involved with his case. Do you understand?" When Garrick didn't answer, Drury let go of the door and spun to face him. "Do you understand what I'm saying? Unless Kane requires you for anything, stay clear or you could prejudice his case."

"I know how it works, Ma'am." He mentally kicked

himself for the sarcasm that leaked into *ma'am*, but Drury didn't seem to notice, which was unusual for her.

"The Crime Commissioner is breathing down my neck already." Drury kept a close, friendly relationship with Commissioner Scott Edwards. In his sixties, he still had a way with the ladies, although Garrick suspected he was gay. The Commissioner was an elected figure charged with overseeing the Kent Constabulary, and he had friends in high places. Drury was adept at manipulation in order to get her own way, so for Edwards to be pressurising her meant Kane's investigation was being critically watched.

"You didn't answer my question. Why me?"

She yanked the door open and walked through. "Because you've been requested."

They entered his old incident room, and Garrick was pleased to see his team was all here. DC Fanta Liu flashed a thin smile from behind her computer terminal, then nervously looked at the others. DC Wilkes gave a curt nod, and Chib failed to look him in the eye. The uneasy, frosty atmosphere was palpable. Only DC Harry Lord looked pleased to see him. He no longer walked with the crutches after being struck by a car driven by a suspect, but he still had a slight limp. He raised a coffee mug in a salute.

"Good to have you back, sir," he said firmly.

Garrick opened his mouth to reply, but his throat was dry. The odd atmosphere in the room had thrown him off kilter. With nobody forthcoming about the kidnapping, he turned to the evidence wall.

There was a single photo in the middle.

Frowning, Garrick hurried over, almost tripping over the foot of Fanta's chair. The image was one he knew. He tapped the picture and cast his eyes around the room.

"Is this our missing woman?"

Chib finally looked him in the eye and nodded.

"Yes, sir."

Garrick turned back to the familiar image of Molly Meyers taken from her glamorous BBC headshot and wondered what the hell he had been pulled into.

4

DS Chib Okon took up the briefing after a nod from Drury. Garrick tossed his coat over the back of a chair and sat opposite Fanta. He leaned forward, propping his elbows on his knees as he listened, but a part of him became detached as he soaked in the subdued atmosphere and the way people deliberately avoided looking at him. It was like being a friendly ghost. Only Fanta kept twisting in her seat to glance at him – but suddenly stopped and kept her eyes on Chib. It was almost amusing watching the young Asian woman wrestle with her instinctive gregariousness. She laced her fingers together and forced her hands to sit on the desk in front of her.

"Molly Meyers has been missing for just over forty-eight hours," Chib informed him as she indicated a map of Tunbridge Wells on the wall. A building on Mount Pleasant Road had been circled. "She was last seen leaving the BBC building at 5:28 pm."

Two days... Garrick had been struggling with his own personal crisis to pay attention to the details, but hadn't

Drury mentioned that Molly had called that day, then stopped? That was uncharacteristic for the plucky reporter, so he made a note to double-check.

"Colleagues said she was meeting a contact for a story she was pursuing. She was excited about it, but nobody knows what the story was. We know she parked at the Torrington Car Park here." Chib put a pin in the map. "And ANPR confirms she left six minutes after leaving the office. Then, we don't know. Her colleagues didn't hear from her the next day, but that was nothing new. Only today, when she missed a meeting and didn't answer her phone, did a production assistant grow concerned."

She put up another picture taken from Facebook. It showed a shade-wearing Molly and a stubbled guy in his late twenties, with a long face sporting highly defined cheekbones and combed back jet-black hair. He oozed a distinct Italian vibe. He had his arms around her as she took the selfie against some summery mountain peaks.

"Tito Russo. An IT consultant, Italian, and he has permanent citizenship here. He was Molly's partner for three years, but they had split recently. When we contacted him, he said he hadn't heard from her. Didn't know she was missing. They'd split up, and she was blocking his calls."

"Do we know where he is?" Garrick asked.

"Glasgow, with an alibi."

Chib took a step away from the board in a manner to suggest she'd finished her presentation of the facts. Puzzled, Garrick looked around the room to see who was stepping up to continue the narrative. Nobody moved.

"Well, I can see you're all dumbstruck and awed that I'm back so soon, so perhaps one of you can enlighten me about what makes this a kidnapping and not a missing persons case?"

Still, nobody stirred. Then Drury stepped up to the evidence wall.

"At two o'clock today, I received an email from Molly's account." She nodded at Fanta.

Fanta's fingers clacked across her keyboard, and the email appeared on the TV mounted next to the evidence wall. There was a photo attached. Taken from the waist up, Molly Meyers was gagged and bound to what appeared to be a chair. She was peering directly at the camera, but her normally big inquisitive eyes were half closed in pain, or distress, or both. The background was out of focus, so it gave no hint of where she was being held. The last time Garrick had seen her, she'd was her usual self; an attractive, young, dynamic redhead who he'd helped, and even come to put up with, if not respect. After all, it was his own case involving a murder and an art dealer that had captured the public's imagination and cranked her career up several gears. Her expression of helplessness made him feel wretched. A hand-written sign had been hung around her neck, the text of which made him feel worse:

Tell David Garrick and his team to come and find me. I will be dead in 72 hours x

Garrick's cheeks flushed hot, and he felt all eyes turn on him. He still hadn't moved from his chair.

Drury stared unblinkingly at him. "Now you see the urgency about having you back."

The tone of the message chimed with the scrawl written on the wall above Dr Harman's head. It took Garrick several attempts to speak, as his mouth was suddenly dry.

"It's the same person..."

Drury shook her head. "What did I tell you about this, David? Weren't you listening?"

"Now I'm forbidden to follow a hunch?" he snapped back.

"I want proof, not hunches."

Garrick bolted to his feet so suddenly his chair rolled back on its castors and slammed into the desk behind, causing Fanta to jump.

"How can it not be?"

"The handwriting analysis isn't conclusive. Perhaps a copycat...?"

"Amy's death hasn't made it into the news yet. Who would know the details?"

Drury held up both her hands to calm him down. "We've been through this, David. if it is connected, then you can see how you investigating this is... sub-optimal. You're emotionally involved, which is going to cloud your decisions. I'll be frank, I don't want you on this." The other detectives didn't know where to look as their Super vented. Drury tapped the message on the screen. "But *somebody* does, which puts it out of my hands."

Garrick looked around. His team was finally breaking the wall of shame and looking at him. He circled a finger around the room.

"What about them? Didn't you assign them to DCI Kane's investigation?"

Drury nodded towards the email. "It was made clear this was to be you and your *team*. If it makes you feel any better, they all volunteered for this."

Garrick cast his gaze around the room again. There were faint glimmers of smiles tugging at DCs Lord and Wilkes' eyes. Fanta gave a thumbs-up. Only Chib didn't make eye contact.

"This is about as wrong as it gets," Drury continued. "But we have no leads, a ticking clock, and a motive that seems to orbit you."

Garrick joined her at the evidence wall and peered closer at Molly's picture.

"What if I refuse? Kane can handle it. Or Chib?" He gestured to his Detective Sergeant. "She's more than capable. Totally trustworthy."

"I can't make you do this," Drury said in a cold, low voice that made it clear that he had no option. "If you do, and it goes wrong. It won't just be your career thrown out of the window. I'll be out right behind you. And if you succeed, then Ollie Kane will be getting all the plaudits. This is a zero-sum game. It also must be a low-key operation. Fortunately for us, the BBC take the kidnapping of their staff very seriously, so they won't be making any noise about this. From this moment on, we're all forced to play this out."

Garrick's legs trembled, forcing him to lean on the edge of a table. For the last few days, his old migraine had been ominously silent, as if swept away by his grief. But now the tumour was awakening, and he could feel the painful warnings.

"And because of the intricate nature of this situation, you'll have to report directly to DCI Kane."

Garrick looked sharply around the room, expecting Oliver Kane to step into the limelight. There was no sign of him. Kane was a London Met detective, but of equal rank to Garrick. Having him as his de facto Super was a kick in the nuts, a complete outrage. But he checked himself. Now wasn't the time to launch into an argument. A woman's life was on the line. He rapped a knuckle against Molly's picture on the monitor.

"What did digital forensics glean from this?"

Fanta spoke up, reading from the few notes that had appeared on the HOLMES case file. "There's been no attempt made to remove any metadata." Emails, photos, in fact almost all kinds of computer file were crammed with markers such as the creation time and date. "It was taken seventeen minutes before the email was sent, using Molly's own phone."

"How do you know that?"

"Remember when she shot that video of you diving out of the hotel window?" Garrick couldn't forget, and still bore a few slow healing bruises to remind him. "She sent you the video. The metadata matches. That's the good news. The bad news is that there is no GPS data linked to the image and no sign of her phone being active on the network."

Garrick nodded thoughtfully. "So this was either taken in a location with no phone signal, or it was on flight mode so it couldn't access the GPS." The first scenario indicated either luck on the perpetrator's front or careful planning. The second alternative represented the devious planning of somebody who wouldn't leave anything to chance.

"And before you ask, I've contacted the phone company to find out where it was last used," said Fanta with a trace of smugness. "We're waiting."

"Ask them for the blackout data." Garrick didn't feel the usual thrill he got when he bamboozled Fanta. She shrugged, so he continued. "I want to see the areas her phone carrier *doesn't* receive a signal."

"They could be underground or in a shielded building," Wilkes said as he latched onto Garrick's train of thought. "Like a factory."

Garrick nodded. "Look into any likely structure in the blackout areas. And not just Kent. Surrey, Essex, Sussex. She's had two days to be moved." She could even be on the other side of the country, he thought ominously. "But what I'm curious about is the seventeen minutes between taking the picture and emailing it. That suggests travel."

Fanta gave a low whistle under her breath. "Seventeen minutes from a signal blackout still covers a huge distance."

She was correct, but Garrick didn't have time to dwell on the negatives. "Anything else from forensics?"

Fanta glanced at the report on her screen. "A filter and the camera's flash were used, so they can't tell if it was artificial or natural light."

The difference between underground and a place with windows, Garrick thought. The kidnapper really was being careful.

Chib took up the briefing. "We've started tracing her movements from the car park. There are a lot of videos to still gather and trawl through, so we'll need some extra people for that."

Garrick glanced at Drury, who gave a gentle nod. Ordinarily, she would have resisted the mere thought of financing extra people, but Garrick sensed the life of a journalist was thought to be worth more than an ordinary member of the public. At least in Drury's career stakes, and with the Commissioner watching her every move.

Chib continued. "I've sent forensics into her office. They have a hot desk policy, so no one individual has their own desk. But that means everything is stored on the server."

"And her house?"

"A team is on their way there now."

Garrick clapped his hands together and rubbed his palms; more to channel the pent-up energy he was feeling than to galvanize the team. "Right, Chib, me and you are going down there now." Chib nodded, but she didn't look pleased with the prospect. "Harry, I want a timeline up on the wall, starting a month before now. Her ex, their relationship, her contact with our cases, her gym routine. I want it up there in glorious technicolour."

"Yes, sir."

"Fanta, keep on top of digital forensics and hurry the phone company."

"What about me?" said Wilkes.

"I want you to find her car. What did she drive?" Garrick stopped himself as he remembered seeing her in it once outside a hotel. "It's a new Beetle. Where the hell is it? Start interviewing anybody in her workplace. Somebody must've got a sniff of the story she was working on."

The team moved silently about their tasks, without the usual banter and grumbling. That alone was enough to unnerve Garrick. He was watching Chib retrieve her jacket and car keys when Drury moved by his side.

"What if we find nothing?" she asked quietly.

Garrick looked at her and gave a thin, humourless smile.

"Of course we will. If the kidnapper wants to play a game, then they would've left something for us to follow. It's not a question of *what if*, it's a question of *why*?"

His migraine took that moment to gnaw at his temples. With it came the dark thought that if the miscreant wanted to hurt Garrick, he would've gone after Wendy. Molly had been specifically targeted for one reason only - to make a big splash in the media. The question of *why* remained. Would her reporting about her ordeal make bigger waves than news of her death?

Garrick had less than seventy-two hours to find out.

5

After setting Molly's address in the car's GPS, Chib drove a little faster than her usual caution dictated. Neither she nor Garrick spoke a word as they pulled out of the police station gates. The fact her Nissan Leaf was electric further added to the painful silence. Chib was normally circumspect when it came to conversation, but Garrick had always felt comfortable and at ease with her. Finding out anything personal was a chore, and something he had chipped away at over the last few months. By the time they joined the M20 eastbound, Garrick could take the silence no more.

"Everybody seems happy to see me." From the corner of his eye, he saw Chib grip the steering wheel a little tighter, but she kept her eyes on the road. "You, especially."

He took some satisfaction in noting her discomfort. She licked her lips and answered in a quiet voice.

"It's a little difficult, sir. For all of us. We know what happened to you."

"Difficult for *you*? Oh, I'm sorry…"

"Nobody knows what to say." She glanced at him but couldn't maintain eye contact, which was just as well as the road was busy. She was hoping Garrick would pick up the conversation, but he stubbornly remained silent. It was several seconds before she continued. "DCI Kane gave us complete access to his case files. One thing we had to do was look into the relationship between you and…"

She couldn't bring herself to say, 'the deceased', and Garrick found he couldn't either. The words tumbled from his lips before he could stop them. "My therapist."

Chib nodded. "Nobody knew."

"Of course not. Anyway, you read her reports. Apparently, I'm sane."

"Which is how we found out more about your sister."

"Don't tell me nobody knew?"

"We'd all heard rumours. Stories. Some people respected your privacy, so nobody wanted to look too deep."

The words 'some people' rankled him. He had his suspicions about who fell into which camp, but he decided it best to let things slide.

"Great. Everybody is tiptoeing around me to avoid the elephant in the room. The two elephants, if you count Amy. Three, if you ask why somebody has got it in for me. What is it you want to ask me?"

"Pardon?"

"If everybody is watching their Ps and Qs, then they're obviously embarrassed about saying something wrong. And that includes you. So, what is it you want to know?"

Chib shrugged and looked at him sidelong. "I don't… I don't know." She laughed at her own hesitation, and Garrick felt the atmosphere thaw a little. "I suppose I want to know the same things you do. Why and who? And the same goes for Molly's kidnapper. Do you really think they're linked?"

Garrick stared out of the window, watching the green motorway embankment pass by with almost hypnotic regularity. Chib and the team were working under him now, but for a few days, they were at DCI Kane's behest. They had a foot in his investigation, the one Kane had only shared whispers and hints about. It wasn't unreasonable to assume they, or at least Chib, being the DS, had been briefed at least a few more layers deeper than Garrick could reach. That put them in a difficult place in discussing anything that Kane may see as compromising his own case. But Garrick didn't care about that. In fact, he felt himself bucking at the rules with each passing hour. On a professional level, he understood the need to keep him out of Kane's investigation, but being placed away from the answers he sought was painful. He didn't want to place any of his team in an awkward situation by demanding answers, but he had no intention of ignoring the fact he needed to dig deeper. Much deeper.

"To me, the *who* is obvious. The *how* and *why* are puzzling me."

"I assume you think it's John Howard."

"Don't you?"

"A dead man? I was there, sir. I saw what happened."

Garrick drummed his fingers on his leg. "What did you see?"

"The fire. You, smashing through the window and falling into the snow outside. I stayed with you while the ambulance arrived. They came a minute ahead of the fire brigade, by which time the fire had really taken hold."

Garrick had been unconscious, but had read the report.

Other than thanking Chib after he'd been discharged from the hospital, they hadn't spoken about the traumatic event.

Chib continued, her eyes firmly on the road. "Some bloke across the street helped me drag you away from the flames and gave me some blankets to put over you and under your head. Nobody could get close to the shop."

"Which means you never saw John Howard inside."

"No. But they found his body and made a positive ID from dental records." She glanced at him, remembering the case they investigated about a body found in an art dealer's home. A body they had erroneously assumed to be the art dealer himself. "And if you're thinking about Derek Fraser—"

"Which proves the lengths people will go to disguise a body's real identity."

"Which implies John Howard premeditated pretending to burn to death in his own home. That's ridiculous."

Garrick said nothing. He wouldn't put anything beyond the serial killer's nefarious planning capabilities, although a small, logical part of his mind was desperate to stick to the facts. However, Chib's reaction to his theory was openly dismissive. He couldn't work out if that was her opinion or the line Kane's investigation was taking. In which case, did they have another suspect in mind?

"Did you know he was in Illinois the same time Emelie was murdered?" he said quietly. "Do you think *that's* a coincidence?"

There was no hesitation in Chib's reply. "Not at all."

Garrick made a mental note of how assured she sounded. He gestured to the road ahead.

"Since you don't share my suspicions about Howard, who do you think is behind Molly's abduction?"

"I think that's a little more clear cut. Aside from what

happened in your home," she faltered over the words, once again dancing on eggshells, "you've been in the public eye quite a bit over the last few months. I don't think there is another detective the public could put a name to here, or anywhere in the country right now."

Garrick couldn't disagree. He recalled how he'd been recognised in Pizza Hut while on a date with Wendy. After a clip of him tumbling off a hotel conservatory went viral – a clip recorded by Molly Meyers – his face had been plastered across social media.

"Now if I was somebody with issues," said Chib as she sped past a Romanian lorry, "and wanted to be famous, then you and Molly make an excellent pair."

"You think this is some twisted publicity stunt?"

"Like those shooters in America. They seem to happen almost every day because somebody wants their fifteen minutes of fame."

"I think it might be because they have gun laws that belong in a third world country," huffed Garrick.

"It boils down to the individual," said Chib. "Who ever heard of a criminal worried about breaking one law in order to break another? If you're going to do something so obscene as kill, I don't think breaking stringent gun ownership laws would bother you too much."

"So the motive is fame?"

"Could be. Or perhaps she stumbled across a story that threatens to expose somebody? Or an ex-lover, or there's a colleague jealous of her sudden success. Success that was driven by you. Maybe it's somebody with mental health issues. I would suggest any of those is a stronger line of enquiry than chasing a dead man."

"Bottom line is that you think the kidnapper dragging me

into this is a publicity stunt? That's quite coincidental, considering the timing with Amy…"

"You've made it very clear to me that you don't believe in coincidences. I happen to believe in them. The world is a strange place. Strange things happen."

"Except strange things happen to me *all the time*."

In all his time living in Kent, David Garrick had never heard of Stelling Minnis. In his mind, it sounded like a location in the Lord of the Rings, but it was a small, unremarkable village in the heart of the Kent Downs. Molly Meyers lived in a bungalow on Bossingham Road, the main thoroughfare that cut through the village since Roman times. The marked police van in her driveway made the house easy enough to identify as they approached.

"Nice to see they're keeping things low-key," muttered Garrick as they pulled up behind it.

The bungalow sat several yards back from the road, with a five-foot hedge offering some privacy. Her neighbours on either side were six yards away, blocked by a hedge taller than Garrick. A rosy-faced Police Officer greeted them. She was supervising a locksmith who was drilling through the front door lock.

"We should be inside in a minute," she assured them.

Garrick took in the white painted home. There were a few hardy plants in the front garden, which looked as if they'd been resident for years. A patch of grass was shin high. He couldn't imagine Molly as a gardener, and it had an air of neglect about it. There was no garage, and no sign of her Beetle.

"Is this hers or rented?" he asked Chib.

"It's in her name," she confirmed. "No mortgage. Looks as if she inherited it. The deeds come from a Meyers."

"So, our Molly wasn't struggling to make ends meet." Garrick circled the building.

They had passed several quaint-looking farm cottages and bungalows on the ride in, but Molly's property gave the air of the runt of the litter. It was small and unloved.

The open sides offered easy access to a small rear garden with more uncut grass. A small shed was locked only by a latch. Inside were a few rusting garden tools in a bucket, a shovel, a manual lawnmower, and a racing bike with a flat tyre and patches of rust tarnishing the frame.

Garrick completed his orbit around the building by passing the rubbish bins at the side of the house. A green one for recycling and a grey one for everything else. Garrick fished a pair of blue latex gloves from his Barbour's pocket and rolled them on. He opened both bins. The refuse one was a quarter filled. Garrick knew from living alone that it would probably take a month for her to fill it, so it probably hadn't been emptied for a while. He quickly shut it to block the smell. The recycling was quite full. There were a few torn printouts, rinsed clean yogurt pots, plastic bottles, and cans. Most of the recent additions were newspapers from the weekend, he noted. There was nothing that immediately begged for attention. He closed that too, deciding to leave the examination to some poor sap in forensics. By the time he re-joined Chib and the officer, the locksmith had the door open and was already heading back to his car.

The décor inside was certainly not what Garrick expected from Molly. An old sofa, armchair, and empty mahogany crockery cabinet further suggested that the young reporter had inherited the house from her mother. The only splashes of modern life were the forty-inch TV hung on the wall and an internet router flashing in the corner. The living room stretched back to incorporate a dining table covered in a variety of newspapers, and a large bay window looking across the garden. A musty smell lingered in the air. Nobody had been here for days.

Leaving the police officer guarding the door, Chib searched the other rooms. A kitchen, equipped from the eighties, lay through one door.

"Sir, there's a bowl in the sink," said Chib, popping her head around the door. "Looks like the remains of cereal and milk in it. Otherwise, it's all pretty normal."

She headed down a short hallway. A cupboard in one wall was crammed with coats, shoes, and a hoover. Other doors led to a bathroom and the bedroom.

Garrick took stock of the living room. He could hear the occasional squeaky hinge of wardrobe doors opening, or the scrape of the bed being rolled aside. Such hasty searches seldom revealed much useful information in a kidnapping case. Already it was clear to him that Molly Meyers hadn't been abducted from her home. There were no signs of a struggle. Nothing appeared to have been quickly put back in place. The newspapers on the table were dated the morning she went missing. A pile of bills was stacked on the corner. He used his index finger to fan the pile a little wider. Amongst the usual junk mail was a water bill, an envelope printed with theatre artwork, and one that he guessed came from the bank. There had been no mail on the front doormat, but deliveries, especially to small rural villages, had been cut back in recent years.

The last time Molly Meyers had been here, she hadn't been in a rush and there were no signs of urgency. It felt normal. And that bothered him. He had only got to know her recently. She was enthusiastic, energetic, and opportunistic.

In his view, the home didn't fit her lifestyle. Organised wasn't a word he associated with her.

Viewing the room with a fresh perspective, he saw the remotes for the TV and Sky box were on the empty coffee table. Arranged parallel to the side with a hint of obsessiveness. Curious, he turned the TV on. It went straight to a Tom and Jerry cartoon. Energetic music blared out as the wily mouse got the better of Tom by ramming an ironing board down his throat. Garrick was surprised such violence wasn't banned in today's woke culture; he'd always loved the cartoons as a child. This was the last channel she had been watching. He struggled to see Molly Meyers sitting here and laughing at cartoons.

He cast his eyes about the room again, analysing the sense of order that wasn't a characteristic of Molly. Chib entered the room.

"Nothing jumped out at me, sir. I didn't see a laptop or any car keys."

Garrick's gaze fell on the dining table, and he was struck by two things. Out of the four chairs tucked around it, two had been drawn out at opposite ends, as if a pair of diners had recently sat down to face one another. But these had been drawn out at perpendicular angles, not angled as would suggest somebody had sat there. And the newspapers themselves were neatly aligned, not stacked, or overlapping, as he imagined a keen reporter quickly reading through the main points would leave them as she discarded one to read the next.

"Almost like a museum display," he muttered.

Chib followed his gaze and quickly latched onto his line of thinking. She took a picture on her phone. Garrick scanned the headlines, trying to see if there was any connection, but he drew a blank. As the cartoon music built to a crescendo, he looked back at the letters. He fanned them fully out on the table and picked out the colourful theatre envelope. Pinching it between his thumb and forefinger, he held it up to Chib.

"What were you saying about coincidences?"

Chib's eyes widened, but she didn't say a thing. Clearly emblazoned across the envelope was the logo for the *Garrick Theatre* in London. The slapstick antics of the cartoon cat and mouse filled the silence as Garrick put the letter back down. Then he lifted the copy of The Sun and peered underneath. There was nothing there. Next, he checked The Mail, then The Guardian – and his hand froze in place.

Underneath lay a mobile phone and an Apple Watch. He tapped the phone's screen and a picture of Molly Meyers appeared. It was a close-up of her face. Her eyes wide with fear as she stared at the camera; her mouth gagged. The phone overlaid the current time, and Garrick was very conscious as another minute ticked by.

6

Forensics were called and prioritised, but Garrick had no time to hang around and wait for them to arrive. Chib examined the watch.

"Her last run is timestamped eighty-three minutes after she left the office."

"Which means from Tunbridge Wells to here, she would have come direct. Then headed out on her run. Hardly the act of somebody who felt threatened."

"Unless she was forced to come this way." Chib waggled the Apple Watch. "Have you used one of these before?"

Garrick harrumphed. "Does it look like I do?"

"They monitor heart rate, your pulse, everything. They're very cool. They can also track your GPS position."

Garrick's eyes widened. Chib tapped the phone and the screen instantly unlocked. She exchanged a meaningful look with her DCI. Phones were notoriously difficult to unlock in cases, often requiring a passcode or biometric data such as a fingerprint or facial ID. In a few instances, they'd been lucky in the past, but neither of them doubted accessing this phone was a stroke of luck. Molly Meyers was the sort of person to have every security element enabled. Somebody *wanted* the police to access this.

It took Chib seconds to local the Strava app.

"This is a very cool app," she said. "I've used it myself. The US army got into trouble in Afghanistan when they issued fitness trackers to their soldiers. All the tracking data showed their regular exercise routes, which they realised could be used by Taliban snipers."

A few taps later, and a map appeared. It was of the immediate area. A red line showed Molly's route from her house to a destination close by.

"It doesn't return from there," Chib pointed out. "So, it was turned off—"

"Or she's still there," Garrick intoned.

"Shall we call for an armed unit?"

Garrick shook his head. "It's too easy. This is..." he glanced at the envelopes on the table, "pure theatre. She won't be there. The kidnapper just wants *us* to be there. Come on."

Outside, Chib unlocked her car, but Garrick marched past, holding the phone in one hand as he watched a little icon on the screen mark his location.

Chib indicated to the car. "It's not far, sir."

"And we may miss something along the way if we drive."

Garrick turned left at the gate and walked briskly down the road. He heard Chib sigh and lock the car door as she hurried after him.

"We could be walking into a trap of some sort," she said nervously.

"This is a game the kidnapper wants to play. We won't get

very far by bending the rules. And after all this, I don't think he'll be so clumsy as to end it in some naff ambush."

"You've heard of the game, *Mouse Trap*, haven't you?" Chib muttered.

The road ahead continued, with a forking branch to the left. Garrick held up the phone and moved it slightly. The map spun around as it recalibrated. Molly's red route took a sharp hairpin bend to the left, away from the road, where a path cut through a narrow strip of grassland running behind the homes on Bossingham Road. It was down this path Molly had gone.

"I wonder if this is her regular route?" said Garrick. "She has the watch, the app. She obviously looks after herself."

"Let me see." Chib took the phone from Garrick as they walked down the grassy arcade. There were a few trees, and the space was wide enough to feel pleasant rather than claustrophobic. Chib navigated her way through several options. "I can't see any previous saved runs. Maybe digital could pull up a history of her movements."

"If she had been forced to make this run, what does that tell you?"

"It tells me she wasn't expecting to be kidnapped."

Garrick nodded. "It also suggests that she was hoping to meet somebody or was picking up or dropping off something that she deemed important."

"A lead for her story. Unless she has a dark secret, and this is blackmail."

"Blackmailers seldom kidnap their victims."

They reached the bottom of the pathway. It curved around to the right and onto the end of a dirt road that had been carved from the chalky dirt. As the crow flies, they were about one-hundred and thirty yards from Molly's house, although the indirect route had taken them almost three times that distance. Garrick and Chib glanced from the destination on the phone to the end of the road ahead. A huge windmill stood at the corner.

"That's where she went," Chib confirmed.

As they drew nearer, a sign welcoming them to Davison's Mill declared it to be closed. The four-storey windmill was a handsomely restored wooden structure, with brown horizontal panels tinged green with moss. Four white wooden sails blossomed out, creating a picture-perfect image of the English countryside. A building to the side of the gate was a small museum that promised visitors a history of the mill, its renovation, and importance. It was closed, too.

Chib zoomed in on the map as far as it would allow her. "It looks as if she went into the mill, not the museum."

"Let's go." Garrick clambered over the fence; aware he was already panting from the short walk. He thought back to the several times Wendy had asked him to join her on a hike. He regretted not taking her up on the offer. The unprovoked memory gave him a sudden pang of longing. He was missing seeing her. The last few days of messaging had failed to sate the need to see one another, and with no time to spare while the search was on for Molly, he now couldn't even afford a quick phone call.

He hopped to the ground on the other side of the gate and offered his hand to help Chib – but she had already vaulted over it, using only one hand for balance. They followed the gravel pathway past the museum as it led towards the windmill. There was no sign of any passing vehicles on the road beyond. Just the stillness of the country air. A crow cawed nosily from a nearby tree. It felt for a moment that they'd taken a step out of time.

"Hello?" Garrick shouted. His voice fell flat in the fields around them. "Police!"

Next to him, Chib tensed, as if expecting an attack.

Nothing stirred.

"What happened to the element of surprise?" Chib whispered.

Garrick indicated to the phone. "We've been handed an invitation. The only ones surprised to find us here are me and you."

The entrance to the windmill was elevated from the ground, with a white wooden handrail circling the first floor. A small brick building stood adjacent, and the path ended at the steps leading up to the windmill's entrance. Gravel crunched underfoot as they approached. Garrick swapped a wary look with Chib as they ascended the steps. He sucked in his breath, then pushed the door.

It swung silently open.

A quick glance at the lock revealed it had been forced. Inside was utter darkness. Garrick activated the torch on his phone and swept it around. He'd didn't quite know what to expect. A huge wooden shaft ran down the centre of the building, connecting the sails above to an enormous set of cogs on the ground that powered a pair of grey millstones. It put him in mind of being inside a clock. A narrow walkway was bolted to the walls and circled the mechanism in levels all the way to the top. On the opposite wall, a ladder accessed the immediate level above.

"Call forensics." Garrick took a step inside. The wooden floor creaked under his weight.

"Um, sir. I don't have a signal here." Chib held up her phone so he could see.

Garrick checked his own. "Me neither. I'm sure I had one at the end of the road."

Chib took a step back, but then hesitated. "I think I should stay until we know what's in here."

Garrick shook his head. "Time's ticking, Chib. I'll be fine."

He didn't feel fine as he walked further inside. The hairs on the back of his neck rose as each floorboard trilled a note of its own as they bore his weight. He angled his light up to see if he could illuminate anything more. Instead, the machinery cast deep shadows that danced across the walls as he circled towards the ladder. It added a sense of dizzying movement, which he found uncomfortable. His eyes flicked to the door behind. He couldn't see Chib, so assumed she'd left to make the call. As he watched, the door slowly and steadily swung shut, blotting the light from outside.

He reached the foot of the ladder and craned his neck up. It was incredibly humid. They may be heading into autumn, but the days continued to be stuffy and close. He wiped the sweat from his brow with the back of his hand. There was a window midway up the windmill, but the shutter was clamped firmly closed, allowing only thin spears of light inside. He strained to listen, but could hear nothing. Even the sound of the crows outside had been muted.

There was a faint musty smell, and he wondered when the last time the mill had been opened to the public. How long had the kidnapper planned to use this location? Had it required careful preparation, or was it a spur-of-the-moment decision?

With the only light coming from his phone, Garrick had to angle it to the side, dowsing himself in shadow as he gripped the ladder. It squeaked with each step as he ascended into the darkness.

His heart was in his mouth. Every sound amplified. Curiously, there was no sign of his migraine. He wondered if it was because he was running on a potent cocktail of adrenaline and fear? His hand stretched for a rung that wasn't there. He'd reached the top.

Garrick scanned the torch around. He was now above the hatch cut through the first-floor walkway. He tentatively pressed his foot on the floorboards and was reassured by the firmness of the wood. It looked reasonably new, not the rotting spars he'd feared. They'd obviously renovated the interior to the same high standard.

He involuntarily gasped as something brushed his face. He lashed out with the phone, knocking aside a thick cobweb that adhered to his fingers. It relentlessly stuck to his skin until he rubbed them hard against the wall to peel the grimy webs off. He swept the light across the platform, which circled a quarter way around the building and ended in another ladder leading higher up.

Blood pounded in his ears. He stopped to carefully search for anything he may have missed. So far, there was no sign that anybody had been here for weeks or even months. The thought that this might be some sort of elaborate red herring struck him, although he couldn't see why an egotistical kidnapper would do such a thing.

Garrick hurried to the next ladder and shone the light upwards into another dark void.

"Hello?"

His voice didn't carry far, as it was absorbed by the darkness. He'd called out more for his own peace of mind rather than expecting an answer. He was relieved not to have received one.

On the next ladder, he placed his foot on the second rung

and lifted himself slowly through the hatch, letting the torch lead the way. Another walkway curled around the wall. The roof closed to a pinnacle two floors above, with more gears and wooden shafts bolted to the ceiling. They connected to the windmill's rear fantail mechanism that entered through the roof.

He snapped the torch back down to the walkway. At the end was a large, crumpled canvas sheet, about the same size as ones used to cover hay bales. He had automatically dismissed it at first glance, but now it seemed out of place in the immaculately restored structure.

Garrick pulled himself through the hatch and onto the platform. Heights had never bothered him too much in the past, but with the dark void to one side, he felt a tremor of vertigo. Wood groaned with each step. There were more cobwebs up here in the rafters, and he had to bow his head to avoid them. After about twenty paces, he reached the canvas and knelt.

Now he was close, he could see that the sheet was covering something about the same size as him. He gripped the edge and slowly lifted it up, angling his phone underneath and bracing himself for what he would find...

7

The canvas sheet was old and brittle. As Garrick raised it, the harsh crinkling noise from the fabric made it sound as if the entire platform was about to give way. The light from his torch bobbed, making him aware that he was trembling.

Raising the sheet by just a foot revealed what he feared most. A hand. The skin was bluish-grey, and the nails cracked and dirty. The thin, long feminine fingers were clenched in a fist and free of any jewellery. Even without lifting the sheet further, he could see a red plastic tie had bit deep into the wrist and bound it to the nearest handrail support post.

He was too late.

Garrick felt sick. His breathing was shallow, a reaction from years of hanging around dead bodies. He had no wish to inhale the stench of decaying flesh, but it had the adverse effect of making him lightheaded. He braced himself for the horror of what lay beneath.

Still crouched, he resisted the urge to yank the sheet away

like some elaborate conjuring trick, just to get it over with. Instead, he slowly lifted the canvas to reveal the body.

Only there wasn't one.

The arm extended to the shoulder – where it had been brutally carved off. The severed limb lay across the walkway, and Garrick thought it was, if it was possible, more repulsive than finding a corpse. He was so shocked that he lost his balance and slipped onto his arse. The back of his hand holding his phone painfully clipped the handrail, and the phone dropped from his grasp – and with it his only source of light.

Garrick watched the light spiral down the central shaft and heard it strike the floor where it extinguished, plunging him into darkness at the top of the windmill in the company of a severed arm.

Chib returned minutes later, although it seemed like an eternity to Garrick. She retrieved his phone and joined him up on the platform to see his gruesome discovery. The warm atmosphere was cloying, and Garrick had no desire to stay inside much longer. He hurried back down the ladders, outside, and all the way to the entrance gate to catch his breath. He had been sweating so profusely that he took off his Barbour only to find his shirt beneath was heavily sweat stained around his chest and armpits.

Chib joined him as he leaned against the gate.

"I'll call this in," she said after casting a sympathetic eye over him.

That meant one of them had to stay at the scene to guard the evidence, while the other search for a phone signal again. Garrick looked at his phone. The screen was fractured from the fall, but it still worked. He could just see he had no signal. He nodded his head in the direction of Molly's bungalow.

"You go. Fetch your car too. I've done enough bloody walking for today."

Chib nodded and climbed over the gate.

"One thing, sir. I don't think that's Molly Meyers." Garrick's brow knitted in confusion. She pressed on. "The flesh looks far too deteriorated, considering when she went missing. And she's five-four? From the length of that arm, the victim was maybe half a foot taller."

She started jogging back the way they had come. Garrick had noticed the texture of the skin, but analytical reason had abandoned him as he sat there in the dark. It hadn't occurred to him it might not even be Molly, which raised *many* other questions.

He looked around the site. There was nobody around, yet he couldn't shake the feeling that he was being watched. He rubbed his head, massaging the growth the doctors had found under his skull. His private physician, Doctor Rajasekar had cautioned that he might experience hallucinations if it grew even a little larger, and there was no doubt he had recently experienced some discrepancies with reality. Was this new feeling just another side effect?

A loud cawing from behind made him flinch. He turned to look back at the windmill. Four large crows had perched on the roof. Part of him wondered if they were lured by the smell of decaying flesh from within.

The other part wondered if they were really there at all.

Davison's Mill became a bustling centre of activity once an army of police vehicles turned up. The lane leading up to the gate was crammed with police and forensic vehicles, while the forensic team had erected a white tent in the field so they could rapidly process the evidence they'd found.

DCs Liu and Wilkes had been drafted straight into door-to-door enquires at the impressive properties that surrounded the windmill, while uniformed officers spread out from Molly's bungalow, calling house-to-house, and combing through the hedges and grass verges for any clues. Although it was vital to keep Molly's name out of the enquiry, it was impossible for it not to spread across the village, especially since an incident response vehicle had been parked in her driveway for most of the afternoon.

Garrick stood in the forensic tent as the arm was retrieved and placed into a refrigerated box so it could be examined in the morgue. He was impatient for answers. The SOCO who retrieved it confirmed it was unlikely to be Molly Meyers, as the flesh had been dead for at least four days.

Back at the station, DC Lord had waited anxiously for the kidnapper to make contact and explain the rationale behind the sickening new find, but no such call came. That convinced Garrick that there was a clue right under their nose, and it was one that was quickly revealed.

"These look like hacking marks to me," said the SOCO, who was sweating heavily as the humidity in the tent increased. He indicated the end of the upper arm, which had been severed at the socket. "My money's on a meat cleaver."

The refrigerated box sat on top of a foldable metal table. A toolbox of various medical cutting equipment lay to the side. Three portable lamps positioned around the table added to the daytime heat.

"Was she alive at the time?" Garrick asked.

The man shrugged. "I can't tell that. But she has something in her hand."

Garrick frowned as the officer placed a scrunched-up ball of paper onto the metal tabletop. Garrick carefully unfolded it, using gentle pressure from his little finger to smooth away the creases.

It was a page torn out of a notebook, with words written in block capitals:

RAISE YOUR HANDS IN PRAISE,

FROM YOUR PAST TO THEIR FUTURE,

WITH GOOD ADVICE, THE PATH ONCE BEATEN WILL BE REVEALED AGAIN,

AND WITH IT THE MANY BECOME WHOLE.

"I guess that means something to you," the forensic officer said with a frown.

Garrick reread the words and was filled with a sinking feeling.

"No," he said. "It means absolutely bugger all."

Fanta and Sean returned from their door-to-door rounds, only to report nothing suspicious had been seen.

"The museum is run by volunteers," Fanta explained. "And for the last week, people have either been ill or on holiday. They had no visits booked, so it's been empty for the last five days."

"There are no security cameras here," Sean added. "And none of the houses around who have them saw nothing suspicious. We're gathering the footage, but nothing covers this section of road."

Garrick sighed. "Yet somebody broke in. Placed a severed arm and hid it to look like there was a body, then left without being noticed. They may have kidnapped Molly at the same time. Was this part of her usual run?"

Fanta shrugged. "Nobody we spoke to seems to remember her running this way."

Garrick tried to imagine her last moments here. "We know she left the office. Got in her car in the car park and drove here. From the time leaving the car park to the one on her run, she wouldn't have had much time to go anywhere else. She went straight out for a run to this place and never returned."

"She must've been meeting somebody," said Sean.

"Her kidnapper, it seems." Garrick's frown deepened. "Who then returned to her house to place her phone and Fitbit on the table for us to find."

"The GPS on her phone had been switched off after her run," said Fanta. "And the SIM was removed so it couldn't be tracked."

"Our kidnapper is very well prepared," muttered Garrick.

"He has a good grasp of security and police procedure," Chib added.

"Are you saying that the meeting here was simply to set up a clue for you to follow?" said Fanta. "That seems... overkill. If you pardon the expression."

"Which then leads to recovering a body part and *another* victim and this message." He offered them the crumpled note found in the hand. It was now encased in a transparent plastic evidence folder.

Sean took it, and after reading, he passed it to Fanta. "What does this mean?" he asked.

"It means somebody has far too much time on their hands," Garrick muttered. He glanced at his watch. It was now pushing 17:30 and so far, they had achieved little in tracking down Molly Meyers. "She drove home. The kidnapper met her here, then returned to her bungalow. I'm supposing that's when her car was taken."

"Kidnapped in her own car," Fanta said almost to herself.

"Like she said, this is a lot of effort to go through," said Sean, waving his hand towards the windmill. "Is it supposed to prove the kidnapper is ruthless and will harm Molly if we don't play ball? I still don't get why her?"

Garrick shook his head. That question was nagging him, too. He had no doubts the kidnapper and Amy Harman's murderer were one and the same. Even without evidence, it was clear. In his mind, the only real question was, *where* was the suspect? The *who* and *why* were self-explanatory, even if Chib thought his theory was pure fantasy. His musings were cut short when the forensic officer loped over, drinking heavily from a plastic water bottle.

"We got word through from the prints we took from our Cousin Itt—"

"Who?" asked Fanta.

The forensic guy looked at her in surprise. He held his hand out and waggled his fingers. "You know. Cousin Itt from the Addam's Family."

"No. Itt was the one covered in hair," said Sean.

"No, Itt was the hand! In fact, in the proper black and white show, it was a whole arm."

Fanta's frown deepened as Sean shook his head. "You're wrong. The hand was called The Thing."

"What the hell are you talking about?" Fanta snapped with more anger than Garrick had seen before. He was impressed; her outburst had defused his own. The last thing he needed right now was to be seen as losing control.

"A TV show..." mumbled the embarrassed SOCO. "Doesn't matter. My point was the fingerprints aren't logged anywhere. We ran her blood but couldn't find a match. So, she's a Jane Thing... um, Doe." He took another swing from the bottle as a distraction.

"At least that shows Molly is okay for now," said Sean.

"Only if she's happy being in the company of a madman

who hacked a woman's arm off," said Fanta sharply.

Sean remained tactfully silent, and the forensic officer spun around to head back to the tent. At that moment, Garrick's phone rang. It was DC Lord.

"Hey Guv, I'm still at Meyer's office. I found something you should look at."

Garrick watched as more forensic officers entered the windmill. Every square inch would be swabbed, brushed, and analysed for the smallest clue. Garrick had little faith they'd find anything. He wondered what Kane had found at Amy's murder scene, or had that been forensically wiped clean, too. That would be evidence he wouldn't be privy to, but if there was anything, it could prove relevant to his case. However, if Chib didn't think they were linked, he doubted DCI Kane would think that either.

"Can't you send it to me?" Garrick replied. "I'm going to be tied up here all evening."

Lord lowered his voice. "I really think you should see for yourself."

The words were weighted, although Garrick couldn't fathom why. "Okay, Harry. I'm on my way." He hung up. "Where's Chib?"

"She's at Molly's house, overseeing that and the door-to-door," said Sean.

"Tell her I'm going to see Harry at the Beeb." He took the plastic evidence wallet containing the crumpled paper and handed it to Sean. He'd taken a photo on his phone, but the words were already burned into his mind. "Forensics haven't been over this yet. See what you can find out. And get some handwriting analysis and find somebody who likes bloody Dan brown books and cryptic crosswords to see if they can make sense of it. Fanta, you're driving me."

8

G arrick would have preferred to drive to Tunbridge Wells alone and stew in his thoughts. He could've taken the moment to call Wendy in the vain hope of a private phone call, but DC Fanta Liu's presence prevented that. While requisitioning a police vehicle would've been an option, he was counting on Fanta's natural eagerness to loosen her tongue about her brief stint under DCI Kane's wing.

"Is everything alright?"

As an opening conversational gambit, Garrick knew it was awful, but the last week had frayed his poor social skills to near nonexistence.

Fanta glanced sidelong at him. As usual, she was speeding her Polo a little too fast for comfort. An empty can of Red Bull rattled around his feet, colliding with a discarded packet of Quavers.

"Fine, sir."

Garrick understood her well enough to know the use of formality meant she was far from relaxed. With her driving,

Garrick wasn't at ease, either. His left hand gripped the plastic grab handle near his head to brace himself as she took a turn in the narrow country road a little too fast.

"Oh. Just the way you snapped at that SOCO was a little unlike you."

"He was being an arsehole! I was thinking about what Molly must be going through. It's horrible."

"I don't want to imagine."

"I just thought it was because you were stuck back with me. I'm sure everybody was hoping working with DCI Kane might have provided a career bump. What with him being Met and all."

He was surprised to hear a snort of laughter from Fanta.

"You're not *jealous*, are you, sir? I never thought you'd fancy being all hoity-toity in the Metropolitan Police Force." She articulated the Met with a cod posh-English accent worthy of a Monty Python sketch. Against his mood and better judgement, Garrick chuckled.

"Don't you think I'm good enough to be a big city player?"

"You never struck me as the type."

Garrick forced himself not to chase that conversational rabbit; knowing Fanta, they could waste the entire journey in a rambling discussion that wouldn't lead anywhere. Fortunately, it seemed to have put her on the groove he wanted.

"I was left juggling the loose ends of the Will Sadler case, with the solicitors demanding all the evidence yesterday." The actor was facing a lot of sexual abuse charges, and the big Hollywood studio that had once supported him had turned a legion of top-priced American lawyers on him in a desperate bid to distance themselves from him. Arrogant, pushy lawyers from both sides always added to the stress of tying up a case.

Contrary to just about every police show Garrick had watched on TV, the moment when the troubled detective cracked a case, it didn't end there. Carting somebody off in handcuffs often wasn't even the midpoint in real life. The officers involved were responsible for presenting, filing, and delivering the evidence when it went to court. Although the case had happened at the start of the year, he and his team had spent months preparing paperwork for the trials of three guilty parties who had been involved in the John Howard case. While Kane was investigating the killer himself, Garrick's team had to tie up the surrounding crimes they'd uncovered. It was all very tedious, and they were due in court later that month. God only knew if all the evidence had been collated correctly. It was not unknown for cases with cast-iron evidence to be thrown out because a process hadn't been followed correctly.

"And then DCI Kane started placing everybody in silos." Fanta shook her head in annoyance. "How is anybody supposed to talk to anybody else?"

"Silos? What do you mean?" The unorthodox structure of Kane's investigation was already ringing alarm bells.

Fanta paused as she pulled onto a busy A-road – then sped up so quickly Garrick was pushed back in his seat. The engine roared like a beast. Fanta's voice never rose above a casual level.

"Kane's lot were looking into John Howard himself..."

"Jesus, Fanta, what have you done to your car?"

That got a smile from her. "Cool, isn't it? Sean pimped it up for me."

"You've turned into a bloody boy racer."

"Girl racer," she corrected. "Anyway, there was somebody dealing with his international movements who we weren't allowed to talk to. The girl from Staffordshire was nice. She was dealing with poor Eric's case."

Eric Wilson had been Garrick's old DS. When Garrick had been on compassionate leave because of his sister, Wilson had been seconded to an investigation in Staffordshire and replaced by Chib. Wilson had been killed in the line of duty, and it was later revealed that the investigation was linked to John Howard.

Fanta continued. "And that military woman was weird. So up herself. Didn't even get to know her name. And we had to..." she lapsed into silence and flicked a glance at Garrick.

He barely noticed. John Howard had been in the military and dishonourably discharged. He recalled being told something about crimes during the Falklands conflict, but was curious why there was a military liaison circling the investigation. His inner monologue finally caught up with what Fanta was hinting at.

"You guys had to look into me."

Fanta didn't look happy as she nodded. "No one knew about you and Dr Harman. Not that we should've," she quickly added. "And we'd all heard rumours about what happened to your Emelie. It wasn't difficult to link that with Howard's visit to the States."

"Did you feel you were close to cracking Amy's killer?"

"No. Kane was always telling us to keep an open mind." She suddenly lowered her voice. "Harry thinks it was somebody on the inside."

Garrick's blood ran cold at the thought there was somebody *within* the force who may have been responsible. The single comment suddenly unleashed his migraine, and he clutched his forehead with his right hand and squeezed to massage the pain. Fanta's eyes were on the road as she over-took a line of lorries, so she didn't notice.

"I mean, somebody who could access your house like that time and time again…"

She was on a stream of consciousness, unaware of what Garrick did and didn't know. Already he'd learned the killer had been in his house. The times his front door had been left open, the inconstancies with his surveillance camera, all incidents he had assumed were the fault of his own mental state…

"Even Sean thought it must be somebody in the know after he spoke to that Range Rover dealer. I didn't even know you could buy a car with bitcoin! To be honest, I didn't even know it was real money. Even the dealer thought it was sus when he was told to deliver the car to the middle of nowhere. And this was all the way back in January. Oh, by the way, it's still in the pound, and I'm still looking to trade this in if you don't want it." She shot him a hopeful glance. "It's registered in your name, so you *are* the legal owner…"

Garrick found his voice as she finally paused in her torrent.

"Other than to mess me up, why would *anybody* buy an expensive car and deliver it to my door? What've they got to gain?"

"It makes you look corrupt, is what it does."

That hadn't occurred to Garrick. Now several thoughts were branching in his mind. She'd said it was bought in January, when Howard was still, officially, alive. Just as he was killing the asylum seekers, and framing several people around him, had he originally intended Garrick to be one of his scapegoats? Obviously, Howard dying in his own shop would've derailed his plans, but *somebody* had continued them – delivering the car and killing Amy Harman. Posting an empty envelope from America that had been sealed by his sister, or more accurately, the sealing gum contained traces of her DNA. This all involved a second participant. For Garrick, that felt too complicated for a man like John Howard. Then again, he obviously didn't know the man as well as he thought he did.

He tried to pull his mind back to see the bigger picture. If Howard was somehow still alive, delivering the car just before murdering Garrick's psychologist in his own home would certainly make him seem like a distinguished, but corrupt copper who'd turned on the young doctor. It was a story the media would certainly jump on. But not Molly Meyers. She would've surely seen through such a thinly veiled set-up. Was that why she was kidnapped?

He circled back to his original thought that she'd been abducted to make a splash across the media. The severed arm added to the fantastical, making it more front-page worthy...

And harder to keep quiet.

Everything Howard or his accomplice had done was carefully choreographed. Planned many months in advance. Every angle appeared to have been covered. They would have known that an active kidnapping would have been kept from the press, especially if it concerned one of their own. By adding another victim, the police would have their hands full trying to stop leaks. It reminded Garrick of an old spy mantra he'd read in a book: sow discord and constantly attack with misinformation. That left your opponent off-balance. It felt like the sort of thing a military man would do.

"You said there was a woman from the Staffordshire force down here?"

"She was working with Eric," she said softly.

With events galloping along over the last few months, he'd ignored the fact Sean, Harry, and Fanta had worked a little with his old DS Eric Wilson. At the time, he'd been slightly surprised none of them had attended the funeral, but in retrospect, they were in the middle of a murder case, although DCI Kane had attended. He now suspected Oliver Kane may have warned the others off. Garrick thought Kane had been searching for somebody at the funeral itself.

"She was chatty," Fanta said. "She was working with Sean when he was killed. That was when they discovered more of those lamps were being shipped out."

Once again, Garrick felt the floodgates of information open. Information that he'd been deliberately shielded from. He had dozens of questions but feared that any one of them would remind Fanta that she wasn't supposed to divulge anything to him about Kane's investigations. She clearly thought he knew it all already.

The lamps John Howard made were macabre creations with shades made from the skins of his victims. Kane had told them they'd found more, including books bound in human skin, but he shied away from the details. Now Eric Wilson had been involved with the John Howard investigation even *before* Garrick had uncovered it. That forced him to do some mental chronological ballet.

The first victim he and Eric had discovered was Galina, an Iranian immigrant who'd had a patch of back skin removed. It was the same time Garrick had been told about his sister's murder and he'd been taken off the case.

The timing of the two events now resonated with meaning for him.

When he'd returned to work, Eric had been seconded to Staffordshire. Somebody must have linked Galina's skin removal with the lamps being shipped up north. Although no connection with Howard had yet to be made, Garrick now wondered why Drury hadn't pointed out the nature of his ex-DS's secondment.

Months later, Kane had shown him an out-building on a farm that John Howard had used to butcher victims. But the three girls that he knew Howard had killed had all sported increasingly confident signs of being skinned. He'd naturally assumed Howard was gaining confidence in his grizzly craft, but if he'd been doing it for months before, then that suggested either Howard himself had been learning the art from *somebody else*, or he had a *protégé*.

Either way, it wasn't a big leap to assume either would carry out the wishes of their deranged friend.

The pain in Garrick's head felt as if he'd been physically struck. He needed to see his doctor and had another important MRI scan booked in a couple of days' time. But with Molly missing and every second precious, he'd have to postpone it. His own health would once again come second to work. It would probably kill him... if Fanta's driving didn't do it first.

She pounded her horn.

"You moron! Learn to drive!" she yelled as she cut up a huge fourteen-wheel French lorry in order to make the turn-off she'd been about to overshoot.

9

There was a lot less space in the BBC Tunbridge Wells studios than Garrick had expected. With the radio and small television studios below, he was greeted by a production assistant who couldn't have been over twenty and sporting acne blotches that bordered on physical assault. They went to the first floor and into a cramped office where two members of the production team attempted to go about their business, while DC Harry Lord sat at a computer, reading through emails.

Harry sipped from a mug of coffee, an essential prop he found wherever he went, and waved Garrick and Fanta over.

"Take a seat, if you can find one."

With the hot desk principle, space was at a premium. The few desks available with computer terminals were devoid of paperwork or any of the usual office cluttering. It was also scarce on seats. Fanta took the only free chair and was about to sit until she caught Garrick's eye.

"Here you go, sir." She rolled the seat next to him.

Garrick sat in it and was alarmed by the creak from the metal frame as it took his weight.

Harry pointed to the emails on-screen. "This is Molly's inbox. Everything's stored on the server. Journalists don't have their own computers."

"These are her work emails, not her personal ones?" Fanta asked as she leaned between the two of them.

"Correct. I can see here she's forwarded a lot of messages to her personal Gmail address, but I can't access them."

"We found her phone at her house," Garrick said. "But all her emails and log-on details had been erased."

"I found several that... well, you judge for yourself." He looked up at the two staffers at their desks and waved his hand for attention. "Excuse me! Can we have a bit of privacy for ten minutes?"

Garrick got the impression DC Lord had prearranged their departure as they quickly locked the screen on their work terminals, took their phones and left the office, quietly closing the door behind them.

"Right," said Harry, loudly cracking his knuckles.

Fanta winced. "Do you have to do that?"

Garrick saw Harry was about to reply, so quickly cut in. "What did you find?"

Wordlessly, Harry double clicked an email and angled the monitor so Garrick could read it more easily.

The brief introduction established a casual rapport between Molly and her correspondent as she nudged for information. Then it continued straight into the meat of the message:

I can confirm the file you want exists, but I can't access it, never mind release it, as it's marked Official-Sensitive and is covered under the Official Secrets Act. An MP enquiry into the

offenses was conducted on August 3ʳᵈ, 1982. Predictably, the find-
ings have been kept classified, but Second Lieutenant John Howard
was dishonourably discharged immediately afterwards. Unusu-
ally, there was no official reason announced, although it came with
all the usual penalties, pension rescinded, etc.

Garrick had assumed Molly was researching her story back in February when the incident with John Howard occurred, but checking the date on the email showed it was sent a week ago. Of course, he should've known that she hadn't even crossed paths with him before the summer. It was his next case that had helped propel her to the lofty heights of the BBC. "Why was Molly trying to reopen this story?"

"Maybe she got wind of Kane's investigation?" Harry suggested.

"But she's particularly focusing on his war record," said Fanta, casting a meaningful look at Harry.

Harry didn't meet her gaze. He just nodded at the screen. "Carry on reading."

Garrick looked at the sender's email address before he did. *Sfoss41@aol.com* address didn't give too much away.

I can't give you anything on the record, but there is a lot of
disturbing detail in that report that some would call torture, but it
reads so much more than that. Corporal Evans and Corporal
Ryman, who served in his unit, were also discharged. I don't know
what happened to Ryman, but the file was amended two years
later to note Evans had suffered psychologically after the war and
had committed suicide.

The entire investigation was conducted by the Military Police,
but when the three accused returned to the UK, the Met monitored
them for a period of three years before closing the case.

"Monitored," intoned Garrick. "They were keeping these three under surveillance. What the hell did they do out there?" Some light was shed on his question as he continued scrolling down.

Like I said, I can't give you details. Maybe you can push some buttons at the Met. What I want to tell you – and off the record – is that you were right in your reference to the term 'Murder Club'. It sounds like a bad 80s movie, but I think it may be relevant to your story.

Best of luck,

S. Foss

Garrick leaned thoughtfully back in his chair. Why was Molly Meyers chasing this story now, and what exactly had she stumbled across? John Howard's military service, combined with Fanta's revelation that there was a military liaison helping DCI Kane out, confirmed there was a much larger investigation happening under his nose. One that he'd help uncovered and was now intrinsically connected to.

"We should be tracking down these Foss and Ryan characters," Harry said, breaking Garrick out of his daydream.

"Yes. Of course," Garrick's head swam, and he found it difficult to focus on a course of action. Was he tired or overwhelmed? "I keep going back to why she was looking into this now. It's feeling like she may have poked a stick into a hornet's nest."

Harry scrolled to another email. "Yeah... and with that in mind..." he doubled-clicked a message and indicated Garrick should read it.

It was one line that made Garrick's blood run cold.

D Garrick. Medical files attached.

With shaking hands, he opened the attachments. The first was the official report Dr Harman had submitted, that assessed his psychological condition. He had never seen it, but Drury had been pleased with the results. He quickly scanned through it, noting references to the trauma of losing his sister and the strength of his character.

Harry shifted uncomfortably. "There are a few emails there from Flora PD. She was asking for information about what happened to Emilie."

"What did they tell her?" Garrick's throat was dry, so the words came out almost as a croak.

"They stonewalled her pretty good and said the case has now been handed over to the FBI."

Garrick turned so sharply to DC Lord that he caused both Harry and Fanta to flinch.

"It's now a Federal case?" From the little Garrick knew about the American law enforcement system, that meant the investigation was no longer a 'local' Illinois State case, but it had jumped state lines. What had they discovered?

Garrick turned back to the monitor and opened the second attachment. It was an MRI scan. He didn't have to read the notes on the side of the image to know he was looking at the tumour in his own head.

He leaned back in his seat and looked at Harry and Fanta. DC Liu was still reading the information, so it took a couple of seconds for her to process what she was seeing.

"That's you?" she said in confusion. "What happened to your head?"

"It's a tumour, DC Liu."

She mouthed the words *oh shit*, but kept quiet. Harry looked at him with sad, bloodhound eyes.

"And you listened to me whining about a broken leg and a few busted up bones. Sorry, sir."

"Noble battle scars for doing the right thing, Harry," Garrick said quietly. He pointed at the screen. "This is God's punishment for me being a copper."

"How long do you have left?" Fanta looked almost in tears.

Garrick gave her a double take. "I'm not bloody down and out just yet! It could be benign. They're monitoring it. It doesn't mean I'm going to keel over and die while I'm on the crapper!"

Fanta's cheeks burned deep red with embarrassment. "I didn't mean—"

"And nobody knows about this. Not even Drury. There's nothing *to know* right now." Garrick felt a trace of panic. He doubted Drury would take him off the case in the middle of a time sensitive kidnapping, but after that... it could spell the end of his career. He was also aware he'd made it sound as if he expected the other two to conceal evidence during a case; an accusation that could end their careers, too.

"How did she get this?"

"It was sent from Tunbridge Wells Hospital," said Harry. "I thought you should see it before anybody else." He looked guiltily at Fanta.

"But how?" Garrick pressed. "Our Molly is turning out to be a better journalist that I ever suspected."

Once more, the feeling that this was another round in a game solely designed to discredit him, rose its ugly head. Was somebody feeding Molly information and perhaps underestimating her investigational instincts as he had done? Was he being set up? According to the email date stamps, it had arrived two days before the military one. Had Molly turned on the hand that was feeding her the scoop? After all, he liked to think she had some loyalty towards him after all he'd done for her. But if so, why hadn't she come to him directly?

"I'll look into why the hospital sent it," Harry said with the implication he'd be discreet.

"It looks like Molly's big story was all about you," said Fanta as she leaned forward and seized the mouse to scroll through the emails. "Look at the chronology. These earlier ones are about your sister. Then John Howard. And then your personal stuff. She was following a trail. Or being fed it."

Garrick ran both hands across his face and sighed. "I don't know what to think."

"I do," said Fanta firmly. "I saw enough with Kane's unit to know he is convinced that John Howard killed your sister. These emails prove he's been a psychopath ever since the Falklands War. And somebody is very pissed off with you for killing him. If you want this detective's deduction," she indicated herself with her thumb, "I think Molly got in the way of a revenge attack on you."

Garrick and Harry exchanged a look. Harry's eyebrows shot up, and he nodded.

"Against all odds, and I don't believe I'm saying this, but I think she's right. Somebody isn't happy."

Garrick opened the Foss email again and quickly reread it. "We need to find Foss and Ryman as fast as possible." And he should really corner DCI Kane and drill him for information. The only problem was, if Kane was willing to share anything, then he would've done so by now. Which raised another question – why hadn't he? Who did it benefit by keeping Garrick out of the loop?

Before he could overthink it, a new email arrived in Molly's inbox. The subject line made his heart pound: *FAO David Garrick.*

He quickly opened it. There were just two words:

Tick-tock...

Attached was a photo of Molly. It looked to be taken in the same place as before, except her head was now slumped to the right. A knife blade entered the image from the left-hand side and pressed against her throat, drawing a vivid line of blood.

That was not what worried Garrick the most. It was the fact the email had been sent to Molly's own mailbox the very moment they had been looking through it.

He looked around the empty room, wondering just how the kidnapper knew what they were doing...

10

G arrick couldn't go home, both physically and emotionally. While the bloodied evidence from the killing had been removed from his house, Superintendent Drury didn't want Garrick returning without twenty-four-hour protection, which she was not willing to authorise. Having one copper watch his hotel was one thing, and Garrick had discreetly sent them packing days ago.

Not that Garrick particularly wanted to return home. He doubted he'd ever want to return there after what happened. He still had another seventeen years on his mortgage, but was prepared to take a financial hit just to get rid of the place. In all the years he'd lived there, he'd barely made a dint personalising it. He had forged no particularly fond memories. It'd just been a house that he lived in.

And now it would forever be the house where Amy Harman had been murdered.

The thought of returning to his hotel brought with it a feeling of wasted time. He needed to rest, and his team was already fatigued, yet there was little to do but wait for information to come in. However, he was painfully aware that it was time that he couldn't get back. Time Molly Meyers was rapidly running out of. Instead, he headed back to the station and sat in front of the evidence wall. He planned to sleep there until the case was concluded.

His team seemed to think along the same lines. DC Liu had returned with him, followed thirty minutes later by Harry, who'd made a detour and arrived with a party-sized box of Dunkin' Donuts, coffees, and a matcha tea for his boss.

Chib and Sean turned up within minutes of each other, having left the SOCO team wrapping up the huge search in Stelling Minnis. Chib had returned home to get changed and arrived with three blankets and two pillows.

"We've all got to catch some shut-eye," she said to Garrick as she helped herself to a chocolate cream doughnut.

As the team assembled around him and delivered updates, Garrick didn't move from his seat, where he was slumped like a surly teenager, staring at the evidence wall. He'd printed out an enlarged photo of the note found in the mutilated hand.

RAISE YOUR HANDS IN PRAISE,

FROM YOUR PAST TO THEIR FUTURE,

WITH GOOD ADVICE, THE PATH ONCE BEATEN WILL BE REVEALED AGAIN,

AND WITH IT THE MANY BECOME WHOLE.

The line *from your past to their future* rankled. He knew it was written specifically for him, but the meaning continued to elude him.

"The neighbour saw Molly arrive home at about 18:50," said Chib. "She said she looked hassled, but then again, that wasn't anything new. And she was putting her bins out about five minutes later when she saw Molly go out for a run. With the nights closing in, it was getting dark. A few minutes later, somebody further down her street thinks he saw Molly's car leave but didn't pay any attention to the driver."

"A few minutes?" said Garrick. "There's no way she could have run there and back so quickly."

Chib nodded. "Which suggests her kidnapper took her car shortly after she left the house, then intercepted her in it."

"Mol went straight home to change," said Harry, noisily slurping his latte. "So she already knew she had a rendezvous."

He told everybody about the emails they had found on the BBC server, and Molly's investigation into John Howard. Fanta placed the names Ryman and Foss on the evidence wall. Garrick was silently thankful that Harry didn't go into any details about exactly *what* Molly had uncovered concerning Garrick's medical condition.

Chib looked thoughtful as she helped herself to a strawberry sprinkle.

"Molly starts looking into a story about your sister." She looked sidelong at Garrick. "Which leads her to the Flora police investigation and the inevitable John Howard connection."

"So it seems," said Garrick, casting his hand in the air. None of the threads were connecting into anything coherent for him. "And that pissed somebody off enough to kidnap her."

"A kidnapper that we now have every reason to assume is linked to Amy's death," said Chib.

Garrick wagged a finger at the new names on the evidence wall. "And these two are our gateway into that." He fixed Chib with an unblinking look. "I need to know where DCI Kane's investigation is regarding them." Chib shifted uncomfortably in her seat. "I know you lot were examining Amy's connection with me. And that's fine. That's your job. I've got nothing to hide." He knew that was a lie, but after flicking a look at Fanta, he pressed on. "And I know there is a military police liaison who has been brought in. Who is she?"

Chib shook her head. "DCI Kane compartmentalised every strand of that investigation. None of us were told the full scope of it."

"Which is a rotten way to conduct police work, wouldn't you say?"

Harry snorted. "None of us were impressed with it. I felt it was us versus them when it came to the crunch. Kane would get all excited about a lead and bugger off for a day or two. When he came back, nothing relevant was ever channelled to us."

Despite his fatigue, Garrick was feeling volcanic. Kane was treating him and his team with disdain. Worse, he was probably withholding evidence that could help them track down Molly Meyers.

"So we have a possible reason for kidnapping Molly," said Sean, "but without a ransom, we don't have an endgame. Why do any of this? If the goal is to humiliate Garrick, I mean, the Guv, sorry sir..." Garrick waved the *faux pas* aside. He really didn't care. "There are a lot of easier ways to do it."

Garrick had considered the act of simply releasing his medical records could have screwed up his career. But this was something John Howard had crafted and put into action long before Garrick had been diagnosed. This was a much deeper level of hatred, or sheer evil, that was beyond him.

Garrick stared thoughtfully at the ceiling. "The email

from Foss mentions something called the 'Murder Club'. What is that?"

"I did a little search on that," said Fanta. "Nothing was flagged up. On HOLMES, on the internet. Chatrooms. Nothing."

"Oh, I received the blackout information from Molly's phone provider. I got it here." Fanta put up a map of the South East and zoomed in on Kent. There were plenty of black patches scattered across the county, including Molly's home village of Stelling Minnis. "Without a starting point and some timings, it's not very much use right now."

Garrick sighed. "Where did we get on Amy Harman's movements prior to her death?" he asked. Chib glanced at the others. Garrick sighed. "Come on. We all think there's a connection. I'm not asking you to steal the file from Kane's investigation. Just share what was discovered."

For a moment, he thought nobody was going to speak up. Then Fanta broke the silence.

"She was last seen by her secretary the evening she was killed." Fanta did a fine job of not hesitating or inflecting the wrong words. She delivered the statement as if Garrick had nothing to do with the case. "At 6 pm, she left her office here in Maidstone. Went to her car and drove home, leaving the secretary to lock up. All we uncovered at the time was that she never made it home."

Garrick frowned. "To know where she parked, where she lived, all takes a little more effort than simply stalking her at work. What about her other patients?"

"She had fourteen active ones and, I think it was something like twenty-six that were in various states of being closed." Fanta bobbed her head, indicating she wasn't certain of the actual figure. "We interviewed them all. Four of them had violent pasts, but all of them had alibis."

"What about her car? Where was it found?" Something Kane had told him was vying for attention.

Fanta summarised from the report in front of her. "In a ditch on a B-road three miles from your house. It had been pushed in, and an attempt had been made to cover it over."

"Just like Emelie," he breathed.

"What?"

"You've read the Flora police report on my sister. Her DNA was found in a car that was dumped in a ditch. The indication was she was alive beyond the ranch killings. There were traces of other victims, too. It's a bit of a parallel."

"Or a copycat," said DC Wilkes. "You get a lot of that in the States."

After a moment's thoughtful silence, Fanta resumed summing up Dr Harman's situation. "After she left the office, there was no sign of her until approximately 11:36, when you found her. Her time of death had been placed at nine. So that's five and a half hours of missing time, and midway through she was killed. Most of the wounds on her were probably inflicted at the scene." Fanta's voice finally broke with emotion, but she quickly rallied herself. "There was some bruising indicating she had been gagged and her hands and feet tied. But that's all."

Chib cleared her throat. "Sir, I know there are many parallels here, but we're not trying to solve Dr Harman's case."

Garrick shot her a dark look, then stood up and prowled the room. While the others were slumped in seats and visibly exhausted, he felt the need to keep moving to prevent his anger from building. He hoped DCI Kane didn't make an appearance because he was sure he'd lunge for the man.

"At some point, Amy's killer intercepted her before she reached home. Somewhere so off the beaten track she could be gagged, bound, and her car taken, with nobody seeing."

"I think we all agree there is a connection," said Chib in a firmer tone. "But we are lacking proof and veering on chasing the wrong case. Molly is missing. Not Doctor Harman. The Super made it very clear what our priorities are."

Garrick saw everybody tense. His DS had openly challenged him in a case that was proving to be deeply personal. He felt a flicker of respect for her.

"The voice of reason, as ever, Chib. Quite right." He pretended not to notice everybody visibly relax. "But we can't side-line the case completely. I want you to keep it front and centre. Keep drawing parallels. If our kidnapper and killer are one and the same, then we just need to look for a common MO between them. Two pieces of disparate evidence from separate cases might just suddenly be what we've been missing."

He focused on an image of Volkswagen Beetle that had been hung to represent Molly's missing car.

"Somebody knew Amy's movements exceptionally well. I bet they knew Molly's, too. Were there any people working at their offices, I mean maintenance and such?"

Fanta shook her head. "Dr Harman's receptionist said the only person to come in fixed their systems a few days earlier. Their phone and computer network had been buggy for days."

A distant memory scratched Garrick for attention. It was something minor; something that had irked him... but he just couldn't bring it to the fore. Then it struck him.

"Did anyone track down the repairman?"

Fanta shrugged. "I'm not sure. It doesn't seem like they have."

"I made a call to her office, but the receptionist said she never received it. I thought that I was the one getting confused and hadn't made it after all. What if somebody had access to her systems? They could access my patient records and delete voice messages from me."

"That's a shot in the dark," said Chib.

"We're in the dark on this whole case. Ask forensics to run a check on Molly's computer at the BBC and Harman's work machine."

Chib frowned. "What exactly are we checking for?"

"A virus, malware, whatever. Specifically, look for the same problems on each." He forced a smile. "Humour me, Chib."

She signed, which triggered a yawn. "OK, I will."

As the hours drew on, activity inevitably slowed to a crawl. Garrick repeatedly told Fanta and Sean to go home, but they resolutely stayed at their desks until they could no longer fight sleep. Sean tilted his chair back and was asleep with his feet on the desk. Fanta wrapped herself in one of Chib's blankets and slept with her head cradled on her desk. Garrick didn't blame them for wanting to stay, but conversely, tired detectives were of no use to him, especially as the last few hours had generated no new leads. Harry and Chib had fielded SOCO reports which showed no signs of forced entry into Molly's house, and they'd found so much DNA in the windmill that it was going to be time-consuming to log and eliminate the museum staff. Garrick doubted the kidnapper would have left any of it. Even more frustrating was the fact that nobody knew who the arm belonged to. Garrick was certain it wasn't a random addition. It was a clue; just one he didn't understand.

It was just past midnight when Chib sauntered off for coffee and an extremely long bathroom break, over which he thought it best not to query. Harry was nodding off at his desk. Every time his chin hit his chest, he'd jolt awake and pretend that nothing had happened. Garrick stared at the words that had been clutched in the disembodied hand. His mind was fudge, unable to connect any of the phrases together. He had to sleep but was certain that he'd be awake throughout the night, fretting that no progress had been made and time was running out.

However, that didn't fit in how he saw the kidnapper's plan unfolding. Why go to all the lengths that had been made just to impose an arbitrary time limit with some abstract clues that he couldn't solve. Even if the others were right, and the culprit was enacting a dead man's plan, it was still a plan dependent on *him*. He suspected that no matter how slow he was in solving the case, the kidnapper would follow his pace.

Of course, if he was wrong, Molly would die because of him. And that wasn't a risk he was willing to take.

He had thought 'Raise your hands in praise' was somehow a reference to the severed arm and hand, but the plural had thrown him off that line of reasoning. Whose limb was it? He drew up the ongoing forensic report. It concluded that it was several months old and molecular damage revealed that it had been stored in a deep freeze. It could have come from anybody...

He leaned forward in his seat. Whatever fatigued line of perception he'd crossed, he was thinking about himself, that he was central to the unfolding events. Everything appeared to be arranged with such precision and malice that using a random victim, somebody without a link, no matter how symbolic, seemed to border on incompetence.

So it was nobody he knew.

But what if it was somebody connected tangentially to his past?

"Harry?"

Harry Lord's eyes flicked open. "Mmm?"

"We didn't have any matches on that severed arm, did we?"

"Nothing on any database here." Harry yawned and stretched his arms. The muscles in his shoulder blades clicked.

"How about the States?" Harry looked at him in some confusion. "Contact Flora PD, or whoever we have at the FBI. Ask them to run DNA comparables on any of the other victims at the ranch where Emelie was killed."

Harry's bleary expression was replaced with surprise.

"How could that be possible?"

Garrick bobbed his head thoughtfully. Fatigue was replaced by his mind revving on all cylinders.

"*'From your past to their future'*. What if that's telling me I need to look at events leading to this moment..." He trailed off as another notion struck him. "Oh, shit..."

"What?" Harry stood up and joined Garrick at the evidence wall. He followed his gaze to the printed message. "What am I missing?"

"You're missing nothing, mate." Garrick ran his fingers across the message. "I'm the blind one. Of course! He wants me to look into my past. What led me to reveal John's crimes?"

"Galina, Jamal, and Sihana," said Harry as he searched for the Flora PD contacts. None of the team would forget the names of the three young immigrants who John Howard had butchered.

"*Raise your hands in praise*... just like you do in church. Our Lady of Good Counsel was the Roman Catholic church in Hythe. Good counsel... good advice..."

"Shit..."

"We need to get down there straight away."

11

Had Garrick been left to his own devices, he may have driven his car straight through the church's front doors to gain access. DS Okon was her usual sensible self and made sure they had all the correct permissions to get access. That wasted almost two hours, and by the time they'd reached the church, it was close to four in the morning.

Father McConnell was a barrel of a man, with a bass-laden voice to match. After multiple attempts to telephone him, it had taken a uniformed police visit in the dead of night to wake him. Despite claiming to be a man of the cloth, he'd been unable to disguise his annoyance at being woken up. His temper was compounded by the fact he'd been ill for several months and, after a recent operation, was recovering from colon cancer. Outwardly, at least he seemed to still be a fit man.

He found his spare set of keys and joined Garrick and Harry at the red-bricked Church of Our Lady of Good Counsel in Hythe. Every step across the small car park at the back, he grumbled. He muttered as he jangled the bunch of keys in the door and, after jiggling it back and forth, it found the bite and unlocked. He opened the door and took a faltering step inside. Garrick almost walked into him as the priest stopped.

"What's the matter?"

"The alarm's not on. That lad's forgotten again!" Father McConnell's hand patted the wall until he found the light switch. Garrick heard a couple of clicks, then a sigh. "Blinking lights are out, too."

"Excuse me," said Garrick as he shoved past the priest. He'd had the presence of mind to leave the station with a hand-lamp and clicked the chunky power button on. The harsh white beam, more suited to illuminate roads and warn traffic to slow down, cut across the lines of pews. Harry joined him, armed with another lamp.

The curved wooden ceiling beams gave the illusion that they stood inside a giant ribcage. Shadows danced across the bright yellow walls and the bare white stone altar. A golden cross hung from the ceiling, catching the lights as the beams scanned the darkness. They both took a step down the aisle, their footsteps echoing in the stillness. The shifting shadows made the saintly stone figures either side of the altar appear to hunch and writhe in anticipation. Garrick struggled to find anything peaceful or reassuring in the dark church. It felt more like stepping into a nightmare.

Father McConnell and the uniformed officers who had escorted him remained at the entrance as DCI Garrick and DC Lord slowly walked further inside. Like the rhythmic swaying of a metronome, their light beams swept along the pews to the left and right.

Despite the eerie atmosphere, Garrick was beginning to

fear that this was a red herring, or worse, a complete blunder on his behalf, fuelled by tired, muddy thinking.

Then the beam fell on a bare foot poking from the shadows of a pew to Garrick's left. He stopped so suddenly that Harry, who was looking at the other side, shouldered him. Harry was about to mumble an apology when he saw what lay at the end of Garrick's beam. Swinging his own light cast the remaining shadows away and revealed an entire naked leg that had been hacked off just under the thigh. Congealed blood had pooled around the stump to form a gruesome halo.

Pre-dawn light struggled through the layer of grey clouds above Hythe and offered just enough illumination for the SOCO team to cordon off the church grounds. Fortunately, the church was at the corner of two quiet roads, one side of which was a row of garages. At such an unsociable hour, it had taken just over two hours for the first members of the team to assemble. By now, the adrenaline kick of finding the severed limb had peaked, and both Garrick and Harry were crashing. They had been awake for almost twenty-four hours and could not push themselves any further.

Chib, Fanta, and Sean arrived to take over the operation. They'd stayed behind at the station, slumbering as Garrick and Harry sneaked out in the dead of night. The officers who had brought Father McConnell to the church would take Harry and Garrick back to their respective homes and hotel, but first Garrick had to endure the forensic team's fiercely jovial and energetic auburn-haired lead investigator as she walked out of the church and headed straight for him with a wide smile.

"I was so stoked when I heard this was one of yours, Dave," she bawled in an Australian accent that was far too loud for the time of morning. "I missed the windmill but heard about it when I was on a B&E. It's so bloody boring just sweepin' for prints. I know when it's you, things get a bit more interestin'!"

Garrick could barely keep his eyes open. "Happy to entertain you, Zoe." The fact he could remember her name was a miracle. He often had trouble when he wasn't tired.

"Well, it's a bloke, but I reckon you got that from the hairy leg."

Garrick had been too tired to notice. Zoe pressed on.

"And I reckon it was lobbed off around nine, ten hours before you found it. My lads'll narrow that down. It was sawn off," she added as an afterthought.

"Was he still alive?" Harry asked in a quiet voice.

"Can't tell, but with that amount of blood, I'd say if not, then recently dead. And he wasn't killed here. That happened someplace else. Which makes sense. You don't wanna be haulin' a corpse around if you're just using a leg."

Garrick knew this was critical information, but his mind refused to process it. He headed for the police car.

"DS Okon's in charge. I'm dead on my feet, Zoe." He instantly regretted his phrasing. He opened the car's rear door and hesitated before climbing in. "Keep an eye out for any message."

"What sort of message?"

"A note. A..." he couldn't think of anything else. "The killer is leaving a trail. No matter how cryptic, he'll have left something to point the way."

He didn't catch Zoe's parting words. He just gave a small wave of the hand in farewell and sat in the car. Within seconds, he was fast asleep.

After just over six hours sleep, Garrick felt supercharged

when he awoke in his hotel room. The stale smell was becoming noticeable even to him, so he cracked the window open a little and put his rubbish bin out in the hallway. Then he remembered putting his phone on silent shortly before crashing on the bed. He checked it to find he'd missed dozens of emails. There were far too many to assemble the status of the case quickly and coherently, so he called Chib for a swift update. Walking to the station, he noticed a text from Wendy. He vowed that no matter what, he'd make time for her today. He just didn't even have time right now to click on her message to read it.

He called Chib as he walked.

"Forensics ID'd the body," she said with almost no preamble. "Father Cillian Byrne."

Garrick stopped in his tracks. The priest had helped to unlock the John Howard case, even if it had been via a frustratingly circuitous route.

"He'd taken over while Father McConnell was recovering, and he hadn't been seen since mass the previous day. Parishioners said the church was closed yesterday with a note on the door saying it was because of illness."

Garrick remembered Cillian being a thin man, but not one so feeble that he couldn't defend himself. It also marked the first male victim. A shift in operation, if John Howard had somehow risen from the grave, and a definite change of tact for someone carrying out a dead man's wishes.

"Next of kin have been notified, and DC Wilkes is down at his house with forensics. There's no sign of forced entry."

"This is a blatant revenge attack," said Garrick. "Father Cillian helped us solve the case." The reality was that he'd pointed the way to Stan Fielding's farm. Fielding was a racist and ultimately arrested for drug trafficking, but he was also being set up for John Howard for the murders of the immigrants. John Howard had *wanted* Stan Fielding to be arrested. It had been blind luck Garrick had later uncovered his friend's secret passion.

"And Molly was trying to expose it all," Chib added. "It's not about *you*, sir. It's all about John Howard. Although..." She trailed off.

"What is it, Chib?"

"We've identified the other victim." She waited for a prompt, but Garrick was too tense to react. She eventually continued. "Harry Lord put a request in with Flora PD last night to identify the severed arm. They came pack with a match: Ye-Jun Joh. She was one of the victims found at the ranch when your sister was..." again she trailed off.

Fragments of memory surfaced. Something about there being several other dismembered victims. One of them was a Korean student who'd gone missing a fortnight earlier.

"That settles it," Garrick said quietly. "It's all connected, for sure. Either John Howard is alive and well and doing his best Jack the Ripper around Kent, or somebody is fulfilling this whole elaborate scheme for him. I don't know which is worse. The psychopath, or the psychopath's apprentice."

The words written on the note were burned into his mind. Now they were starting to make sense. Especially the latter lines:

WITH GOOD ADVICE, THE PATH ONCE BEATEN WILL BE REVEALED AGAIN,

AND WITH IT THE MANY BECOME WHOLE.

The path once beaten... that had to refer to the John Howard case. And now it was being revealed once more. It was the final line that chilled him.

"*And with it many become whole*, Chib. Different parts of different victims all trying to point to some conclusion."

"That begs the question of how many more victims the killer's planning to make."

"Something tells me that Molly Meyers is going to be the last one." *Or it's going to be me*, Garrick mentally added.

"I'll get Wilkes to draw up a list of all the people interviewed in the original case. Uniform can check up on them."

"Do it." Garrick didn't feel it was the right thing to do, but in the absence of any proper direction, he couldn't afford for the team not to explore every nook and cranny. The killer's plan was far from spur-of-the-moment. "How did that arm get over here?"

"John Howard had a dark shipping network," Chib pointed out.

"Which I'm guessing DCI Kane knows about." The silence on the line felt awkward. "Come on, Chib, I know you're not supposed to talk about his cases, but we have crossover here." After another pause, he snapped. "Fine! I'll call him myself."

Chib smoothly shifted the conversation. "Zoe's team worked all morning on piecing together every bit of information they had on Father Cillian. From the estimated time his leg was amputated to when it was found, her team has created a *killing circle*."

"What the hell is that?"

"They've zoned out just how far away the amputation needed to occur in order for the limb to be left in the condition it was."

"That's a really smart idea."

"She emailed it to you."

"Did she find any other message?"

"No. Not yet. What time will you be in the office?"

"I'm not sure." Since he'd heard the latest victim was Father Cillian, he had stood in the street and debated what to do. As they continued talking, he had doubled-back to his hotel and reached his car. He said goodbye to Chib and climbed inside. The Land Rover started on the second attempt. He was no longer going back to the station. His Detective Sergeant was paying despicably honest adherence to the rules by not divulging anything for Kane's investigation. While she was technically doing the right thing, it was hampering his search for Molly. He had to take matters into his own hands.

Perhaps it was paranoia, or the dull throb from his head that the co-codamol he'd taken when he awoke had failed to suppress, but he thought that Chib had more loyalty to DCI Kane than himself. Perhaps it was because she was eager for promotion, or maybe because they both came from the same London cop pool. He couldn't say, but that was the reason he couldn't tell her where he was going to. He wanted to arrive in Ebbsfleet unannounced.

He made one other phone call for back-up.

What he was about to do could ruin his career – if it wasn't in tatters already.

12

North Kent Police Headquarters was a bespoke modern white stone and glass building that was the antithesis of the Serious Crime Unit's current home. While most of the department had transferred to this new hub, Drury had kept the Maidstone base almost as a rebellious outlier post, which is just the way Garrick liked it. It may be a draughty, cold office, with temperamental lighting and heating, but it gave the sense they could operate more independently. Even if that was only an illusion.

While a flash of his ID card had seen him through to the car park, the electronic entrance system in the lobby meant he couldn't simply march into DCI Oliver Kane's office and demand to speak to him. Especially as he was, technically, still a person of interest in Kane's investigation. Since he had surfaced on the scene, Kane had made a point of turning up out of the blue to question Garrick, always trying to catch him when least expected. At one point, Garrick became convinced that the detective had been following him. Even using a cloned number plate to do so – which would be illegal in any investigation.

Now Garrick was going to turn the tables. In his heart, he knew there was little he *could* achieve with this approach. And with Molly's life on the line, this could easily be seen as a colossal waste of time. But he was following a hunch - and hunches had sustained his career this far.

"Am I going to get into trouble for this?" said Fanta, next to him.

He'd called her immediately after hanging up from DS Okon and told her to meet him here. Aside from the need for a reliable car, he wanted somebody he could trust and who had inside knowledge of Kane's investigation.

"You're just following orders."

"That didn't work out as a good defence for those Germans," Fanta muttered, peeling the wrapper of a Twix with the exaggerated slowness of somebody trying not to make a noise, but succeeded in drawing it out so long that it became irritating.

"For the record, I draw the line at asking you to conduct war crimes. Just keep your eyes peeled."

Fanta had told him the team had visited Kane's incident room on the third floor. Garrick had been to the building a few times and knew that security IDs were required to get through the lobby gates and access certain levels. They'd parked several bays diagonally down from the black Hyundai i40 Saloon Garrick had seen Kane driving.

Fanta continued grousing. "We could be here all day. It doesn't feel as if we're helping Molly."

Garrick shot her a stern look, which she refused to meet.

"If you want to return to the office, then feel free to take my car." He was relying on Fanta's desire to conduct field work to keep her quiet, and it worked. He sighed and softened his voice. "We've got nowhere tracking down Foss or Ryman, have we?"

"Sean submitted requests to the Home Office and directly to the Army for release of their records, but he has heard nothing back."

"Exactly. And I think Kane knows who they are. All we need are their details." He could see from her expression that she was still unsure. "Look at it this way. We're chasing a kidnapper. We're following the clues he's laid down from the windmill to the church and are now scrambling to find out where the next step is going to take us. Do you see the problem?"

"We're wasting time?" She ate the first Twix finger in two bites and chewed thoughtfully. "And we're chasing. We're not getting the jump on the kidnapper."

Garrick tried not to smile. Her knack of thinking outside the box was something he appreciated and was keen to encourage.

"And this is not just about Molly Meyers. This goes back to Emelie. It goes to Eric Wilson's murder. I know you didn't get to work with him much…"

"I knew him well enough to like him," Fanta said with a rare hint of sadness. She'd joined the team about six months before he had been seconded.

Garrick watched her devoured the second chocolate finger.

"I wasn't hungry. Thanks for asking," he said. He hadn't had time to have breakfast and hadn't eaten since Harry Lord's midnight doughnut feast.

Fanta was lost in thought and ignored him. "You think

that if we find Ryman and Foss, then we can get ahead of the kidnapper? Ds Okon doesn't think so."

"Exactly. I've asked her to lean on Kane, but she won't. I think she's afraid of him."

Fanta shrugged. "She doesn't particularly like him. She hated having to work with him again."

Fanta opened a plastic bottle of Coke Zero and whimpered as it frothed and spilled over the neck and dripped to the floor.

"Dammit!" She placed the bottle in the cup holder and searched for a tissue to wipe her hands and mop the spill on the floor. She didn't notice the atmosphere change in the car.

Garrick finally found his voice and tried to sound as casual as possible. "Work with him again? That must've been a pain."

Fanta found a tissue and dabbed the coke from the floor matt. "Yeah. She wasn't too pleased."

Garrick was suddenly walking on eggshells, as he didn't want to raise Fanta's suspicions.

"How long were they in the Met together?"

"A couple of months, I think. God, now my fingers are sticky." She scrunched the tissue and stuffed it in the door pocket, which was overflowing with crisp and chocolate bar packets. From the depths, she produced a hand sanitiser and squirted it in her palms.

Garrick's mind was buzzing.

DS Chibarameze Okon had replaced DS Eric Wilson while Garrick had been on compassionate leave because of his sister's death. Superintendent Margery Drury had never adequately explained why Wilson had been seconded. Over the last few months, Garrick had learned that Wilson had been sent to Staffordshire to work on a case involving illegal imports and exports. The same network that had been ship-ping John Howard's macabre human skin lamps to twisted buyers around the globe. That's what had got him killed.

Then it hit him. That's how the severed arm had made it into the UK. A sickening pre-planned shipment. It wasn't human trafficking, but in some ways something much more perverse: *corpse trafficking.*

Had Eric Wilson uncovered it?

Again, there was a lack of details concerning how he died, which wasn't unexpected in an active investigation. But Kane had indicated that he'd known more when he'd turned up at Wilson's funeral. Garrick dropped the pieces of his mental jigsaw into place, trying to form a picture, but of *what,* he didn't know.

It made sense that Wilson had been seconded because he and Garrick had found the body with her skin removed. Somebody, possibly Kane, had hoped this knowledge may be useful in a separate case. At that stage, nobody was aware John Howard was the man responsible. Chib had replaced Wilson. That was standard practise, but now it appeared Chib had come from Kane's operation too. Was that merely a logistical appointment placed on a national police force that was starved of resources? After all, she'd made no secret that she'd come from London. Or was it more than that?

Had Kane *deliberately* placed Chib as a mole within Garrick's team?

He knew that was a wild accusation. Chib was a superb detective. She'd saved his life. She was constantly on the ball and never complained about anything. And yet...

There were signs, hints, that all wasn't quite right. Nothing he could ever point to, but when combined, they added fuel to his new suspicions. Chib was reticent when it came to talking about her personal life. She was engaged but didn't wear a ring and never spoke about it. She had revealed almost nothing about her past career and remained aloof with the rest of the team. Not negatively, but just enough to make him think twice. From the moment she'd met him, she'd aimed to please. Even giving him his preferred matcha tea from their very first encounter. Something she'd only know about if she'd been told... or read a report on him. It would also explain how Kane knew *exactly* when to turn up to talk to Garrick...

Now he was sinking into the quicksand of paranoia. His doctor had warned him that some of the side effects of the tablets she'd subscribed may affect him this way - and that was before he'd told her about the subtle hallucinations he'd been experiencing. He rubbed his temples, massaging the now-gentle throb of his migraine. Accusing his own DS of spying on him was stupid, unproductive, yet oddly seductive...

He slid the passenger window down to help air the stuffy car and clear his mind. Fanta was diligently watching the entrance to the building, so he took his phone from his Barbour's pocket and checked if there were any updates on the case. That's when he remembered the text from Wendy. He read it, hoping for something pleasant to take his mind off the dark thoughts swamping him.

ARE WE BREAKING UP?

He felt sick as he reread the line several times. He'd been too tired, stressed, and preoccupied to speak with her recently. Scrolling through his previous replies, they all sounded terse and distant. No wonder she was upset. He quickly typed a reply:

NO!!!!!

He sent it, suddenly feeling foolish that he'd used too many exclamation marks. Then he added that he'd call later, no matter what was happening.

Fanta suddenly spoke up. "Sir, look."

Oliver Kane walked from the building in deep conversation with a woman in a smart black suit. Her long dark hair was tied in a ponytail, and she had lupine features that he found not unattractive. A laptop case was cradled in one arm.

"What's the plan?" Fanta whispered unnecessarily. "Do we jump him and bundle him in the boot?"

"Let's save the waterboarding for later. I want to follow him, then find a place for a little chat." He watched as they crossed to the Hyundai and continued talking. "Any idea who that is?"

"That's the woman from Military Intelligence."

Garrick's stomach suddenly flipped as *she* opened the Hyundai and sat in the driver's seat. Kane nodded goodbye, then hurried across the car park to a dark blue Toyota Rav 4.

"I thought you said that was his car?"

Garrick thought back to the time – the only time – he'd seen Kane *in* the Hyundai. It had been when he'd been cornered in a rainy Sainsbury's car park and Kane had told him about Eric Wilson's death. He hadn't paid too much attention at the time. He'd just cracked the Derek Fraser case and been told of Eric Wilson's death, so he had a lot to preoccupy him. But in his mind's eye, he now saw DCI Kane had exited and entered his car through the *passenger* door. He'd never seen the Hyundai's driver when it had trailed him and Chib, nor had he seen Kane around the Chilston Park Hotel when the Hyundai had been parked there during the Fraser murder case. A chill ran down his spine.

It meant DCI Kane hadn't been tailing him. Military Intelligence had.

He put his hand on Fanta's as she reached for the ignition key.

"I thought we were following him?"

Garrick shook his head. "Change of plan. Follow her instead. But don't start until they're near the gate." When he'd called Fanta, he'd forgotten that Sean Wilkes had tuned-up her engine so that it now sounded as if the God of Thunder resided in her exhaust pipe. It was hardly the stealthily tailing he'd wanted. For once, he wished he was in Chib's silent electric car. However, he now suspected that Chib would either refuse to entertain his plan or sabotage it...

Fanta waited until both vehicles were at the gate before turning her engine over. It growled unnecessarily loudly, and she slowly pulled out of the parking bay. Kane was the first through the gate as the barrier raised. DC Liu kept a respectful distance back as they followed the Hyundai out of the gate and onto Thames Way in the opposite direction Kane had taken.

The Hyundai picked up speed as it went straight on at the roundabout and headed towards Ebbsfleet International train station. The woman obviously thought speed limits were for lesser mortals, but luckily Fanta wasn't too keen on them either and did an admirable job at keeping up, yet maintained a discreet distance. However, Garrick winced every time her exhaust crackled and snapped with the slightest acceleration. She'd assured him that it was a desired feature, rather than a mechanical problem.

Further navigation around the knot of roundabouts leading from the station found them on the A2 and speeding towards London. Most of the way, the Hyundai kept in the outside lane and pushed eighty miles per hour. They only slowed as traffic became congested on the approach to the M25 turn-off, but once they'd moved past that, the woman was in a hurry once more.

"Don't get too close," Garrick warned as the car's engine roared unnecessarily. Fanta eased off the pedal but kept the Hyundai in their sights. Ahead, they glimpsed the distant towers of Canary Wharf as they approached London.

Then the Hyundai suddenly indicated and made a sharp left across the three lanes of traffic and took the slip road off. With a quick-check over her shoulder to check her blind spot, Fanta followed – just making the exit in time. Garrick gripped the handle above his door to brace himself, but said nothing.

The Hyundai was at the top of the slip road and indicating to take the first exit on the roundabout. Fanta had been forced to mash the accelerator to turn off in time and now sped towards the rear of their target, who was taking the turn at a leisurely pace. Fanta slammed the brakes to prevent them from rear-ending. By the time she reached the roundabout, the Hyundai was already speeding onto a second roundabout. Fanta sped towards it – but they lost sight of their target.

"I think you may have spooked her," said Garrick.

"I couldn't help it!" Fanta snapped defensively.

"No. You did great," Garrick assured her. "Although this may not have been the best car to blend in."

By the time they reached the second roundabout, the Hyundai was nowhere to be seen.

"Dammit!" Garrick craned his head to see if there was any sign of the black car. "Go around. We may just—"

"I think I've found her," said Fanta.

Garrick was about to ask where – but noticed she was staring in the rear-view mirror. He craned around to look out of the back window. The Hyundai was now behind them and flashing its headlights.

"Busted!" said Fanta, with more than a hint of irritation. "What should I do? Burn off?"

Garrick indicated to one of the turn-offs. "No, pull over down there. It looks like she wants to talk."

Oakfield Lane was at the edge of a housing estate. Fanta pulled up just outside a small parking area with a row of convenience shops to the side. The Hyundai pulled up behind them. Garrick watched in his wing mirror as the woman got out of her car and slowly approached him. She didn't appear to be afraid of facing her pursuers, especially as the car looked like it belonged to some Chav boy racer from the outside; Fanta had even left the engine running. Although, Garrick noticed the woman had her phone in her hand, angled in just such a way that she could video the encounter. He rolled his window down.

The woman peered in. Her stern expression flickered with recognition when she saw Garrick.

"David. You could have picked a less ostentatious car in which to follow me," she said.

"I was just saying the same thing," said Garrick with a wry smile.

The woman peered across at Fanta, who was doing her best to hide her face by looking away.

"Ah, DC Fanta Liu. Are you aware there is something wrong with your exhaust pipe? It's making a terrible racket."

Fanta gave up her nonchalant act and stopped the engine.

"You seem awfully keen to speak to me, Detective."

"You're a difficult woman to make an appointment with."

Since they'd lost any advantage, Garrick decided not to hint at how little he knew about her. "And since you'd inspired me by following me around everywhere, I thought I'd return the experience."

The woman smiled. "Well, now you have me."

"I need everything you have on Foss and Ryman. The ones mentioned in John Howard's discharge case."

She stared at him with wide, grey eyes. He'd expected hostility. Instead, there was only curiosity.

"You can ask DCI Kane for them. Although–"

"Although that would mean seeing the evidence he has on an investigation involving me. Awkward, I know. However, they are government records that I need for a completely different case. The kidnapping of Molly Meyers. And I really don't have time for formal requests. Your office hasn't even acknowledged that we've asked for them."

"We're not in the habit of acknowledging *anything*."

"Molly's life is on the line. I could explain the line of enquiry I'm pursuing, but I won't insult your intelligence, because I reckon you already know."

"You understand confidential government documents can't just be released willy-nilly."

"Then when Molly dies at the hands of her abductor – which will be the end game – then I'll be happy to publicise how Military Intelligence and another police investigation decided that her life wasn't worth cutting through bullshit bureaucracy."

"I can deny everything. I don't exist."

"DCI Kane does, though. And, as much as I hate to play games, sometimes I'm forced to. And when I do, I like to cheat and break the rules." He pointed to the dashboard. His mobile phone was propped up against the windscreen. Fanta hadn't even seen him put it there. "And this conversation is being videoed. So, for somebody who doesn't exist, you look fabulous on film."

Once again, if she was annoyed, the woman hid it well. She gave a half-smile.

"I think Oliver is wrong about you." She winked at him and sauntered back to her car. Fanta looked between Garrick and her mirror.

"That's it? She isn't going to do anything?"

"I have a feeling that was a compliment."

An email suddenly arrived on Garrick's phone. It was the address for *Susan Foss*, and it was just on the other side of the Dartford Crossing in Essex. He looked up to see the Hyundai pull past them; the woman gave a friendly toot of the horn. Garrick showed Fanta the address on his phone.

"It looks like we finally have a lead we can follow."

13

As they crossed under the Dartford Tunnel and neared Susan Foss's address on the outskirts of Basildon, Garrick received a call from Chib asking him where he and Fanta were.

"We've made a breakthrough on tracking down Susan Foss. She's the one who sent the military intel to Molly. We're just arriving to interview her."

"Digital forensics came back." Chib sounded a little put out. "You were right. They discovered the same piece of malware on Molly's work terminal at the BBC and the receptionist's machine in Dr Harman's practice. It mirrors the user's screen so a hacker can see whatever they see and download files straight from the network. This one is relatively new, but not uncommon. Virus scanners should prevent it from infecting a machine, but theirs didn't. Which meant somebody accessed both machines and turned off the virus protection before installing it. Once it was on, it wouldn't be spotted unless somebody was really searching for it."

"So somebody must've physically installed it?"

"That's right. And according to Dr Harman's secretary, they had an engineer in three weeks before her disappearance because their phone and internet were up and down. We're already searching camera footage."

"That's great news, Chib. Keep me posted."

He hung up as they pulled up outside an unassuming semi-detached house in a quiet suburban lane.

"This is her house," Fanta confirmed.

If Susan Foss hadn't been expecting any visitors, then the barking engine of Fanta's car would certainly have raised the attention of the entire neighbourhood watch. They approached the house.

"DCI Liu, I'm ordering you to crush your car when we get back."

"I keep telling you I'm happy to trade you for that new Range Rover you don't want."

"You can have my current one."

"You'd have to pay me to take that piece of junk off your hands."

Fanta thumbed the doorbell before Garrick could answer back. A dog barked from within. Seconds passed and Fanta was about to ring again when a voice sounded, urging the dog to shut up. Then the door opened a fraction, a chain preventing it moving further. A crescent of a woman's face appeared with a shock of grey, frizzy hair hanging in front of her eye. She looked Fanta up and down, then scrutinised Garrick.

"Good afternoon–" Garrick began.

"No! I don't have time. It's my birthday, and I'm celebrating a blood transfusion!"

"I... er..." Garrick had been mentally preparing his introduction, favouring a friendly approach. Now the door was already sailing closed. He jammed his foot into the gap to stop it.

"If you don't move that foot, my dog'll have it!"

Garrick searched in his pocket for his ID card. "We're police detectives, Mrs Foss, and we need to urgently speak with you."

"You're not Jehovah's Witnesses?"

Garrick found his card and held it up. With remarkable speed, Susan Foss snatched it from his fingers and scrutinised it with a closeness that betrayed her myopia.

"I assure you that's genuine, and I haven't seen Jehovah for a long time. Although he knows I could do with his help right now."

He'd moved his foot when presenting the card, and now the door slammed in their faces. Fanta was about to say something irritatingly sparky, but Garrick was saved when he heard the chain slide off the latch and the door opened wide. This time Susan Foss was faintly smiling as she returned Garrick's ID card.

"Sorry about that, Mr Garrick. I've had my fill with the God Squad. The pests won't leave me alone. Please come in."

"This is DC Liu," Garrick said, allowing his junior to enter first.

The short hallway was lined with colourful artwork of the sort Garrick approved of – detailed and easily identifiable landscapes.

"Did you paint these yourself?" Fanta asked.

"I did. Turned into quite a hobby since I retired."

"You've retired already? You don't look that old." Despite the grey hair, Susan Foss had the advantage of smooth, glassy features.

"I took early retirement as soon as they let me." She ushered them into the kitchen, where a little Yorkshire Terrier sniffed around their feet and its tail wagged with increasing enthusiasm. Susan gestured to a table. "Sit. Coffee?"

Garrick was about to refuse, but Fanta beat him to it. "That will be terrific. The old man isn't so keen on coffee breaks."

Garrick frowned at Fanta, then saw Susan smiling as she moved to a De'Longhi coffee machine. Fanta was settling into her easy-going rapport that put her interviewees at ease and her superiors on edge.

While Susan made three lattes using the Nestlé pods, which she inserted into the machine, Fanta fussed over the dog, who then leapt into her lap and insisted on a head scratch.

"Seb's taken a shine to you. He normally only lets Nolan do that. That's my husband, but he's not here."

"Sorry to hear that," Fanta said solemnly.

"I'm not. It lets me paint in peace." She glanced at a clock on the wall. "But he'll be home at six." She carried the cups over, placing them in front of the detectives before sitting with her own and holding it with both hands for warmth. "So, how do you think I can help you?"

"We're investigating John Howard."

Susan nodded. "About time. I saw it on the news. You're the one who got him."

Garrick nodded. "Yes."

She nodded her emphatic approval. "Well done. He should've been locked up years ago. When I saw the news, I was expecting you to show up then. Imagine my surprise when nobody did. Only recently a young reporter has been chasing it."

"Molly Meyers."

"That's her. I told her I was more than happy to spill the dirt on him, especially because the police didn't seem to do any digging around. The definition of incompetence..." She suddenly chuckled. "Not you two, of course. You caught him. I meant the military. They wouldn't share anything, even if it was in their own best interests."

"We saw the files you sent, Miss Meyers. Can you clarify just how you were involved in the disciplinary case?"

"Disciplinary? It was a court martial. And I doubt there was anybody involved who didn't wish they could put a bullet in all their heads. Evans, Ryman, and Howard. Mores the pity we couldn't. I was a psychologist for the military, mostly dealing with post-traumatic stress disorders. After the Falklands Conflict, there were several lads suffering. Some of the things that happened out there..."

She sipped her coffee and gazed thoughtfully into space before continuing.

"On the whole, the Argies didn't want to be there. They were young men dragged into a conflict by a dictator. Some of the officers were abominable. They even tossed people they thought were spying from helicopters. Nasty pieces of work. Goose Green was nothing short of a concentration camp. People starving. But like I said, I blame the officers, not the poor buggers forced to fight. Then there was our little trio."

She snorted derisively and sipped her coffee again.

"I'd rather spend time with Galtieri than those three. Howards was a Second Lieutenant responsible for Ryman and Evans. I really can't guess how they got into the Paras.

They must have lied through every psychological test thrown at them."

"I wasn't aware Howard was a paratrooper," Garrick said, although it made sense.

"They were black stains on the Third Battalion. The military wanted them brushed under the rug and I reckon their fellows in arms would've like to have pushed them under a tank."

"What did they do, exactly?" Fanta asked. She was rubbing the dog's head so slowly that he was falling asleep.

"They killed prisoners. Not shooting them in the back of the head sort of thing. Full on torture. Not as part of some black ops intelligence gathering or covert operation. And not just soldiers. We suspect some civilians too. British ones. We don't know how many, as it was difficult to prove. That's how they slipped free."

"There was no evidence?"

Susan pulled a face. "Eyewitnesses, body parts found, and a few corpses retrieved. Evans had seven fingers he'd hung from a string as a keepsake. They were only arrested on circumstantial evidence, and the court martial relied a lot on hearsay and third-hand testimony. What sold it to me was the consistency of all those stories. There was no real deviation from one to the other. Those three men were as guilty as hell. You could see it on their faces. Howard was practically smiling all the way through the trial like a smug dickhead."

"Because he knew there was no real evidence," Garrick said quietly.

Susan gestured with her hand. "Exactly! Other than a dishonourable discharge, what could the military do to them? Nothing."

"So they walked away."

"Unfortunately, yes. During one of my assessments, Corporal Colin Ryman mentioned something they called the Murder Club. Their little trios' secret pact. Of course, he denied they actually did anything. Claimed it was all hyperbole to gear themselves up for shooting the Argies. But again, you could tell *that* was the lie. Other squaddies had heard about it. It became a bit of an urban legend, to be honest. I suppose that's why Top Brass let it slide."

"How were they caught?" Fanta asked, taking a sip of coffee.

"Evans' necklace thing was discovered. Then a farmer had accused them of abducting and killing his daughter. They blamed the enemy soldiers, of course, but this was after they'd surrendered. You must remember, at that time, nobody wanted bad news stories. We'd just won a war single-handedly. The yanks didn't bother helping. None of Europe did. At home, the military and Thatcher were heroes. Her poll ratings had tanked before the war, but off the back of victory she was re-elected. Naturally, the government and the military didn't want any black stains to mar victory, so everything was quietly swept aside, and documents were made inaccessible."

"They were deliberately hidden?" Garrick asked in surprise.

Susan chuckled. "No, worse than that. They were filed away with so much red tape they'd never surface again."

Garrick took a sip of coffee and immediately regretted it. He'd avoided the drink since Emelie's death, and the sudden bitter taste felt as if his tongue was being stabbed with pins.

"And the three of them integrated back into society," he said.

"After their court martial, that was the end of it. If you saw the intel I gave Molly, then you'd have seen I monitored them afterwards. I was one of the few vocal ones insisting they spend time behind bars. I was essentially given six months to prove they were guilty."

"An impossible task with all the evidence left behind in the Falklands and a trial held in secret," Garrick said sympathetically.

Susan sighed almost mournfully. "It was my biggest failure. Who knows how many more deaths that led to?"

Neither detective wanted to interrupt Susan as she silently stared into her cup, lost in recollection. After almost a minute, she continued.

"Evans was the weakest link. He was the one I thought I could crack." She glanced at Garrick. "Please understand my job was to prove their guilt, not to treat their mental state."

"Of course."

"He was suffering from PTSD. He developed a hand tremor and had difficulty associating with his family. His wife left him after a month of returning and reported him for physical abuse." She met Fanta's gaze. "This was the early eighties, so reports of domestic violence were largely ignored by the police, or they were treated as the usual rough and tumble of married life."

"So nothing happened to him?"

Susan shook her head. "He broke her arm. Smashed her nose quite badly, but he didn't even get a slap on the wrist. He couldn't hold down a job and soon found himself sleeping on the streets. It was difficult to keep track of him. Then, about five months in, he killed himself. Threw himself off a bridge in Newcastle according to official reports. Which was a shame, because I think I was finally getting him to open up."

"What about Howard and Ryman?" Garrick prompted.

"They continued to deny everything and pointed out that Evans was a nutter, and everybody knew it. They claimed that if anything had happened, it was Corporal Evans acting alone."

"They were setting him up as a scapegoat."

Susan finished her coffee in a single gulp and tapped her index finger on the table as if nailing the point down. "Now you see it! And this is what I told my superiors at the time. As far as we could tell, the three of them hadn't kept in contact, but we hardly had the resources to keep them under surveillance. It was as clear as day and night to me that Howard and Ryman became increasingly confident as Evan's mental state deteriorated. But if you want my ex-professional opinion, he wasn't suicidal."

Garrick put his coffee aside and leaned his elbows on the table. "Are you implying that Corporal Evans may not had committed suicide?"

"I'm not implying it. I'm telling you. And I had good reason to believe that. I reported my suspicions upstairs, but they wanted something other than speculation and circumstantial evidence. But with no perceived crime, the Newcastle Police Force wasn't willing to investigate, and the Military Police considered the case closed."

"One less hassle for them," said Fanta.

"Precisely." Susan leaned back in her chair and stretched her arms out. She looked like a woman finally un-shouldering the burden of the world. "A month later, my investigation was wrapped up. John Howard and Colin Ryman walked free; in fact, they were already building a new life for themselves, as if the Falklands had never happened. And my services with the military came to an end."

"They never asked you back for any other cases?"

Susan shook her head. "I was an outside consultant. Several of my peers continued to be asked back, and I had expected to get occasional cases. But no, not me. I worked for social services for a while, then started my own private consultancy, but truth be known, the whole Murder Club affair had squashed my desire to practice. In fact, my faith in humanity was practically extinguished. I was so happy when Molly wanted to reopen the case. Of course, I don't have access to any of the records, and the government won't release anything so embarrassing."

Garrick leaned back in his chair and drummed his fingers thoughtfully on the table. "You are aware John Howard was killed during his arrest?"

"I saw the report and was so delighted. I hope he suffered."

"Which just leaves Colin Ryman as the sole survivor. It's important we find him as soon as possible."

Susan flicked her hands helplessly. "I wish I could help. I never tried to keep up with what either of them was doing. Although, I kept an eye on the papers for anything that sounded like their handiwork. I can tell you that Ryman moved into security work, using his para training to lure in some high-profile clients so he can't be difficult to track down."

Garrick continued drumming his fingers, stopping only when Fanta gently nudged him with her foot under the table.

"Mrs Foss, everything we are discussing is strictly off the record and confidential." She nodded her understanding. "Molly Meyers has been kidnapped. We believe it's, in part, linked to her trying to uncover what John Howard and the others did. We have precious little time to track her down.

Anything you can offer is welcome. I don't care about speculation or evidence. I just want to save her life."

Susan Foss's eyes grew wide in shock as Garrick spoke. She scratched the side of her hair and looked around the room as if seeking answers.

"Colin Ryman is the only one of them alive." Garrick nodded and let his fanciful theories about John Howard's resurrection slide. "Other than him going off and doing security work... around the Stevenage area," she added, "then there is little else I can suggest."

She put her head in her hands and repressed a loud, dry sob.

"This is all because I fouled up."

"Mrs Foss, this is not your fault at all," Fanta assured her, reaching across the table to lay a consoling hand on Susan's arm. In doing so, the terrier slipped from her lap with a little yelp, then trotted to his food bowl to save his pride.

"It is my fault," Susan insisted. "Evans admitted the whole thing to me, only I thought I was being clever by using it to rat out the other two. He admitted that their Murder Club was real. And I let them get away with it."

14

_____

Susan Foss tapped her pen on the table to an irregular tattoo. She knew she shouldn't because the sound would carry through the Formica table and be amplified on the cassette recorder. She continued anyway because it was clearly irritating the man sat opposite.

Simon Evans had been on edge since he sat down in the windowless office. His face was heavily tanned and the wiry growth clutching his chin was at least three weeks old. He stank, too.

It had taken her two days searching the streets of Newcastle to find him. With an A-Z in one hand, swiftly purchased from WHSmiths, she had tried soup kitchens, the Salvation Army, and visited every group of homeless she could find. Eventually, somebody had recognised him – a fiver was a handy jolt to anybody's memory – and she tracked Evans down, sleeping on a wooden pallet amongst the dumpsters behind Woolworths. He'd been pleased to see her for a change.

On the way to the office, which she had purloined from

Social Services, he'd dragged his heels until she agreed to buy him a cheeseburger and fries from Wimpy. She'd made him wait outside as she ordered it to take-away.

The office that she'd requisitioned was little more than a couple of plastic chairs and a desk, but that's all she needed. The other two suspects had been easy to trace and interview, one in Herts, the other in Kent. But after discovering Evans' wife had thrown him out after he punched her, the ex-para had gone to ground. She watched as he stuffed the meal down in front of her, ketchup dripping down his chin. Lettuce slopped on the table, which he scooped up with dirt-encrusted fingers, which he then licked clean. As she studied him, she swore something moved in his hair. She tried not to think about it.

Despite initially being glad to see her, Evans retreated into his shell as she began questioning him. He refused to acknowledge that he'd struck his wife, but Susan had seen the broken arm, black eye, and bruises for herself. She had no sympathy for the pathetic man sat across from her.

He bobbed his head, eyes darting to the left and right, as he continued to side-step her questions. He was jittery and nervous, which is why Susan decided on a new course of action. If he wouldn't play ball with the gentle approach, she'd irritate the crap out of him and enjoy doing it. The tapping pen seemed to be his trigger.

"It's a shame to see you like this," she lied gently.

"It's temporary," he muttered. "I'll be back on me feet soon."

She noticed his eyes kept darting to the black plastic tape recorder at the end of the table. The play and record buttons were down, the C-90 cassette could be seen whirling away as its built-in mic recorded every word.

"I'm surprised you fell off your feet. The other two are doing brilliantly." It wasn't a lie, but she couldn't help sweetening the pill. "Both of them said leaving the military was the best thing they did. They're earning a ton now. And Colin's gone and got himself one of those new Ford Sierras. Nice car. Better than my old thing." She enjoyed watching him squirm. "But like you said, you can probably get back on your feet. Have you heard from them?"

Again, he glanced at the tape recorder and grunted something unintelligible.

"I'm going to have to be honest with you. What happened in the Falklands, well, they're doing a convincing job at laying it all at your feet."

He stared at her. For the first time, there was a hint of fear in those bloodshot eyes.

"We all know there's guilty and there's *guilty*. I've seen the closest friendships break up when real things are at stake. A bunch of mates is one thing, but losing your car, house, family, all that money... well, they're very different stakes, aren't they?"

His eyes darted between the rapping pen and the recorder. Susan gave a sigh that she hoped wasn't overly-theatrical and took a packet of Silk Cut from her purse. She'd stopped smoking months ago but kept them handy, just in case. And right now, they served a dual purpose.

"Want a cig?"

Evans nodded and took it from her with trembling fingers. Susan lit it with the plastic lighter she also kept with them. She knew her husband would smell it on her breath later and hated the thought of letting him down. She reluctantly put them back in her bag as a cloud of smoke grew around Evan's head and masked the scent of sweat and dirt.

He leaned back in his chair and his shoulders sagged a little, but still his eyes strayed to the tape deck.

"I know life on the street isn't a charm, but prison isn't built for the likes of you, Simon. You'd soon be missing your freedom. Even if that's eating from a bin and pissing on your shoes to keep your feet warm. I can see Howard and Ryman got lucky finding a fall guy like you."

She let the words linger... then slowly reached across and stopped the tape recorder. Evans gave her a sharp look.

"This thing is a legal requirement, as you know. Everything we talk about when it's not running is, well, let's put it this way. I could tell you I was the one who really shot John Lennon, and it wouldn't be admissible as evidence. Whatever you say can't be used against you. But it can help me find leads on other people who are taking you for granted." She leaned forward slightly, sitting upright, and made sure that she didn't show the slightest hint of repulsion or fear. "You're not innocent. I know about maybe a fraction of what you've done, but it's enough. The others, however..."

Evans' gaze slid from her to the glowing red coal at the end of his cigarette. He rolled it in his fingers, now looking thoughtful.

"You can't bang me up without evidence."

"You know that. And a war zone is a brilliant way to hide it."

The para smiled as he accepted the compliment. Now the tape wasn't recording, his arrogance was rising.

"Them other two killed for fun. John said for art, but he is a bit of a snob. It's a kick. Like a drug. You don't need coke to get a high." He raised his eyebrows. "I have some standards."

"You were better at it. Is that what you are saying?"

She was relieved when Evans slouched back in his seat

and took a long drag on his cigarette. Caution was now being overridden by sociopathic pride.

"It's not better, luv. Like I said, it's a rush. And it was people who deserved it. Bloody Argies? And once we were up in Glasgow. There was this Paki kiddie-fiddler. He died slow, one piece at a time." He pointed the cigarette at her. "A public service."

That was news to Susan. She made a mental note and regretted she couldn't write it down. "And the young girl in West Falkland?"

"That was Howard. He has a thing for girls. Not, y'know, fucking them. Just hearing them scream and cry. I don't like it too much." He shrugged. "Each to their own."

"I need proof they're as sick as you say they are."

"We don't leave proof. That's the idea behind the Murder Club."

"So that was a real thing?"

Evans laughed. "It's not like we made badges and membership cards, or had secret handshakes. They kept talking about some old film in which two strangers met and killed each other's victims so there was no connection and they both had perfect alibis."

"Strangers on a Train."

He nodded. "It was black and white. John had this idea that there were more like-minded people around. Collectively, we could set things up, and who would know? John was smart about it. He didn't want people with a grudge, like in the film. And no psychos, either."

"So that's how you operated? The three of you covering for each other."

"The plan was to go wider. Ryman knew a couple of

people in the States. Typical John had somebody in a high place. Propper Jack the Ripper style."

As the cigarette burned down to the orange filter, he took one final pull on it before stubbing it out in his fries container. He propped both elbows on the table and held his head in his hands.

"I saw it as improving society. Like I said, I was getting scumbags off the street. The other two were out of hand."

Susan was struggling to get her head around a killer with morals.

"Then don't take the fall for them. Tell me something that will bring them crashing down."

"We don't leave evidence. We know all the tricks, that's one of the rules. But I reckon if you go after John's man upstairs, that'd open pandora's box."

"Do you have a name?"

"Did he?" asked Garrick. He had barely breathed as Susan recounted her story.

She nodded. "But he wasn't stupid enough to give it to me."

Garrick swallowed his tart reply.

"He planned to, though. He wanted assurances he wouldn't be charged. Impossible to guarantee, of course, but a deal could've been done. He was murdered three days before I was due to return to Newcastle when he was going to name names."

"Which is why you think Ryman and Howard threw him off the bridge?"

"There's no question in my mind that's what happened. Of course, I lack proof. Just as I lacked proof for anything he said to me because I stopped the tape. That's what haunted me. If I'd left it running, then maybe I could have got some sort of official confession from him. Or if I'd been smart enough to think of having a Dictaphone or something hidden away. Remember, this was the eighties. Nothing was small and easy to hide."

"What about this kiddie-fiddler he mentioned?"

"Again, back then DNA profiling was *just* beginning to bear fruit with the arrest of Colin Pitchfork."

Garrick knew the landmark case well. Pitchfork had raped and murdered two girls in Leicestershire. Another suspect, Buckland, was about to go down for the crime until DNA evidence from semen pointed the finger conclusively at Pitchfork.

Susan continued. "There was a rumour that an Asian man had raped several girls the year before in Glasgow. He went missing, and then it became an urban myth. If Evans was telling the truth, he'd also made the point that they didn't leave evidence lying around."

Garrick motioned to stand. "Well, at least you have given us a very useful lead on tracking Colin Ryman down."

Fanta didn't move as she spoke up. "What about the Man Upstairs? Did he give any hints about who that was?"

Garrick sat back down and waited for Susan to answer.

"That's the odd thing. It was after I handed in my report of that very meeting that Evans was killed."

"If you're right about that being the handiwork of the gruesome twosome, then how did they know Evans had spoken to you in the first place?" Susan raised her eyebrows, encouraging Fanta to continue. "With no recording, there was only you and whoever read that file."

"And shortly afterwards my case was closed, and I was never asked to return for any consultancy work."

"Almost as if you were blacklisted."

Susan nodded in agreement. "Of course, that makes me sound terribly paranoid."

"Who above you would have read that report?"

"We are talking Military Intelligence. The cult of secrecy. I submitted my findings to a department. After that... who knows?" She paused for effect. "I've been spending many years stewing over this and occasionally I dug around. I made a list of people I know were serving in Intelligence at the time and have since left to go on and do other things, including die."

Garrick was feeling the prickling sensation that important strands of a case were finally tying together.

"What did you do with that list?"

"I knew I couldn't do anything with it. I didn't know what to do, especially after seeing Howard's death on TV. But I knew I had to get the word out there. I was going to send it to you as the lead detective on his case, but then, you could be as corrupt as the next man. No offence. Then I noticed a reporter who knew you. Somebody who had some common ground and couldn't be previously involved in any of this..."

Fanta couldn't suppress a gasp of surprise. "Molly wasn't looking into the story – you gave it to her!"

Susan nodded sadly. "And now I fear history is repeating itself, and she will be killed because of me."

15

Tick-Tock.

There hadn't been a reminder since, but Garrick was painfully aware that, with every hour, the kidnapper was expecting progress. The major problem he had right now was the investigation lacked focus. It was a sprawling mess that ultimately sat on his shoulders.

Was there really an influential figure hovering over all of this, or was Susan Foss leading them down a blind alley?

But if she was on the right track, that explained DCI Kane working with Military Intelligence. Did they know who it was, or were they still searching?

That raised the question of why DCI Kane hadn't interviewed Susan Foss. If Garrick could so easily be given her address, and Molly Meyers had been investigating the same track. Had Kane already discounted the idea and moved on? If so, that was detrimental to Garrick's own time-sensitive mission. Kane's strategy of working his multiple angles in secret was hampering the search for Molly Meyers – and Garrick hated the fact that his sole focus was being pulled in multiple directions: could he trust Chib? Was Kane hoping to achieve something by leaving Garrick in the dark – or was he trying to hide something... or somebody?

Garrick's temples throbbed from the conflicting theories and the growing paranoia that was enveloping him. Perhaps there was a simple solution to it all, but he just couldn't see the wood for the trees.

After all, he was the one at the heart of it all.

His sister. Dr Amy Harman. The murdered Korean woman. Father Cillian. They all orbited him.

Hearing his sister breathe his name down the phone after her death. The letter sealed with her DNA. The bizarre gift of a brand-new Range Rover.

All designed to make him appear as a crank, increase his paranoia, or discredit him. Perhaps all three. An elaborate game with him as the central piece... or the fall guy. Concocted for some ill that Garrick couldn't fathom.

It was too much of a distraction. Every clue, every lure pulling him in the wrong direction. Perhaps that was the plan – a trail of bodies that led to ultimate humiliation. He returned to Thames Way to pick up his car and sent Fanta back to Maidstone with her focus on tracking down Colin Ryman and the other names Susan Foss had provided.

He spoke to Chib but didn't fill her in on the new revelations. The slower that piece of information circulated back to Kane, the happier he'd be. He pressed her about any more evidence found regarding Father Cillian. She had been making progress with DC Wilkes in highlighting possible places where he could've been killed, using the forensic team's kill map. It still covered a large area of Kent and into East Sussex.

He was feeling terrible about fragmenting his own team,

but he needed various lines of enquiry dealt with laser-like precision.

Wendy's text message kept popping into his mind while talking to Susan. It was an unwelcome distraction, and it was unprofessional to deal with personal problems, but this one was hampering his thought processes, and it had a quick fix. All he had to do was turn up and speak to her. Ten minutes, and then he would have a clear focus for as long as he needed.

Checking his watch, he reasoned she'd still be in school and that he could make it there just as the kids were leaving. All he had to do was drive there with the same recklessness Fanta had showed.

Garrick raided his memory to recall the school Wendy worked at, and eventually the name surfaced in his mind. He arrived at three fifteen in time to be caught up in the tail end of the parental pickup. Garrick found a visitor's parking spot and stretched as he climbed out. He ran a hand through his stubble and realised he hadn't shaved nor changed his clothing since the start of the case. A quick glance in the grimy wing-mirror showed his hair was poking in every direction. He licked his fingers and attempted to flatten it. He looked terrible.

As he walked towards the reception, he watched the tide of identically uniformed children talking excitedly about their day to their parents, while the older children gathered in knots, laughing and joking. He wondered just at what age the criminal instinct took over and erased such innocence. Although people were culpable at any age... he slammed down on his morbid thoughts. He couldn't afford to sink into such despair. No matter how bleak a case, positivity was the key. Most people on the outside didn't appreciate how vital gallows humour was when coping with deeply stressful situations.

A boy slouched in a chair in the reception area, wearing a sullen expression that showed he was in trouble. The elderly receptionist didn't smile when she saw Garrick coming. She wore a mask that was thankful that the day was already over, but hated that there was still more to come.

"Afternoon." Garrick smiled warmly, but knew his appearance was against him. "I'm here to see Wendy Sinclair."

A frown graced the woman's brow, and she checked the computer. "She's left already."

Had she been so upset she had to go home? That didn't sound like her.

"Oh. OK, thank you." He walked back towards the exit and called Wendy's mobile. It went straight to voicemail. He hesitated as the automatic doors slid open in front of him. He hung up and redialled. The phone carrier's default answer-phone greeting spoke again. He turned around and went straight back to the receptionist, who looked less thrilled than last time to see him.

"Left? Where did she go?"

If possible, the woman's face soured as she shrugged. "She left."

He leaned on the counter between them. "I need to know where she went."

The woman's eyebrow flickered to show that it wasn't her problem. Garrick glanced around the reception and lowered his voice when he noticed that the sullen boy was eavesdropping. He quietly slid his police ID from his pocket and passed it over. The woman inspected it. Evidently, she hadn't seen one before, so couldn't spot a genuine ID from a fake.

"It's important that I speak to her."

"Garrick, eh?" The woman issued a sigh so deep that it sounded as if she was in pain. She slid the ID card back to him.

"She went home."

"Thank you." Garrick turned and marched for the exit.

She called after him. "The caller said you needed to meet her there urgently."

Garrick didn't look back. He sprinted to his car.

Twisting the key in the ignition, the engine resolutely failed to turn over.

"No, no... come on, you piece of junk," he growled.

Another attempt – and the engine spluttered and died. His knuckles were white from gripping the steering wheel so hard. The worst possible thoughts filled his mind. His forehead and cheeks flushed, and a pain shot through his head with such intensity that his left eyelid spasmed. He could imagine the growth in his head bursting from the sudden stress and killing him on the spot. He'd be damned if he let it be the end of him before he had a chance to rescue Wendy.

He tried her phone again – with the same results. She never turned it off, and he couldn't recall her ever complaining about the signal at home.

"Dammit!" he tossed his phone onto the passenger seat and thumped both palms on the steering wheel. "Come on, you bastard!"

He turned the ignition key – and the Land Rover grumbled to life. His eyes widened in relief, but he lost no time in slamming it into gear and pulling away. It was torture to drive slowly through the school's one-way exit system, made worse by the straggling kids paying no heed to traffic and threatening to step in front of his car. At the gate, a parent was making a painfully slow right turn – the same direction Garrick had to go.

Every curse word he knew silently passed his lips. The roads around the school were still scattered with kids, so he didn't dare go any faster. Only when he overtook a bus that was filling with pupils did he speed up. His mobile phone slid off the seat and clattered into the footwell. He didn't care.

Time was already against him.

Seeing Wendy's car parked outside her house was more alarming. It made it more of a mystery as to why her phone was switched off. The car's suspension gave a tortured clang as the front wheel mounted the kerb in his token gesture of parking. He ran to the front door and repeatedly thumbed the bell, then hammered on the letterbox for the hell of it.

His eyes scanned the windows for any signs of movement.

His heart thumped in his chest, and he fought a wave of dizziness that caused him to stagger. He reached for the door for support. He had to get a grip on himself.

Then the door opened, and he almost fell into the hallway – and into a confused Wendy who caught him.

"David?"

She wasn't strong enough to support his weight and staggered backwards, still clutching his arm. Garrick pulled himself together and found he was tightly clasping her.

"Are you OK?" he said with such urgency that Wendy blinked in surprise.

"Me? Are you drunk?"

Garrick let go of her and found his feet. From her reaction, he judged that he must look deranged.

"Your phone is off!"

"My battery died. David... you look terrible. Have you been drinking?"

"What? No. Just not sleeping." He looked around. "Is anybody else here?"

"Like who?"

Garrick closed the front door and checked the lock. It didn't appear to be broken. He poked his head into the living room, then the kitchen. There was nobody there.

"How long have you been home?"

"About forty minutes. After I got your call, the head let me leave early because—"

"I never called you." Wendy's confusion deepened. "Did you actually speak to me?"

Wendy shook her head. "Reception took the call. Bettie said it was you, calling from the station, and you were on your way over because something terrible had happened."

"That's all that was said?"

"After the last week, and the texts this morning..." she stopped. Her eyes were round and moist, but she was too tough to cry.

Garrick sucked in several deep breaths to calm himself. "I need to sit down."

They moved to the living room. Wendy's handbag was on the table next to her keys. Her mobile was on the edge, recharging from the mains. Everything looked the same as it did last time Garrick was here after their date night started to get interesting – then was abruptly cancelled with news of a murder. He couldn't see today getting much better.

Wendy sat on the arm of the chair opposite him and folded her arms.

"David, I'm very confused."

"Me too. Look, I didn't make that call. Somebody else did to lure you back here."

"Who? And more importantly, why? I live here. I would've

been home ninety minutes later. What difference would that make?"

Garrick didn't have an immediate answer. He rubbed his temple.

"Do you have any ibuprofen?"

Wendy popped upstairs and returned with two capsules and a glass of water from the kitchen. Garrick swallowed the tablets and drank the whole glass before sinking back against the sofa.

"First, I have no intention of breaking up with you whatsoever. At all. I warned you that dating a detective could become unsociable, so if you're having second thoughts, then I understand. I hate it. But I understand."

Wendy laughed. When he looked up, he caught her wiping away a couple of tears away. It wasn't a laugh; it was pent-up relief.

"You stupid sod!" she exclaimed. "You had me going there." She moved from the chair and sat next to him. She clutched his arm and leaned against him. "I thought you'd had enough of me." She kissed him on the lips, then pulled away slightly. "Although if you don't do something about the smell, then you will be dumped."

Garrick found his smile as relief surged through him. But it came at a price and made his head swim. The room seemed to shiver, like a motion picture film strip about to break loose from the projector.

"I'm in the middle of a kidnapping case" He knew he shouldn't tell her, but considering the sinister phantom phone call, he suspected that she was being dragged into it. "And it's not pretty, and I don't have time. Not even for this."

To her credit, Wendy didn't ask questions. She just nodded in understanding.

"It's resulted in at least two new murders already. One of which was in my house. She was my psychologist." He caught the odd look on Wendy's face and realised how that sounded. "I wasn't home. She was killed there as a warning against me. The kidnapping, the murders, they all seem connected to me... and my sister."

Wendy's frown deepened. He'd told her that he no longer had a sister, but he'd placed the details aside for a later date.

"She was murdered while in America. Just last year, before Christmas."

"I'm so sorry." She squeezed his arm.

Garrick shook his head. "I promise I'll tell you everything after we close this case. You must understand, Wend. He's coming after people I care about. He must know about us, and he knows where you work."

The severity of the problem slowly dawned on Wendy.

"You think he was luring me back to k... get me?"

"I do."

Wendy stood sharply up and moved to the room's bay window overlooking the street. She peered left and right. "Then why didn't he do something before you arrived?"

"Because he's playing a game to which I don't know the rules. I'm running around blind while he keeps getting the upper hand. I don't want you staying on your own. Can you go to your parents' or sister's?"

"I'm not sure. Paula has her hands full with her son. My parents would let me stay in Rochester."

That was still in Kent, and far too close for Garrick's liking, but he had little choice. "And don't go to school. Take the rest of the week off. Pull a sickie or something. He can find you there. Can you pack some things now?" He patted his pocket for his phone before remembering it was still in his Land Rover.

"I can pack light," she said.

Garrick was taken by her calm assuredness. "Do it. I'll come with you. I just need to get my phone from the car."

Wendy hurried upstairs to pack. Garrick put the front door on the catch and went to his car. It took several moments to find the phone, as it had slipped under the passenger seat and was caught against the metal runner that moved the chair back and forth. He glanced at the fractured screen – two missed calls.

As he turned to go back inside, a vehicle across the street made him double take. It was a white Volkswagen Beetle. Just like Molly Meyer's missing car.

It even had the same registration.

It *was* her car.

16

———

Evacuating an entire street in the small market village of Lenham was the perfect cover to move Wendy out of her house. It was complete overkill, of course, but David Garrick was now beyond taking a soft approach.

He'd called Chib immediately to report finding Molly's car. Before he'd hung up, she came back with a warning not to open it in case it was booby-trapped. The thought had crossed Garrick's mind, but he'd cast it aside. The kidnapper was out for glory, obliterating evidence would be counterproductive. But suddenly uniformed police were descending on the scene, banging on doors, and ordering people from their homes. The Explosive Ordnance Disposal 621 Regiment from the Royal Logistic Corps was flown in from RAF Northolt. And the entire South East media contingent had assembled just beyond the cordoned area.

Chib and DC Sean Wilkes arrived to help Garrick coordinate the sudden mess he'd found himself in. Several times Garrick felt the ground shift under his feet as his head

throbbed and his vision spun. In the resulting mass movement of people, he'd packed Wendy into the back of a police
car and told the officer to escort her to her parents in
Rochester as quickly as possible. She gave him a short kiss
and squeezed his hand as a parting gesture. It went some
way to soothing Garrick's original angst that they may be
splitting up, but any gains were washed away by the killer's
knowledge of their relationship and where she worked and
lived.

Garrick was reluctant to get her involved during his
explanation of events to Chib and Sean, but he had no
choice. Wendy was now embroiled in the case, and there was
no turning back. It was clear that the ruse to make her come
home early from work was designed to worry Garrick and to
lead him to Molly's car.

As he explained to his two teammates, he wasn't sure if
Chib's reaction was a sceptical one or if he was just imagining
it. Was he being too judgemental about her?

The bomb squad arrived in a flurry of blue lights and
Garrick watched from a safe distance as a man dressed in
heavy protective armour cautiously examined the vehicle.
DCI Kane chose that moment to arrive. With a quick glance
between Chib and Kane, Garrick suddenly realised who had
called the bomb squad in. Left to his own devices, Garrick
would've opened the car door himself.

"I suppose I have you to thank for this fiasco?" Garrick
gestured to the squaddie, kneeling at the driver's door.

Kane looked as if he was about to deny it, but thought
better of it.

"You mean protecting everybody from a possible IED?
You're welcome."

Chib purposefully avoided Garrick's bitter look.

"The killer won't blow anything up. You've been watching far too much telly."

"We can't be sure of that. We're talking about a bunch of boys with military training."

"So you had to call out the EOD just to keep your pals in Military Intelligence happy."

Garrick felt a modicum of delight in Kane's alarm as he stared at Garrick, trying to judge just what he knew.

Garrick's temper ran ahead of any feeling of restraint. "And for the record, my report is going to squarely place the blame for all this at your feet, Oliver. If you'd bothered sharing information instead of sitting on it, then we may have already caught him."

Kane did an admirable job of keeping silent, even though he kept motioning to deny the accusations.

The pain in Garrick's head was loosening his tongue. He felt clammy, and his fists clenched involuntarily.

"And because you've been acting like an utter ballbag, you've become complicit in dragging my girlfriend into this. I swear to God, if anything happens to her, I will do you bad. You'll be praying to be paralysed just so you can't feel my fist ram so far up your arse people will think you're my friggin' puppet." Garrick was normally level-headed, but now a thesaurus of profanities was presenting itself to him.

"Are you threatening an officer?" Kane struggled to get the words out. He was used to people lathering on the respect.

Garrick knew he should calm down and be professional. He rubbed his throbbing temple.

"I haven't even begun threatening you, mate. I want to know if you fully debriefed DS Wilson before you tossed him into the fight. Did he really know the scope of what he was doing, or is that what got him killed?"

"Wilson was told all he needed to know." Aware that DS Okon and DC Wilkes were watching, Kane rounded on Garrick to prove his authority. "*Need to know*. That's the underlying motto of my investigation, especially when you're involved, Garrick."

"There's 'need to know', and then there's utter incompetence." Garrick quickly continued as Kane opened his mouth to retaliate. "And, *Detective Chief Inspector*, stop imagining you outrank me." He pointed to the squaddie, who was now walking towards them. "Especially when you turn up to *my* crime scene. *My* case."

"Which one of you is in charge?" the squaddie asked in a thick Welsh accent as he pulled off his helmet. Underneath, his cropped blond hair was damp with sweat.

Garrick turned to face him, surprised the squaddie had done everything in the space of a short argument. "That'd be me." Glancing over the man's shoulder, he saw all four doors, the boot, and the bonnet, were open.

"The car's not rigged. But there's something you need to look at in the boot." He pulled a face but didn't elaborate.

Garrick nodded and followed him. The squaddie stopped halfway to the vehicle and gestured Garrick should continue.

"That's not my department. I'm going back and getting very drunk." He nodded towards the car. "I reckon you should too."

Chib, Wilkes, and Kane caught up with Garrick. He glanced at Kane and considered telling him to eff-off, but restrained himself. Instead, Garrick approached the Volkswagen. From several yards away, he could see several items in the boot. Unlike the classic Beetle, the newer model had the engine in the front, with the rear space offering generous storage. And it needed to.

At first glance, it looked like parts of a mannequin had been neatly arranged inside. But they were not plastic, they were male body parts. A headless torso was in the middle, with both arms removed and laid horizontally underneath. Where the head should be, a single hairy leg had been deliberately placed. As the true nature of the horror sank in, it reminded him of a butcher's display window.

He heard Chib give a sharp intake of breath, and Sean heaved and threw up.

"I think we've found more of Father Cillian," Garrick said quietly.

"Bloody hell," Kane whispered. "This is revenge for leading you to John Howard."

Garrick tore his gaze from the corpse. "Is that what you think?"

"It's obvious."

"The good father led me to Stan Feilding. That's exactly who John was trying to set up for his murders. I caught John because of an accident."

"The report doesn't quite read that way."

"Whoever claims an accident led to victory? The facts are in the report. Maybe the wording was a tad enthusiastic," he admitted.

"So why the hell kill him?"

"So you are operating on the belief that somebody is taking revenge for John Howard's death?"

"Yes."

"Who?"

Kane remained silent. Garrick couldn't decide if it was an

admission that he didn't have a clue, or part of the DCI's imposed veil of secrecy.

"Let me put it another way you'll understand," Garrick said. "This can't be revenge. I thought it was too, but it clearly isn't. All of this took some planning that started with John Howard being very much alive. I don't think he was expecting to ever be caught or killed by me."

"That's your game theory," Kane said disapprovingly.

"Don't you know me by now? This is my ego talking. This is all about me. Father Cillian, Molly, they're just in the way of the star prize."

"Which is?"

"Which is *me*. The one direction this is all heading leads to the killer murdering me. That's the endgame. He's already planned it. The die had been cast. He knows precisely when it's going to happen."

Garrick felt oddly calm about that.

He also knew that if he was to survive the next few days, he would have to go rogue.

He was fine about that, too.

17

For Garrick, the case had become about one thing – tracking down Corporal Colin Ryman.

Find Ryman; find Molly.

He was operating in the realm of guesswork and hunches, but every instinct told him that this was the correct direction. He also knew that Drury would throw a fit if she knew that his focus was straying, even fractionally, away from Molly Meyers.

Drury had been unusually silent since she'd brought him onto the investigation. He suspected partly because the kidnapper had insisted that he lead it. And keeping a step removed gave her denial space should anything go out of hand, which could easily happen in a kidnapping. Not that he could accuse her of such selfish behaviour. She'd put her neck on the line for him many times, and he didn't imagine this case would be an exception.

Returning to the station, the only communication he'd received from Drury followed on from the sudden media flurry surrounding the bomb squad incident. So far, the bomb threat had help concealed what was found in the vehicle. Secrecy about the kidnapping was still paramount while the clock was ticking. Drury's message was succinct:

COMMISSIONER EDWARDS IS CONCERNED ABOUT THE OPTICS.

Rather than demand regular status updates, which would be a waste of time and resources, the simple message suddenly added an inordinate amount of pressure on Garrick. Scott Edwards was Kent Police's Crime Commissioner, a public figure who Drury answered to. In the past, she'd always dealt with him efficiently, although his last case involving a film production had brought with it some unexpected political pressure courtesy of Edwards and his connections in Whitehall. Garrick was no fool; the Commissioner was undoubtedly putting pressure on his boss.

Chib and Wilkes had stayed at the scene as Zoe's SOCO arrived and combed through the vehicle and Wendy's house, just in case the kidnapper had been inside. He already knew far too much about Garrick's personal life, so much so that he must have been under surveillance – and not just from Military Intelligence.

Fanta was on a call, talking so low that Garrick couldn't make out what she was saying as he passed. He looked at his phone as a text from Wendy came in.

WITH MY PARENTS XX

That was a relief. Not that he expected anything to happen on the police ride there. He'd also instructed an officer to discretely keep watch on the house. Even Wendy didn't know somebody would be looking out for her. He typed a curt reply and sent it before it occurred to him to add a few kisses at the end, too. They went separately. Open declarations of affection were foreign territory for Garrick, doubly so when it came to text etiquette. He really needed a crash course from somebody youthful, like Fanta, but the thought of her having such power over him was frightening.

DC Harry Lord returned from the communal kitchen with some fresh brews. Garrick was grateful for the matcha tea as he sank into his chair. The stress was pummelling his shoulder muscles and as Wendy had reminded him, he still looked like hell.

"Have I missed anything?" he said, closing his eyes. His head pressed against the chair's headrest, and he could feel himself slipping towards sleep.

Harry scrolled through the latest logged incidents on their HOLMES system, which hung the various strands of the kidnapping together.

"Molly's ex has been interviewed and eliminated from all enquiries. They parted amicably, and he was at work throughout the time frame she originally went missing. We had officers combing through surveillance footage around Dr Harman's office looking for the technician who may have installed that malware." He put several blurry photographs on the TV monitor. They showed a thin person in a peaked cap entering and exiting. They were all but useless. "It was a woman—"

"A woman?" Garrick interjected.

Harry smirked. "This is the twenty-first century. They can fix computers these days." He'd raised his voice to intentionally get a rise from Fanta, but she was still busy with her call.

"That's not what I meant. If it is linked to the kidnapper, then is there more than one?"

"The secretary says that she was from the usual tech support they've used in the past. Guardian Solutions. I called them. They use freelancers and say they didn't attend the callout because it had been cancelled thirty minutes after being booked."

Garrick indicated the photos on the screen. "These are the best images?"

"Yep. The secretary said it was a woman. Maybe in her early thirties. Red hair. Thin. That's about it. It was the same set-up at the BBC. They normally have their own engineers, but cutbacks mean they must tighten their belts. A call was made. The call was cancelled. This same woman turns up." He showed a few more surveillance images taken inside the BBC building. The woman was very careful to angle her cap towards the camera. "Looks like the same girl to me. Nothing on any cameras outside. Both incidents happened within two days of each other. DCI Kane's team said they'll take it from here and let us know if they find anything relevant to Molly's case."

"I bet they did." Unable to hold back a sigh, Garrick sank back in his seat and sipped his tea.

"I'm missing something..."

"We probably all are," Harry grumbled. No matter how grim the case, Harry had always maintained a degree of optimism, but now he sounded doleful. "We're in a holding pattern waiting for results, reports, or further contact from the kidnapper."

"He's waiting for us to work out the next clue."

"If you ask me, this whole thing is a wild goose chase."

Garrick flicked open one eye to look at Harry. He sipped his tea. "What d'you mean?"

"Exactly that. Moving Ye-Jun Joh's body, or her arm at least, required planning. Killing Father Cillian couldn't have been part of that original plan. It feels more improvised."

"I think he was an unfortunately convenient victim that fit the plan. It could've been anybody connected to me."

"Yes. But in that case, and don't take this the wrong way... well, why not go for your girlfriend?"

Garrick closed his eye and felt the tension in his head increase. He didn't have an answer for that. Surely it would have yielded the same result.

"Perhaps if he'd done that, I would've mentally collapsed and been unable to complete his little game."

Harry made some noises as he thought about it. "I suppose so. Like at the end of that film, Seven."

Garrick had seen the movie a couple of times and vaguely recalled the twist at the end. "He wants me fully operational because he wants me to see Molly die." He opened his eyes to gauge Harry's reaction. "Whatever his end plan is, I can't see how she'll survive. Keeping me alive means I get to suffer for whatever twisted reason he has."

"So, you're practically immortal in this scenario?"

Garrick snickered and closed his eyes. He wanted to share his thoughts about DS Okon and his theory about Colin Ryman, but he feared creating more of a rift in his team. He only hoped the not-so-tactful Fanta hadn't revealed her side mission of tracking Ryman down.

For several minutes, a near-silence descended, spoiled only by Fanta's low chattering on the phone. So far, she had found information on his security company, including several publicity shots of the man taken in the late nineties and early noughties, but nothing on his service record. It was about seven o'clock, but Garrick suspected he could sleep until the morning if he was given the chance. He thought that he'd lapsed into a micro-sleep as Harry startled him by breaking the silence.

"DCI Kane was down here earlier." That woke Garrick up. He opened his eyes and leaned forward in his seat. "I saw him with Drury, and boy, did he look pissed off."

"Was that just before he called the bomb squad on me?"

Harry nodded. "If you don't mind me saying so, I don't really trust him."

"I'm happy to hear that. I don't trust him at all."

"He asked me for a list of what we found in Molly's emails," he said with deliberate emphasis.

"Oh." The idea that his medical records were in DCI Kane's hands made him feel sick.

Harry gave a faint smile. "We're all tired. I'm not thinking clearly. I may have made a couple of omissions logging the evidence." Harry tried his best to look contrite. "I mean, I should really double-check I haven't left anything out. But with time against us..."

Garrick was relieved as he read between the lines. "That's completely understandable. And nobody could fault any of us for minor oversights."

"My thoughts exactly." There was something else on Harry's mind. He looked at the back of Fanta's head, his mind working on how to articulate it. Finally, he spoke up. "Fanta mentioned Eric had been seconded by DCI Kane."

"That's right. It turns out there were ties with John Howard up north."

Harry nodded. "I did some digging around with Cathy. She's the girl in Kane's team from Staffordshire," he clarified, after noting Garrick's look. "I reckon she fancies me."

While happily married, Harry enjoyed flashing his charm and dousing his testosterone like an amorous Tom cat. He seemed to improve with age – the reverse from Garrick.

Harry continued. "She let bits slip. When we found the

Korean woman's arm, they were able to match its DNA to the crime scene where Eric was killed."

"I thought there had been no matches?"

Garrick had constantly drawn a blank when asking about what happened with his DS. He sipped his tea and found himself more attentive than ever.

"The case file is protected, as it's open with Kane's investigation. I didn't want to ask Cathy to do anything dodgy, so I went through the back door, so to speak. I called SOCO."

The forensic officers operated independently from the police, although they worked within the security framework that each case required. Harry knew this as well as Garrick did. Except, judging by the tight smile spreading across his face, the Detective Constable was apparently savvier at exploiting loopholes.

"Since Ye-Jun Joh is also connected to our kidnapping case, they released *all* the files they had."

"The full case?" Garrick was impressed by Harry's ingenuity. While the official police file on Eric Wilson's death would have the detail about what had happened, the newly liberated forensic files would have been used to round out that report.

Harry finished the last dregs of his coffee as he nodded. "Her DNA was found in an empty refrigerated flight box in a warehouse in Shrewsbury. The sort of box used to carry medical samples around. Because nobody had thought to match it to your sister's case, it remained unidentified until the limb turned up in the windmill and we'd already made the American connection."

"What did you find out about Eric?"

"That's the thing. The report says he was the one who found the case. It also references that it was there he was stabbed and killed. His blood was on the scene and there was mention of repeated frenzied stabbings through his kidneys."

The image repulsed Garrick. "He was stabbed in the back?"

"I reckon caught unawares. So I had a thought. I asked the lab to check if they found for any traces of *Eric's* DNA on the retrieved limb."

"And?"

"Bingo."

"So, Eric found the limb and then was probably killed by our kidnapper."

"It's circumstantial, but it fits. And from what Cathy said, it was a close thing. Backup arrived within minutes, so the killer didn't have time to wipe down the crime scene. They took what they could and ran."

Garrick mused the possibilities. None of it immediately helped located Molly, but they now had an extra location to help track the culprit's movements – even if it was months ago. The more points of interaction they had, the more it'd help narrow their target. Had DCI Kane made the same connection? Was he already several steps ahead? Or had he overlooked it?

Then there was the mysterious woman from Military Intelligence. She had willingly turned over Susan Foss's details, so why hadn't she or Kane followed the same line of enquiry? They may not have known about Susan Foss reaching out to Molly Meyers, but a diligent background check on John Howard and his Murder Club would have surely revealed the connections.

Then Evans' claims that there were people in higher power who were part of the twisted club suddenly came to mind. Were they within Kane's investigation? Obscuring facts and sowing disinformation?

It was an absurd notion. It verged on conspiracy theory.

And yet...

That was a rabbit hole he couldn't afford to jump down. Tracking down Colin Ryman was already uncomfortably close to veering away from Molly's case. John Howard was part of the scope of Kane's wider investigation. Garrick, his sister, and Eric Wilson were just smaller incidents within the whole. As much as he hated to admit it, that was DCI Kane's remit. He just had to find Molly.

He was so impressed with Harry's lateral thinking that he imparted his suspicions about Chib snooping on Kane's behalf. He got as far as opening his mouth when Fanta turned in her chair.

"Sir, I've found that address you wanted."

Garrick was about to ask what address, when he remembered that she was looking into Colin Ryman's past, and he'd instructed her not to tell anybody. He patted Harry on the arm as he rose from his chair.

"Great work, Harry. See what else you can unearth." He crossed over the Fanta and leaned on the back of her seat so he could read the address she had on the screen.

"That list of names Susan gave us is useless," she said. "They're either dead or had such secret jobs I can't find anything about them. But I found this on Colin Ryman. He moved from Stevenage fifteen years ago."

Garrick used her mouse to highlight an address. "This is where he lives?"

"Totally. And not that far away."

Garrick tapped a business name above Ryman's name. "Where did you find this?"

"That's the name of his security company, according to Companies House."

Garrick stared at the name *Guardian Solutions,* and any thoughts of fatigue vanished. That was the problem with cases working in separate silos – there was no overlap of information.

The sense of creeping paranoia was alive once again. He felt in his pocket for the co-codamol container. He was going to have to take more if he was to get through the evening, but he couldn't remember if he'd exceeded his daily dosage.

The more fragmented the case became, the more information would be overlooked and the harder it became to solve. It was almost as if somebody was engineering it to be so.

He decided he would confront DCI Kane... just as soon as he'd tracked Colin Ryman down.

18

"Why are we doing this again?" Fanta whispered.

"Because he's the last surviving link between John Howard and this 'Murder Club'," said Garrick as he wiped the condensation forming on the inside of his windscreen so he could see the house across the street.

"What I mean is, why are *we* doing this?"

"Surveillance. To check if he's home."

The address just outside Sevenoaks was a plush neighbourhood with houses exceeding the reach of Garrick's salary. How a disgraced army corporal from Stevenage could've fallen on his feet so grandly was beyond him. He was learning that crime really does pay. And it paid handsomely.

According to Guardian Solutions' tax return, Colin Ryman's company was turning over approximately £2.2 million a year. How much of that was actual profit, Fanta hadn't been able to deduce on the drive over. Although she noticed that for several years, it had been operating at a loss and had very few assets. They only used freelancers, and the call centre that took their calls was a business based in India that served hundreds of companies.

The mock Tudor frontage hidden behind the high hedge and gates screamed privacy. But even in the dark, closer inspection revealed the lack of care from the overgrown foliage. The grass they could see in the occasional glare of passing vehicles was straggly and overgrown. As they watched, an upstairs light clicked on and remained on for the next twenty minutes. It was dark at 8:30 in the evening as autumn encroached. Garrick watched as another two lights came on downstairs.

"There's nobody home," he said confidently.

Fanta frowned. "Why do you think that?"

Garrick pointed to the downstairs windows on either side of the house. "Did you see those lights come on downstairs?" He waited for her to nod before continuing. "They came on at *exactly* the same time. Timing switches. People always set them for the same time. Leaving a minute or so between them would look more natural. And the curtains were already half-closed."

Fanta looked impressed. "You should've been a detective."

"So my careers teacher said. Come on, let's take a look."

He opened the Land Rover's door and was already out before Fanta registered what he'd said.

"Take a look at what?"

Garrick slammed the door and hurried across the road to the gate. Fanta huffed and reluctantly followed.

"What're you doing?"

Garrick tested the gate. "Checking the property is secure." He rattled the gate. It was firmly shut.

Fanta quickly caught up with him, talking in an overly

loud whisper. "Did you say he'd made his money in security?"

"A lot of money by the looks of things."

"Then won't he have the best security? Why do we have to check it?"

Garrick knelt and pushed his arm through the bars. He felt for the steel arm that pushed the heavy iron gate open and closed and ran his hand along it until he touched the covered motorised assembly.

"Better safe than sorry," he grunted.

"What're you doing?"

"Gates like these are a bugger when the power goes. They're stuck closed."

"The power's on."

Garrick blindly felt around the plastic cap on top of the case. He unscrewed it until it slipped from his hand and fell into the darkness. His fingertips prodded around until he touched a lever. With a little effort, he flipped it a hundred-and-eighty degrees. There was a metallic groan as the tension bar that firmly kept the gate shut, folded. He straightened up and looked at Fanta.

"Just as I thought," he said with a smirk. He planted the flat of his foot against the gate and applied pressure. It slowly swung open. "It's unlocked." He stepped inside.

"Can we do this?" said Fanta in alarm. The sound of an approaching car made her look down the road as a pair of headlights turned the bend three-hundred yards away. Knowing she looked the picture of suspicion, she followed him into the driveway.

Garrick was already casually walking to the front door. Fanta glanced at the sabotage gate assembly. The light from the passing car illuminated the red emergency handle Garrick had released.

"I don't think this is legal," Fanta hissed.

Garrick stopped at the front door and shot her an annoyed look.

"Since when did you become such a killjoy? Besides, we're probably on CCTV."

"Are you going to boot the door down?"

"Really, DC Liu. You have some peculiar ideas..." he trailed off as he shoved the front door and it creaked open. He exchanged a look of surprise with her. "This is very suspicious."

As he pushed the door, he was struck by a flashback of his own front door left open. He'd convinced himself that his condition had made him forgetful, but forensics had assured him that his door had been opened by a duplicate key. Where the killer had got that, he couldn't guess. The image of his own house, moments away from discovering Amy Harman's mutilated body, was so real and visceral that he wobbled backwards. He felt Fanta's hand support him in the middle of his back.

"You okay?"

He nodded. "Fine. Just a little tired." He stepped inside, fighting the dizziness that threatened to overwhelm him.

The illuminated square entrance hall had a staircase to one side curling to the first-floor landing that crossed to the opposite side of the house. There were doors in each of the walls, leading deeper into the building. He noticed a light flashing in the corner of the room – a motion sensor. There was little he could do about that.

"Hello?" He yelled. "This is the police! Your door was open!"

Fanta quietly padded inside, and they listened for any signs of movement.

Nothing.

Garrick moved to the closest door to his right. As gently as possible, he touched the handle and applied downward pressure. It opened without complaint, revealing darkness beyond. He took out his phone and activated the torch. The white LED shone across a marble countertop, a bowl of ill-looking fruit, then onto a kitchen table – and a complete mess. Two of the chairs were toppled on the floor. The table was at an angle, as if knocked aside. Most of the table contents – mats, some letters, and a cup – were scattered, half on the table, the others on the floor.

His light reflected from cutlery in an open drawer. A large carving knife lay across the other implements, as if it had been dropped shortly after being selected.

Garrick and Fanta didn't have to speak. They were both of the same mind: who would attack Colin Ryman, their prime suspect?

Panning the light back to the countertop, Garrick saw several tools laid out as if in use. A small pair of red-handled screwdrivers, a wire cutter, a pair of pliers, and a soldering iron. A roll of solder and blue plastic-sleeved wire stood to one side, with several smaller cut portions of wire strewn around, their coats stripped back to reveal the copper inside.

"Do you hear that?" Fanta suddenly whispered.

Her head cocked back to the entrance hall. Garrick held his breath to listen, but heard nothing. Fanta pointed towards the staircase and quickly crossed over. Garrick followed, and as he did, he caught the faintest noise. Nearing the foot of the stairs, they could both hear quiet sobbing.

Fanta's eyes opened in alarm and, before Garrick could

stop her, she was hurrying up the stairs, carefully balancing her weight on the edge of the bare wooden steps to minimise noise. Garrick tried to hurry, but slowed as each step creaked under his more substantial weight. Ahead, Fanta had disappeared into the darkness.

Leading the way with his torch, Garrick quickened his pace as the steps curved onto the first floor. He glanced up in time to see Fanta switch on her phone's light – straight into his eyes. He hissed and shielded them, but the damage was done. His night vision was now shot.

Fanta swung the light away as she tracked the sobbing to the door furthest away. She quietly approached, sweeping her light across the corridor ahead. Garrick took two steps, then his legs wobbled as another flashback of finding Amy seized him. He stumbled noisily to his knees, catching himself on the banister rail. His head pounded and the image of Fanta, silhouetted in her own flashlight, seemed to distort. He waved his hand to show he was fine as he propped himself up on his knee.

Fanta reached the door. There was no mistaking the sobbing was coming from within. She reached out and gripped the handle. Sucked in a breath. Then pushed it open and stepped inside.

Garrick was half upright when he heard a distinct *tutting*, followed by a whispering voice.

"You shouldn't be here."

Then a thunderous explosion ripped through the air. The flash and debris from the room Fanta had entered struck him across his temple and chest in a wave of heat, and his eardrums felt as if they'd been punched. The entire landing he was standing on collapsed down to the floor below as a blue curtain of fire rolled across the ceiling.

19

Images tumbled together with harsh incongruity. A bright flash from the room Fanta entered. The corridor shaking and twisting underfoot. Then a brief sense of weightlessness as the ground vanished and flames consumed the ceiling.

Gravity reasserted itself moments later. The landing had collapsed where it connected to the room ahead, and Garrick tumbled forward down the inclined slope as debris rained around him.

Then he was suddenly outside the house, scrambling through wreckage and shouting Fanta's name as flames caught the remains of the roof and quickly spread. Garrick had tunnel vision – in his mind's eye, his hands appeared overly large as he clawed chunks of plasterboard aside in his frantic search. He was only peripherally aware that the front of the house had exploded outward into the street, setting off every car alarm and barking dog in the vicinity.

The rising tide of volume became almost deafening until...

He woke in the hospital room.

It was a private ward, and he was lying on top of the bed, still wearing his shirt and trousers, which were covered in black grime and smelled of smoke. His grubby coat was slung over the chair next to him. A nurse in the room flashed a smile as she continued filling in the clipboard she was holding, then moved closer and plucked the thermometer from Garrick's mouth.

"That's fine," she said, making a note of the reading.

Garrick's thinking was foggy, but it was evident he hadn't been unconscious. He had the sense that he'd walked to the bed himself. He glanced at his hands, which were stained black from ashes. A patch of skin had been scrubbed clean and stitches applied to a pair of inch-long cuts.

The nurse continued. "The doctor has read through your medical history, and they need to run some scans. You said you banged your head quite badly."

His mouth was dry as he spoke. "Did I?"

She gave him a peculiar look. "So you'll be staying in for the night."

"What time is it?"

"Ten-thirty."

The last two hours had slipped from his mind.

"The detective who was with me. How is she?"

The nurse's smile faltered, and she didn't answer. She was saved when DC Lord entered the room. He waited for the nurse to leave before speaking.

"The Super has been trying to call you."

Garrick patted his pockets for his phone. It wasn't there. It had been in his hands during the explosion, so he assumed it must be lying in the rubble. He reached for his Barbour and checked the pockets.

"How's Fanta?"

Miraculously, his phone was in his pocket. He'd missed three calls from Drury. When Harry didn't answer, he looked questioningly at him.

"I asked about Fanta."

Harry jerked a thumb towards the door and lowered his voice. "We spoke about that when I popped out." Garrick glared at him until Harry looked away. "She's still the same."

"Which is?" Harry couldn't hide his concern as he looked sidelong at his boss. "For Christ's sake, Harry. I'm feeling totally out of it. Just play along."

"She's still unconscious."

Harry didn't elaborate further, and, from his expression, Garrick didn't want to know more. He swung his feet off the bed and searched for his shoes.

"What did Drury say?"

"Nothing to me. But I think she's handing the case over the DCI Kane."

Like the rest of his clothes, Garrick's shoes were covered in black dirt. He slipped the left one on, which was still laced up. An unwarranted image flashed in his mind of cradling Fanta as he pulled her from the wreckage. She was covered in ashes and lying close to a burning chunk of something.

The severity of the flashback almost jerked him off the bed. He wasn't recalling it. He was reliving it.

Harry continued with more tact than he'd ever displayed. "And she was demanding to know why you and Fanta were at that house."

"What did you tell her?"

"Considering I didn't know, I just said you were following a hunch."

"It was Colin Ryman's address. He served with John

Howard. They had this twisted society thing in the army. The Murder Club, they called it. There were three of them, and Ryman is the last surviving member. I think he's the one who kidnapped Molly."

"When I saw the Guardian Solutions connection, that's what I figured you were doing."

Garrick struggled to unlace the second shoe. "And either DCI Kane knows this and isn't telling us, or he's completely ignorant of the information he's sitting on. Information that would lead us quicker to Molly."

"I really think you should talk to the Super, sir."

"I don't have time for explanations or bollockings. The kidnapper wanted me on this, not Kane."

"But sir–"

"We heard a voice from that room. We were lured in there and then told we shouldn't be there."

"SOCO thinks that was a baby monitor."

Garrick snapped his shoe on and looked at his DC in surprise. "Then he was watching us. What's the radius of those things?"

"They can be accessed over the internet these days. The explosion was from a wired gas cylinder. The front of the house, that room, and the hallway were badly damaged. SOCO says it was a basic booby trap."

"The kind dreamt up by an ex-soldier." Garrick tied his lace. Then he stared thoughtfully into space. "There were signs of a struggle in the kitchen."

"The kitchen was badly damaged by the fire."

"Why booby trap his own house?"

"To hide evidence?"

"Every other incident had been planned and executed without leaving evidence behind. Why wouldn't he have done the same to his own home?"

Harry exhaled a long sigh. "Sir, Drury...?"

Garrick's mind was working overtime. For the first time since Molly Meyers had been kidnapped, he felt as he had the correct strands of the case in his hand, but they were all being incorrectly joined together. He needed more time. As if reading his mind, Harry spoke louder to get his attention.

"We're out of time on this case."

"What do you mean?"

Harry obviously didn't want to tell him as he paced the room. "An hour after the explosion, the Super was sent a severed index finger. It's been ID'd as Molly's."

"Shit."

"My thoughts exactly." Harry wiped a bead of perspiration from his forehead and took off his coat. He tossed it on the bed next to Garrick and paid no attention to the thunk of his car keys inside or the fact his wallet almost slipped from the inside pocket. He was too distracted. Garrick shoved the wallet back in. "She's going to pull us off the case."

Garrick stood up and snatched his coat. "Then you haven't seen me."

"What?"

"When you arrived here, I was already discharged."

"Sir... I'm not exactly a stickler for the rules. But there's a life at stake here."

"There's more than one life at stake, Harry. And having the book thrown at us won't help."

For a long moment, it looked as if Harry Lord was going to refuse to cover for him. Then he pulled a small plastic key card from his pocket and held it between his forefinger and thumb as if it were contaminated.

"Is that why you wanted this?"

Garrick took it. There were no markings to reveal what it was. He caught Harry's eyes narrowing. "A copy of DS Okon's security pass. You asked for it when you called me here."

Garrick took the card and wondered why he'd requested it. His next course of action was to confront DCI Kane... and then he remembered asking Harry to request a copy of Chib's security card. If his suspicions were correct, and she was working for Kane, then it would allow him access to Kane's incident room in Ebbsfleet.

"You don't remember, do you?" said Harry accusingly.

Garrick rubbed his head. To his surprise, the migraine had gone.

"I'm having a senior moment, Harry..."

"You got caught in an explosion. The only reason you and Fanta aren't dead is because the door she opened took the brunt of the blast. You both dropped down a floor as parts of the house fell on you! Is this ringing any bells?" Harry was almost shouting. Any pretence of respect and etiquette had been abandoned. "You both marched in there telling nobody, without telling your *team*." He stressed the last word with emotion. "That was reckless! That's why she's still in a coma!" He jabbed a finger towards the door.

David Garrick met his gaze. The tears straying down Harry's cheeks told him all he needed about the severity of his young DC.

Garrick found it difficult to find his voice.

"I'm sorry, Harry. I didn't ask for this to happen. I didn't ask to be put on this case. But I know, I know with certainty, that I can end it." He was unsure where his confidence was coming from, but he felt it. The tutting and words emanating from the room rose in his mind:

You shouldn't be here.

For once, he believed the message. They shouldn't have been there. They had strayed off the kidnapper's plan. They had lurched too close to who was behind the curtain and pulling the strings. Molly's finger had been a warning to *stick to the game*. To play by the kidnapper's rules, not Garrick's.

But he had no intention of doing that. There was something rotten at the heart of the whole situation, and he was going to find out what it was. He was going to expose the truth – even if it cost him his career.

He turned away from Harry and snatched his Barbour, then walked to the door. He paused before opening it.

"Don't cover for me, Harry. Do what you think is right."

Then he left. He felt his phone vibrating in his pocket as he marched down the hospital corridors, past the reception desk without discharging himself, and out into the car park. He assumed his Land Rover was still back at Ryman's house, and he could hardly taxi his way around Kent.

He took the stolen car keys out of his trouser pocket and repeatedly thumbed the button as he searched for a pair of flashing lights to reveal where the parked vehicle was. The lights of Harry Lord's BMW flashed. Garrick jogged over. He'd slipped the keys from Harry's coat and regretted having to nick his DC's car... but needs must.

From this point onwards, he was playing by his own rules.

20

————

It only occurred to Garrick, when he was driving out of the hospital, that he did not know where he was. Only after catching the hospital entrance in the rear-view mirror as he adjusted it did he see the sign for Orpington Hospital. He waited until he was on a clear section of road before he slowed and quickly texted Harry Lord to apologise for borrowing the car. Texting while driving was an offence, but he'd now broken enough rules for him not to be too concerned. The last thing he needed was for Harry to report his vehicle stolen and the traffic police to pull him over. Text sent, Garrick sped up, once more breaking laws to get to Ebbsfleet as quickly as possible. The finely tuned BMW Series 7 Saloon responded far better than Garrick's Land Rover was ever capable, and the automatic gearbox smoothly slid up through the gears without effort.

Alone, he wrestled to put Amy Harman, Wendy Sinclair, Fanta Liu, or the fate of Molly Meyers out of his mind. The complex intersection of cases had meant he'd strayed from the kidnapping, but by doing so he'd opened the line of enquiry far wider than would have been possible. Molly was his priority. Finding her would unlock everything else – but only if he found her before the kidnapper had a chance to play out his twisted plan.

His hands shook as he gripped the wheel. He wasn't sure why they did, and hoped it wasn't a side effect from any head trauma he'd suffered. Had he lost part of his memory, or was the stress, combined with his tumour, playing tricks on him? Regardless, he had to focus on the information he'd uncovered.

Colin Ryman was at the centre of the kidnapping. Of that, he had no doubt.

The doubts came when he considered if he was acting alone.

The booby-trapped house was primitive, but effective. It felt as if it had been an afterthought because Ryman hadn't taken the idea seriously that anybody would connect him to Molly Meyers. But then there were the signs of a struggle in the kitchen. Scenario one was that he'd taken Molly there first, but that made little sense. But the second scenario was no better – had somebody broken into Ryman's house and attacked *him?*

Molly had been kidnapped because she'd strayed too close to reveal Ryman's identity and making him and the Murder Club public – but this was *after* the series of events designed to taunt Garrick. He still imagined Molly as collateral damage – in the wrong place at the wrong time, thus making her a convenient tool in a pre-arranged plan.

A plan that focused on Garrick.

Colin Ryman's Murder Club connection to John Howard was the obvious motive, but it didn't stack up in Garrick's mind. Why would Ryman conduct revenge on Garrick? Or, more pointedly, why had John Howard unfolded a plan to torment Garrick even while masquerading as a friend? And why was Ryman concluding it now that Howard was dead?

That John Howard had been instrumental in the murder of Garrick's estranged sister was no longer a coincidence. It was the same time the Korean woman was killed, and her severed arm shipped to the UK for someone's macabre pleasure.

But the question of *why* refused to be answered.

As he overtook a taxi, another thought occurred to him. As far as he was aware, John Howard had never been in a relationship. At least, not with a woman. The victims Garrick had been aware of had all been beautiful young women, yet there had been no sexual assaults. Had John Howard been gay? In which case, was Colin Ryman something more? A grieving lover intending to carry out his partner's nefarious plan.

He was clutching at straws. His first instinct was to call Fanta and ask her to dig around Ryman's sexuality. The thought of her lying in a coma made him feel sick. Unbidden, flashes of her unconscious face sprang to mind, matted with blood as she was cradled unmoving in his arms.

A horn from an approaching van made him jerk the wheel, pulling the Beamer back onto the correct side of the road. He'd drifted over towards the oncoming traffic.

Focus.

He stabbed the window button on the door console and was rewarded with a blast of cool air from outside. It helped perk him up.

He was sure that DCI Kane's investigation had the answers. The problem was, they were not connecting the right clues together, or even working on the same case. Kane's secrecy was the kidnapper's friend.

Somebody in a high place...

Susan Foss firmly believed that was why Evans was killed, to stop him from shedding secrets. Her report went up the military chain and disappeared. He suspected that the Military Intelligence involvement in Kane's investigation was a result of this. They were also looking for that person. A figure who wasn't John Howard or Colin Ryman, but somehow affiliated with them. Somebody with enough authority to keep the facts hidden. Somebody who might throw a spanner in the works of any investigation to ensure it was unsuccessful...

Careful...

Garrick was aware his focus was straying into the realms of the tin-hat brigade. Find Molly – find the answers. With this in mind, he parked in North Kent Police Headquarters' car park and surveyed the vehicles until he spotted DCI Kane's dark blue Toyota Rav 4.

Taking a deep breath, and aware he acutely smelled of smoke and sweat, Garrick purposefully approached the entrance. He was walking into the lion's den and all too aware that he might not be leaving any time soon.

It was a mixture of regret and relief that Chib's cloned ID card opened the lobby's security gate. The fact that she had access to this building confirmed that she was working with Kane and had been all along. Recalling that Kane's investigation operated on the third floor, Garrick made straight for the elevators. He repeatedly thumbed the button until a car arrived. When he stepped in, he noticed that a woman had also been waiting just behind him. He gestured that there was plenty of room inside.

"I'll get the next one," the woman said, wrinkling her nose.

The elevator doors swished closed, trapping Garrick in a stench of his own creation. His heart was thumping, but his head felt extraordinarily clear. No aches, no foggy thoughts – just a patchy memory and hundreds of unanswered questions.

The door opened on the third floor and a wide corridor stretched to the left and right, lit by powerful LED lights that replicated daylight. Tinted walls of investigation rooms were only marked by numbers and a secure keypad. A far cry from the draughty Maidstone office that Garrick called home. Room four was diagonally head of him. He braced himself outside the door – then tapped Chib's card on the keypad.

He heard a click from the lock.

With a hesitant breath, DCI Garrick pushed against the door and entered the room.

21

The space beyond was three times larger than Garrick's incident room and populated with a dozen staff. Every wall was filled with pictures, maps, photos of multiple crime scenes, and evidence of all sorts.

A jaded DCI Oliver Kane sat on the corner of a desk next to a large digital touch screen, the sort that belonged in a state-of-the-art classroom, as his DS dragged up pictures of Colin Ryman. Garrick suspected it was his smell that attracted everybody's attention as all eyes turned to him and a deathly silence descended. Garrick was surprised to see a flicker of a smile tug the corner of Kane's mouth.

"DCI Garrick." Kane stood up. "Aren't you full of surprises?"

Garrick raised his hands to impart a witty rejoinder, but he couldn't think of anything to say.

Kane put his hands in his pockets and walked towards him. "I've lost count of how many rules you've trampled to gain access here. I'm at a loss what exactly you want to achieve."

Garrick glanced around and spotted a copy of his own police ID card up there, along with the rest of his team. All except DS Chibarameze Okon. He looked back at Kane and didn't blink.

"Anything you try to do to me right now puts Molly Meyers' life at risk."

Kane gestured to Garrick's grubby clothing. "I think it's too late for that." He cocked his head towards his team, then back to Garrick. "Are you planning to embarrass me in front of my people?"

"No. I'm above that. I don't need to plant moles to spy on fellow officers."

Kane's eyes flinched. He circled a finger around the room. "This is all much bigger than either of us imagined, David. Maybe it's time we talked?" He gestured to an office behind a glass wall in the corner.

It was baking hot in the room. Garrick removed his Barbour and hung it with the other coats on the wall. He glanced around, daring anybody to challenge him, then he followed Kane and the activity in the incident room broke back into a cacophony. The moment Kane closed the door, the silence returned. Garrick tried not to hate him for having a better office than he did. Oliver Kane poured them both a glass of water, then sat behind his desk and placed a finger over his lips in a thoughtful gesture.

"Let me explain about DS Okon—"

Garrick drank the water in several gulps. He hadn't been aware of just how dehydrated he was. He put the glass back down with an overly dramatic thud, which he hadn't intended.

"Chib is at the back of the queue. I really don't care. Molly Meyers is my priority. She should be yours."

"You're chasing Colin Ryman."

"Obviously. And the fact you, Chib, or anybody else didn't furnish us with that information from the get-go is a dereliction of duty. Understand, whatever happens to my career after this, I will be bringing everybody down in a tsunami of public enquiries."

Kane raised his eyebrows in an almost mocking gesture.

"We didn't put too much emphasis on Ryman. Oh, we'd interviewed him, but it was collectively thought that he couldn't be a person of interest."

"He'd booby-trapped his own house as an insurance policy in case people got too close."

"So it appears." Oliver Kane drummed his fingers on the desk and gazed outside at his busy incident room. "But why would he do that?"

"We found signs of a struggle in the kitchen, then DC Liu heard voices upstairs. That's what led us to the room. It seems the voices were coming from a baby monitor. We were lured there. He could see everything we were doing, and the last thing he said was that we shouldn't be there. I'd veered off his plan."

Kane's eyes darted around the room as he pondered just what to say. He leaned back in his chair and ran his fingers through his short salt-and-pepper hair.

"The reason we discounted Colin Ryman from Meyers' case is because he's incapable of doing it."

"I've spoken to Susan Foss. She thinks he's very capable. His little Murder Club. An ex-soldier, a security expert—"

"I don't mean mentally. Up here," he tapped the side of his head, "he's seven levels of cuckoo. A natural born killer.

What you don't seem to have read is his medical record. Two years ago, he was diagnosed with early onset Parkinson's."

Garrick slouched as the wind of indignation was squeezed from him. He only had a passing knowledge of the devastating neurodegenerative disorder, but even that was enough to recognise the extreme acts of brutality they had witnessed would be beyond him.

Kane continued in a low, matter-of-fact voice. "Except it took hold of him quickly. He's at about stage four. He's functional, but not capable of kidnapping a fit woman like Molly Meyers, never mind exiting a crime scene without leaving behind a flake of evidence. As for hacking up Father Cillian, no, that's beyond him."

"Then he has a partner."

"Ryman was eliminated early on. Although, like you, I proposed that idea, too." Kane gestured beyond the office window. "They were resistant to it."

Something dawned on Garrick. "When I saw you at Eric Wilson's funeral, you were looking for Ryman, then, weren't you?"

"To see if he'd show up in the guise of a mourner. It was a longshot, but if he'd done so, then it would have supported my hunch."

"But that was before Molly was kidnapped."

Kane looked levelly at Garrick. He could see in the man's eyes that he'd reached a decision. Kane slowly leaned forward and propped his elbows on the desk.

"David, you're part of my investigation, which is ethically and legally problematic if I divulge too much. It's what makes this whole thing a nightmare to put together." He gestured between them both. "And you and I got off on the wrong foot from day one because of the nature of my primary case." He sighed and rubbed his face. "But we're both going around in circles when we should be moving forward in lockstep. I'm not investigating you. I'm not investigating John Howard."

Garrick jerked a thumb towards the window. "Then what the hell are they all doing out there?"

"Susan Foss's report about this so-called Murder Club vanished. And it would have stayed that way if it hadn't been uncovered by Ms Jackson. That's the woman from Military Intelligence. She grew concerned that it had been closed without a proper investigation. What concerned her most was the idea that Evans, Ryman, and Howard had this little organisation, possibly combined with somebody in power who had covered up the whole affair." Kane sipped from his glass before he continued. "At the Met I was investigating dark web sites where people talked about murder. In the same way gangs recruited kids who stab an innocent passer-by as a rite of passage, well, it turns out that people have dark places to go when they focus on murder."

"Strangers on a Train..." Garrick said quietly.

"You've been talking to our Mrs Foss. Exactly."

Garrick frowned. "I thought she hadn't been approached by you?"

"She had. A while back. But she had nothing new to say that wasn't in her report."

"The one I'm not allowed to see."

"Exactly. The dark web offered an upgrade from the idea of two unconnected people on a train getting away with murder by killing each other's problem. Now it could be done on a larger scale. I'm talking about eighteen people we were tracking in the last eighteen months. A small but dedicated group. When you and DS Wilson uncovered that skinned victim, well, alarm bells rang. We'd seen items for sale on the dark web made from victims. Made to order by people with sick compulsions. When you went on compassionate leave, I approached Wilson to come aboard my team. We'd found a warehouse in Shrewsbury where it appeared orders were shipped to and from. DS Wilson got close... and that's what got him killed."

Garrick toyed with his empty glass. "I wish there was something stronger in this."

"If we were off duty, I'd gladly get hammered with you. When you uncovered John Howard's involvement, well, klaxons everywhere went off. Jackson finally had something to rally Military Intel, and you were suddenly a person of interest, especially considering your connection with Howard and what had happened to your sister."

"OK. That's why I was being followed. But why bother? You had put Chib on my team just to monitor me." Garrick's attitude to Kane had been thawing, but now the iciness in his voice returned with a vengeance.

Kane raised his hands. "What would you have done?"

"I would have talked to me."

"Which we couldn't do because you were a person of interest. Think about it, Wilson, your sister, Howard – all connected to *you*. As I said already, we were working on the assumption there was somebody in power also involved. Could I really trust you or your team?"

"Clearly we can't trust Chib."

Kane wagged a finger. "How wrong you are. Yes, she was put there by me to report on your movements, not about the progress of your cases. And yes, she did... and she hated it. She had nothing but nice things to say about your lot and resented the fact I'd sent her in to keep an eye on you."

Garrick's anger was mollified a little, but he tried not to show it.

"And I see you're not appreciating the scope of my investigation."

"Investigating a person in power. I heard."

"You heard me, but you have your own preconceptions of what power is. Power could be a politician. It could be a DCI or even a lowly constable." He smiled at the look on Garrick's face. "Now, do you see why I had to have somebody I trusted?"

"Are you saying the person who sat on Susan Foss's intelligence report now works for the Force? That would put my team, me included, out of the age bracket of suspicion."

"The entire nature of their club is to recruit strategically."

"And Molly Meyers had stumbled across this. Without realising the full scale of the story. That could damage your entire investigation."

"Yes. Or it could expose who we're looking for... in which case, wouldn't it be best for them to kill the story? Literally."

"It would. But Molly is alive. Why string it out?"

Kane shifted position, but he didn't break eye contact with Garrick.

"Why do you think?"

Garrick felt the chilling reason dawn on him. "To implicate me."

"There you have it. You're not the prize, like you thought. You're a scapegoat. It's almost a sideline to this whole thing, but somebody hates you enough to set you up to take the fall as a serial killer. And what better stooge than a copper? A copper who's been seeing a psychologist. One coming to terms with the grief of his sister's brutal murder. One who may have struck out at those involved in his very own cases.

The media would eat it up. To use a phrase, you'd be cancelled regardless of whether or not you're innocent. And then, the guilty can drift into the shadows and continue what they've always done."

Garrick folded his hands together to hide the fact he was shaking. Kane gave a dry chuckle.

"And the issue I have is that we can't eliminate you from *our* enquires. Whoever is behind this is fully aware of how investigations work. The ins and outs of the legal process. It doesn't matter that you have an alibi when Dr Harman was murdered, because you're obviously working with somebody else."

"Just like Colin Ryman."

"Or *with* Colin Ryman."

Garrick was about to snap back how nonsensical that sounded, but stopped. Kane had a point.

"This second person could be the same woman who put the malware on Amy's and Molly's computers."

"She could be connected or just an innocent thrown into the mix."

"But she was from Guardian Solutions."

"Who confirmed both calls were cancelled. In the same way Foss thinks that Simon Evans was set up because he was going to reveal too much, I think that Colin Ryman is being set up, too. Now he's ill, he's superfluous to the group's needs. He's going to go down with you. David, you're being groomed by people we just can't seem to touch, to take the fall. All roads lead to Rome. And in this analogy, you are Rome."

"If you can't eliminate me from your enquires, why don't you arrest me if I look so guilty?"

"No, David. Unfortunately, I'm on your side. You're more use to me out there, doing what you usually do. Go off the rails. And the thing is, outside of your team and mine, nobody knows you're *here*. Nobody knows if you survived the blast."

"But if the kidnappers have somebody on the inside, they'd know."

"Which would rapidly shrink our search window to just two teams, rather than the entire Kent Constabulary. David, I know how this sounds, but you're better off dead."

A knock on the glass door caused Garrick to jump in his seat. Shit, he was feeling so wound up; it was embarrassing. Kane waved a young man into the room.

"Sir, sorry to interrupt. They've found another body part. And Molly's kidnapper is demanding that DCI Garrick attend the scene."

Kane and Garrick swapped a look. They were both thinking the same thought. Now was the opportunity to turn the tables on the kidnappers.

22

D CI Oliver Kane and DC Harry Lord were greeted at the new location by Chib. Harry hadn't stopped complaining about Garrick's bad faith in stealing his car. Kane had tolerated the constant stream of muttering with good nature, but as they exited from his Rav 4, his patience snapped, and he barked at Harry to shut up.

Used to a more relaxed working environment, Harry kept silent and held up his phone to record every moment of the crime scene as they approached Chib.

"What have we got?" Kane asked as he looked around the large car park. The Londel supermarket sign was still illumi-nated, although the shop had closed a couple of hours ago. The rest of the retail space in Folkestone's Park Farm was empty.

Chib led them to an area that had been taped off between four plastic cones. Beyond, several police vehicles blocked access to the area.

"The head of Father Cillian, left out on display. The

supermarket closed at 10 pm and this was reported at 11:33, so it's a narrow window to dump the head and run."

She stopped several feet from the spherical object that couldn't quite be discerned in the sodium lights. Harry took a few brave steps forward, but he too stopped when he'd seen enough.

"Christ..." Kane muttered.

"This is where we found Jamal's body," Chib pointed out.

The meaning was not lost on any of them.

"*The path once beaten will be revealed again, and with it, the many become whole,*" Harry recited with disgust. "He's building a bloody human jigsaw. We were sent Molly's finger. Does that mean the rest of her is next?"

"Forensics are run off their feet," Chib said, unable to tear her gaze away from the horror. "They're already talking about shipping material to other labs. It's going to slow everything down just when we need to speed up."

Chib's mobile rang. She glanced at the screen: it was an unknown number. She met Kane's gaze, and he gave a subtle nod. She answered it with more confidence than she felt.

"DS Okon."

"I told you I wanted David to be there," came a man's icy calm voice.

From Chib's expression, both Kane and Harry knew who she was talking to. Harry swivelled his phone to record Chib's conversation. She put the call onto her speaker so they could all hear.

"DCI Garrick is in hospital," she said coolly. "He's unconscious and not going anywhere."

"There will be consequences for breaking my rules." The words became almost sibilant with menace.

"He's out of action because of you," Chib snapped.

Her phone beeped as the caller hung up. She flashed a worried look at Harry.

"Did you hear all that?"

"I did, Chib," came Garrick's voice over the AirPods Harry Lord was wearing. He relayed the message. He watched Garrick on his FaceTime connection.

"He knows I'm not there, which means he can see you," said Garrick as he looked at something away from his phone.

"Mmm-hmm," Harry confirmed, slowly panning the camera around the car park.

"But he's not so stupid to hang around."

DCI Garrick had his phone propped on the steering wheel of Harry's BMW. He leaned out of the camera range as he studied the laptop next to him. Over the FaceTime connection, he could hear Harry, Kane, and Chib talking to each other as they spread out across the car park.

Garrick was not computer literate, and loathed having to learn new systems and software, but the program he was using now was surprisingly easy. The clunky icons didn't have the panache reserved for commercial software and betrayed its in-house military origins.

"Okay, Harry, go dark."

Over the phone, he heard DC Lord order all the police units who had turned up to turn off their mobile phones.

Garrick stared at the map on his laptop screen. This handy piece of kit was on loan from Military Intelligence thanks to the resourceful Ms Jackson. It gave a live feed of all the mobile connections in an area. Normally, the police had to request data from phone providers, which could take days to get. The military didn't appear to have such issues regarding data protection and privacy.

The map was focused on the retail park. The fourteen

glowing dots on the screen represented the phones of all the officers who had turned up, and the radios in their vehicles. As preordained, the officers, Kane, and Chib turned off their phones and the police radios – leaving Harry's glowing dot in the centre of the car park.

And one other at the edge.

Garrick couldn't hide the excitement in his voice. "I think it's working. Harry, it looks like there is an active 4G signal in the northwest corner of the carpark."

The dot representing Harry turned in that direction.

"Don't go straight towards it," said Garrick suddenly. "Carry on the way you were walking. It looks like there's a path in the hedge that connects to the housing estate. From there, you can loop back around."

He switched between the dot on the screen and the dark blurry images of Harry running – and swearing - as he followed instructions.

"This is killing my leg," he grumbled. "And you're sitting pretty in my car."

"I'll have it valeted and put in a full tank of fuel when I return it."

"You'd better..."

Garrick had parked a mile away on a side street. The moment he and Kane had been told of the new find they'd hatched a plan. By playing dead, Garrick was suddenly an unpredictable piece in the kidnapper's game. It risked the maniac's wrath, but Garrick hoped that since it was a self-inflicted wound, Molly may not suffer immediately. The baby monitor incident had made him wonder if they'd been watched at every other crime scene. With the malware used to access Molly and Amy's computers, and Ryman's history in security, it was obvious they were dealing with tech-savvy villains. Kane had been the one to suggest monitoring phone signals in the vicinity.

"You're about two yards away," Garrick said as Harry's blip closed in on the phone signal. "Stop. There. Maybe two feet or so to your right and a few paces ahead. I don't know how accurate this thing is."

He'd been given a five-minute pep talk from the technician who'd shown him how the software worked, but Garrick was so focused about not clicking on the wrong thing that the technical details drifted through one ear and out the other.

The sound of branches snapping, and more swearing came from the FaceTime connection.

"Got it. There's a phone zip tied to the tree."

The crunching of more branches followed, then–

"Shit!"

"Harry?" Garrick watched as the rogue dot on his map disappeared.

The FaceTime image shifted as Harry switched to the selfie camera. In the low light, he was difficult to make out, but Garrick could see he was holding up a phone.

"It was on a call, but hung up when I took it."

"He may know we have it... he may think it's a problem. Either way, this is it."

They kept the connection open as Harry re-joined Kane, Chib, and the technician who'd travelled with them. He watched the map light up as the cops switched their phones and radios back on.

The minutes ticked by. "Harry?"

"The nerd has the phone." He aimed his phone camera at a young man in the back of an unmarked van.

Garrick had half-listened as it was explained to him that they needed the phone's unique IMEI number to trace the last call made. They'd employed such technology in previous cases, but never with so much urgency.

There was an audible rise in activity around the van. In the poor light, Garrick could only see merging blurs and couldn't distinguish one voice from the other. Then the image swung back onto Harry's face, illuminated from above by a nearby lamppost.

"They've got a fix on the masts from the originating signal!"

Unlike how tracing a phone call was portrayed the movies, there was *never* any need to keep the suspect on the telephone to trace a signal. Mobile phone data was sent from mast-to-mast and logged every step of the way. The quality of phone calls often dipped in and out of strength as the phone switched to different masts to receive the best signal. The source of the call could be further narrowed by using at least three masts in a technique called triangulation. Garrick was familiar with the logistics. He knew also that it wasn't foolproof.

"He's sending it to you now," Harry confirmed.

Garrick looked back at the laptop on the passenger seat. The map suddenly zoomed out and scrolled as it fixed onto the new coordinates.

Chib's voice came over the connection. "Sir, can you see this?"

The phone's video shifted as Chib plucked the handset from Harry's hand and fixed it on herself. Her eyes were wide in surprise.

"I see it, Chib. The bastard really is playing a game of my greatest hits. I'm on my way."

He stabbed the engine's start button and the six-cylinder engine growled to life. He snapped the laptop lid closed and was accelerating with such urgency that he couldn't make out Chib's and Kane's protests over his phone as momentum flung it from his steering wheel and it cartwheeled into the back of the car.

He knew where Molly Meyers was.

He just prayed that the kidnapper didn't know he was on his way.

23

D riving the powerful BMW through narrow country lanes carried none of the drama Garrick expected. It was more like a smooth magic carpet ride compared to his decrepit Land Rover. That made the onset of his migraine even more unfathomable. What felt like a bolt of electricity shot from the back of his skull to just above his left eyeball with such ferociousness that he slammed on the brakes and skidded to a halt.

The rising taste of bile had him scrambling for the door handle, and he fell out onto his hands and knees to throw up on the grass verge. In the reflected light from his headlights, the hedge in front of him appeared to warp and twist.

"No!" he snarled into the darkness. He didn't need this. He couldn't submit to his own weakness now that he was so close to victory.

His fingers dug into the dry grass and dirt, and he closed his eyes to stop the world from shuddering. Garrick recalled the concern on the nurse's face when she mentioned the scan he needed. He must have suffered some head trauma during the explosion – the fact he couldn't remember it was evidence enough. He lightly ran his fingers through his hair. Other than a horrible greasy feeling that reminded him he desperately needed to shower, there was no tenderness. No signs of a hidden gash in his skull.

"Pull yourself together," he said aloud.

It was an uncomfortably humid September evening, and he was sweating heavily. He inhaled a dozen slow, deep breaths, then opened his eyes. The world was still unsteady but bearable.

He stood – and then staggered. His hand shot for the open car door to steady himself. No poor damsel in distress had ever relied on such an unfit knight in grubby armour.

He sat back in the car and pulled the door closed. Gripping the wheel, he took stock of the situation. He was less than a mile from his destination. DCI Kane and a horde of armed officers were undoubtedly closing in – but how far behind would they be? He thought it unlikely that the unit could get anywhere close for the next fifteen minutes at least, by which time the kidnapper could escape if he knew the authorities were closing in.

Garrick was the vanguard.

For all his many imperfections, he was Molly's best hope.

Despite the urgency, Garrick drove on at a more sedate pace. Partly because the car's powerful engine reverberated through the night and would herald his coming, but mostly because it was painful to concentrate on the narrow road ahead.

Reaching a junction in the road, he pulled over and cut the engine. Pilgrim's Way cut across his path. Three hundred yards further down was a place he knew well - Classic Aero. While the triangulation gave a rough area that encompassed a couple of farms, the renowned aircraft restoration company was a place he'd almost been killed during a previous case. And it lay in a blackout zone for Molly's phone carrier, which was the same one as Garrick, and fell within Zoe's kill zone. The kidnapper was either on a different network or calling via the internet.

As he was trolling Garrick by piecing together parts of his previous cases, the airfield was the most likely venue.

He felt for his phone in the rear footwell. Retrieving it, he noticed missed calls from Chib, Harry, and Kane from before he'd lost his signal. He was on his own.

He climbed out of the car, remembering to lock it and pocket the key fob. He set the phone's torch to a low light and hurried down the lane.

On foot, and in near darkness, the pain in his head eased. As he neared the turn-off into the estate, a cool chill tickled his spine despite the warm air. He had no plan, no weapon, no idea what lay in wait for him. The only advantage he had was that the kidnapper wasn't expecting him.

Or so he hoped.

Digging through his memory, Garrick tried to recall the case notes from the last time he was here. For once, he was thankful that cases didn't simply stop at the arrest. He'd been back to the scene several times, so had the opportunity to view the location in the daylight. It was owned by a family who'd been away during the last incident. Was it likely they had left the property abandoned once again? He'd never interviewed them. That had been left to DC Wilkes, but they came across as normal people who had been shocked to be part of a police investigation. Assuming that they were still home and innocent, then that made the situation even more precarious, as it had never occurred to anyone that there may be more than one hostage.

Moonlight reflecting from white clouds offered a soft light in which Garrick could see the closed entrance gate of the house ahead. A *for sale* sign was bolted to the side of the brick wall. Beyond the wrought-iron gate, the lane lay at a slight angle away from the road. Through the bars, Garrick could see the dark and foreboding silhouette of the house beyond.

He turned the torch light off and kept to the shadows across the lane. The top of the gate was spiked, but the surrounding eight-foot wall seemed to be a more accessible option. From his low angle, Garrick couldn't tell if it was safe to climb or if it was crowned with razor wire, but it was the only way in.

Stomping on the brambles growing on the thin sliver of dirt between the road and the foot of the wall, he blindly reached up and felt the top of it. His fingertips told him it was worse than he'd feared – broken glass. It was a good deterrent, Garrick thought, and one that could see the house-holder sued by a potential burglar who was injured. Well, he could do with the extra cash.

His fingertips traced the glass. Weather and time had blunted the edges. Putting the phone in his trouser pocket, he took off his padded Barbour. While he had been with Kane, somebody had the kindness to clean it with a damp cloth, probably because it was smelling out the incident room. Now he was about to ruin it again as he hung it over the wall. He gently applied pressure and was satisfied the jacket absorbed any potentially painful hazards. With a grunt, Garrick heaved himself up, his shoes scrambling against the wall for purchase. His toecaps caught in several cracks in the crumbling brickwork, and he was surprised to find himself swiftly lying across his coat. The dull pressure of the glass beneath his improvised insulation layer warned him that, blunt or not, his chest and hands would have been shredded by the glass. He swung his leg over to the sound of several small tears in the fabric of his trousers, followed immediately by sharp stings as he was cut. Then he dropped into the darkness below, hoping there was nothing painful to greet his fall.

Gravel crunched underfoot, and he found himself within the estate. He tugged his coat down and slipped it back on. Trying to lighten each step, he hurried towards the house, aware that a simple security camera would undo all his stealthy antics.

There was no sign of life at the house. Garrick assumed the owners had left the moment the for sale sign had been erected. The wide driveway curved to the right, towards the rear of the property, where it widened between several large aircraft hangars in which the previous business had repaired light aircraft and stored a selection of vintage planes. A stretch of grass had served as the airstrip.

Did he hear something?

Garrick stopped. The gravel underfoot was amplified in his ears, and the pause allowed the strains of the countryside to rise from the darkness. A nearby hooting owl caught his attention to the right. Other than that, nothing stirred.

Doubt gnawed at Garrick. He'd been feeling smug at seizing the chance of getting a jump on the kidnapper, but was now fearing that they'd been led on a wild goose chase. John Howard had been his friend, a confidant with whom he'd shared details of previous cases because of the man's penchant to match his deep general knowledge and quirky thinking to help Garrick see evidence in a new light. He'd never suspected that it was because Howard possessed the mind of a calculating killer. As a result, John Howard had seen how Garrick operated. The choices he made, the cul-de-sacs he often navigated himself into, even how Garrick's personal life affected his work. The dead man knew Garrick better than he knew himself.

The deep shadows on the curving driveway ahead forced Garrick to slow down. He didn't want to risk using his torch, no matter how faint the light would be. He followed the turn in between two large hangars. It ended in a long courtyard with a huge barn workshop in front of him, a pair of hangars to the right, and two to the left. A slipway ran to the grass airstrip in the darkness beyond. The doors to the hangars were closed.

Except one.

A crack of light shone through the vertical slit, casting a white line across the courtyard, beckoning – or luring – Garrick inside. He searched for something to use as a weapon. The last time he had been here, the yard was filled with spare parts, junk, and storage containers - all the hall-marks of a busy repair yard. They had gone; the business had been stripped clean in just a couple of months. It made him feel acutely defenceless.

Keeping close to the hangar wall, Garrick edged closer. He reached the gap in the doors and struggled to still his own breathing, which sounded like a ragged siren betraying his position.

He could hear nothing from within.

To add insult to injury, Garrick was unsure if the gap between the doors was large enough to allow him to easily slip through, with an additional two inches around his waist.

He girded himself for the final push. Gone were the dark

thoughts of his illness, the stress of his career, the pain of losing his estranged sister, the sickness he felt thinking of DC Fanta Liu lying unconscious in the hospital. He only had one clear thought.

He hadn't told Wendy that he loved her.

It was a revelation. He cared about her, certainly. Since meeting her on the *Heartfelt* app, she had become the pillar of light and happiness in his life. For the last month, he'd even stopped faffing around with his fossils to spend more time with her.

The sickness he'd felt rushing between the school and her home had been more than concern. Now he recognised it for what it was. Love. He did not know if she felt the same for him, but it didn't matter. Circumstances had made him guarded and aloof for the last couple of weeks, and yet she'd still put up with him.

And now he was walking into danger. He could handle the presence of a man who impulsively killed in the moment, but Ryman was a calculating sociopath. Defenceless and unprepared, David Garrick knew that if his tumour wasn't about to kill him, then the odds favoured an ex-soldier.

Aware he was burning precious seconds, he took out his phone and prepared a text message for Wendy. The words came willingly.

I LOVE YOU. SORRY I NEVER TOLD YOU X

He pressed send. There was no signal, but he hoped it would eventually find its way to her when his corpse left the blackout zone.

He put his phone back in his pocket. With clenched fists, he peered through the gap into the hangar.

24

The vintage aeroplanes he'd last seen here had gone. Their absence amplified the sense of space inside the hangar. A humid haze filled the air; it was a few degrees warmer inside. It was a hundred-foot long with three spotlights; the sort used in photography studios, providing the only illumination in the middle. They focused on a steel-framed chair to which Molly Meyers was bound.

Her head was slumped on his chest. Her wavy red hair was now lank and clung to the sweat on her face. Gaffer tape adhered her arms to the back of the seat and was coiled around her ankles. A pair of black headphones was similarly fixed to her head, with coils of grey tape circling over her head and around her jaw.

Two foldable wooden tables had been dragged to the edge of the light, on which lay a saw, several knives, and a pair of nasty-looking sheep shearing scissors.

Molly Meyers was fifty feet away, cocooned by thick shadows Garrick couldn't see through. He was unarmed and exposed.

He couldn't shake the feeling that he was walking into a trap.

Backup was on the way, but Molly's condition could be deteriorating by the second, so he couldn't afford to wait. The harsh spotlights had triggered his migraine again, and if he stared directly at them, they trembled like a mirage. He grimly reflected that the fifty-foot walk to Molly might kill him sooner than any murderous psychopath.

One last sweep of the courtyard confirmed he was alone. He checked his phone – still no signal.

This was it. Breathing in, he squeezed himself through the gap between the doors.

Inside, he walked purposefully towards Molly. His boots scuffed on the smooth floor, the noise echoing through the empty space. The pain in his head shifted position, now sending sharp crackles down his neck and into his spine as if his tumour was trying to short circuit him.

With every step, an inner voice warned him it would be his last. He squinted against the lights to see what lurked in the shadows. He was halfway across to Molly and still nobody had jumped him. Molly hadn't moved at all and the anxious thought that he was already too late turned his legs into jelly. He had to force each step to get closer.

The shallow rhythmic rise of her white shirt assured him she was breathing. It was damp and speckled with blood, with a dry crimson patch on the floor under her left hand. Even at an angle, he could just see her little finger was missing.

Only ten feet remained.

Garrick glanced behind him. Nobody was creeping up to assault him. Then he became aware of a low, tinny sound. It took him several second to trace it to Molly's headphones.

They were chunky black Bose noise cancelation ones from which he could *just* discern a stream of thrash metal music. He was reminded of US black site torture techniques from waterboarding to playing harsh music to breakdown a victim's mental state. He couldn't imagine the horrors Molly had been dragged through.

Then he was right next to her, and still nothing had happened. He felt a surge of adrenaline – had he really got ahead of the game?

"I'm here, Molly." She couldn't hear him, and the words were more to soothe his own nerves. He knelt and ran a hand over the binding around her left wrist. She sensed his touch and her head moved slightly and she gave a weak, muffled squeal. The tape was too thick to break with his fingers. He remembered the knives on the table and took one. It was a six-inch stainless steel carving knife. It was a little unwieldy for the task at hand, but he couldn't complain.

"You'll be out of here in a moment."

He moved the blade to her wrist, then changed his mind and positioned it to remove the headphones and relieve her of the audio nightmare. Garrick found it difficult to keep the blade steady as his hands shook and his focus shimmered, as if Molly had become a ghost. The razor-sharp point danced too close to her exposed neck for comfort, and he edged it closer to the headphones.

A noise from outside made him jump. The hangar door slid open.

Garrick sprang to his feet, clutching the knife tightly. He braced himself to face the enemy, but found he was shaking and feeling weak. Primal instinct took over, and he suddenly darted between the lights and into the darkness. The sound of the sliding door masked his footsteps. Garrick stopped several yards further into the hangar before realising there was nowhere to hide. He was completely exposed. He spun around; his grip tightening on the blade.

"It's t-time, my dear," the figure said with a prominent stammer.

He was just beyond the pool of light, yet Garrick could just make out he was carrying a tripod with an SLR camera mounted on it. In his other hand, he held a mobile phone. He was shaking as he watched the screen.

"A l-little l-late, but..." he finally looked up – straight at Garrick. But instead of reacting, he smiled and continued towards Molly, unable to raise his right foot with each step, causing it to drag a little. Entering the pool of light, he recognised Colin Ryman, wearing jeans that were a size over, and an old combat jacket. Even from the most recent photographs, Parkinson's had dramatically aged him. The hair at his sides was white, his cheeks sallow and paralysed on the left, and he'd lost a lot of weight. "It's j-just as we p-planned."

Garrick was coiled to pounce – but suddenly understood that he was too far into the shadows to be seen. Just as he'd feared being attacked, the darkness now cloaked him. He had a choice – to wait until Ryman was closer, and therefore an easier target, or stop him now.

Ryman set the tripod down at the edge of the light. His Parkinson's was so severe that he spent several moments struggling to spread the already expanded legs to secure it in place. Even in Garrick's weakened state, the man was no threat to him. But that raised another problem. As Kane had said, the man didn't have the strength to carry out the savage butchery on his victims.

That meant there definitely was a second killer.

With the tripod in place, Ryman ensured the SLR was pointed at Molly and pressed the video record button. He limped closer.

"You w-w-won't have to w-wait too long." He reached for Molly and hooked a trembling finger under her chin to angle her head upward. "You'll f-feel such a r-release," he whispered, then pressed his dry, cracked lips against her gagged mouth. She tried to pull away, but it was a token gesture. "I will m-miss you."

Ryman turned to the table of implements next to him. Garrick immediately regretted allowing the man to get so close to them. With a bellow of rage, Garrick sprinted forward. The audible warning caused Ryman to pause as his hand fell onto a handle of a meat cleaver. Although not in his prime, Garrick imagined his gazelle-like leap from the shadows - when, in reality, it was little more than a barely controlled fall. But it had the desired effect of rapidly closing the distance between the men.

Garrick automatically raised the knife in his hand and thrust the blade down. It wasn't a calculated movement. It was guttural and raw.

The knife slid through the back of Ryan's outstretched hand. Bone cracked under the force, and Garrick felt a jolt as the blade emerged through Ryman's palm and deflected from the cleaver's metal handle. With Garrick's body weight behind the blow, the blade jinked sideways, severing through the veins in Ryman's hand, and continued driving down through the wooden table for several inches. Ryman fell to his knees, dropping his mobile phone, but unable to land on the ground as his outstretched arm was now pinned to the table. He didn't scream. Perhaps he could no longer feel the pain. His one good eye widened in surprise, and he sniggered.

"Colin Ryman, you're under arrest..." Garrick gasped. The words sounded anticlimactic, especially as the suspect was chuckling hard. That's when Garrick noticed the hand with which he'd been holding the phone was now inside his jacket pocket. He slowly withdrew it – revealing a bomb detonator clenched in his trembling fingers. His thumb hovered over the red button at the end. A thumb that was shaking uncontrollably because of his Parkinson's.

"No, no, no, Davey. T-this whole p-place is w-wired."

Garrick was hit by a conflict of emotions. The irony of being at the mercy of a man with Parkinson's and his finger on the trigger of a suicide bomb, and the use of the name *Davey*. Only his sister had ever called him that.

He tried to remember the call he'd received at the start of the year. He'd been sure that it was his sister's voice... but had it been? It was whispered, unexpected. Had his recollection coloured it with Emelie's voice, when in fact it was this piece of filth in front of him? If it wasn't for Molly bound just feet away, Garrick felt he would have pulled the trigger himself.

"We h-haven't f-finished," Ryman purred.

"I was never playing you game." Garrick's hand was still on the hilt of the carving knife. He gave it a twist. Torn flesh cracked and blood trickled over the side of the table and dripped steadily to the floor.

Ryman didn't react. Instead, he smirked. "You n-never had a c-choice." His trigger-hand bobbed uncertainly. "Oops..."

Garrick felt an unexpected surge of confidence. His eyes darted from the detonator to Ryman. This time, *he* smiled and enjoyed the sudden uncertainty in Ryman's eyes.

"You won't pull the trigger."

"T-try me."

"Why end this elaborate plan right now when you're on the cusp of success? You won't do it. *He* won't let you."

Despite his Parkinson's, Garrick swore Colin Ryman's eyes flickered nervously. He was sure he'd hit a nerve. Then the stony façade returned.

"I w-was with E-Emilie."

The mere mention of her name made Garrick's blood boil. That was enough to embolden Ryman. His voice dropped to a conspiratorial whisper.

"I w-was with her w-when s-she cut off her own t-two fingers–"

Garrick hadn't registered taking his hand off the knife, nor his fingers clenching into a fist. It wasn't until he struck Ryman across the face twice, and with such power, that the scumbag's canine fell out. Ryman swayed – the hand holding the detonator knuckling against the floor to support him.

Ryman spat blood and chuckled. "S-she was r-running for her l-life. It was a c-close thing."

Garrick's arm pulled back to strike again – but was distracted by a movement in the corner of his eye. Beyond the SLR camera, the hangar doors slid open even wider. A network of red lasers suddenly combed across the room, highlighted by the humid haze. Several black-clad figures rushed inside with multiple voices shouting at the same time.

"ARMED POLICE! ON THE FLOOR!"

The red threads danced across Garrick and Ryman, who were attempting to stand. He waved the detonator above his head.

Garrick heard one chilling word echo through the hangar.

"BOMB!"

Movement around him appeared to move in slow motion, yet his quivering vision cranked up a gear as if he was witnessing everything on an old movie projector as the film reel jarred loose and was torn up by the mechanism.

The web of lasers swept off him and onto Ryman.

Garrick threw himself at Molly Meyers, his body weight toppling her chair sideways. They both crashed to the ground as hell erupted.

25

T he rhythmic sound of DC Fanta Liu's patient monitor was hypnotic. She lay on her back in the ward, unmoving, just as she had been for the last two days. Bandages covered her face, and a ventilator tube kept her breathing.

David Garrick stared at her with tears rolling unchecked down his face. This was the first time he'd seen her since the explosion, and the only time that her family had taken a break from being at her side. He hadn't wanted to be around at the same time as them because he lacked the courage to explain what had happened. The guilt still made him feel sick.

In some ways, a lot had changed in the two days since Molly Meyers had been rescued, and in other ways, life appeared to motor along as usual.

Colin Ryman had been pronounced dead at the scene. The order to fire had come directly from DCI Kane, who'd feared the ex-soldier would bring the building down on them all. As it turned out, there had been no bomb, just as Garrick supposed. He'd rather be gunned down by the police than face trial.

He and Molly Meyers had been taken to Canterbury Hospital. Molly was in a bad way, dehydrated, starved, suffering blood loss from a severed finger, and her eardrums had perforated under the constant barrage of sound that had broken her spirit.

But she was alive, and Garrick was hailed the hero of the hour, and all he had suffered were half a dozen stitches in his hands, legs, and on his cheek. He hadn't been able to avoid an MRI scan, swiftly followed by a bollocking from his doctor. Doctor Rajasekar had immediately put him on a new cocktail of drugs, the names of which went over his head. They eased the pain, the swelling, and the shaking he'd endured. Rajasekar also confirmed the grim news that his tumour had swelled by a millimetre, and they would have to operate as soon as possible. She had demanded that he stay in hospital for observation, something that he had no intention of complying with.

He hadn't stepped foot across the threshold of Fanta's room. Even unconscious, he feared that the sound of his voice may send her into convulsions. He'd been told that she'd been lucky. The door she'd opened in Ryman's house had effectively taken the brunt of the blast. She'd triggered an improvised explosive built from a gas cylinder; the sort usually purchased to fuel caravans. Without the door in the way, she would have possibly died from shrapnel wounds. The explosion had taken out the front corner of the house. The room had been above the kitchen, and that wing had effectively collapsed with Garrick and Fanta inside. SOCO pointed out that the bomb could have easily been made deadlier by including nails or ball bearings. It seemed designed to destroy the property, not people.

When Garrick could no longer bear watching Fanta's weak heart rate, he left Orpington Hospital and headed to see DCI Kane, this time as a guest in the detective's modern incident room, although Garrick was under no illusion that this was going to be a serious debrief.

The two of them sat in Kane's soundproof office.

"It's a nice feeling to close a case," Oliver Kane said as he stirred sugar into his tea, which was several shades paler than Garrick could stomach.

Garrick shrugged. "My case isn't close."

"You found Ms Meyers. The kidnapper is dead. She has confirmed that was the man who had been tormenting her."

Too many questions were irritating Garrick, but he held back the desire to argue his point.

Kane smiled. "So, congratulations." He gestured through the window. "And it appears mine has also reached its *dénouement*. Which in turn means I have to mop up all your loose ends."

"How so?"

"We found Father Cillian's head in a chest freezer on the premises. Along with Ye-Jun Joh's head. It had been shipped over from the States. You saved Molly's from being the next one."

"Mine would have followed."

Kane didn't respond. He sipped his tea. "As far as we can tell, Mr Ryman moved into the airfield about a week after the business had failed and they'd been forced to put it on the market. Molly was there from day one. She was taken to the windmill. Didn't see the attack coming. He sedated her at first with chloroform, then with *flunitrapam*."

"I saw the condition he was in. He couldn't have knocked her out."

"I'm simply telling you her statement."

"And flunitrapam was used on Amy Harman."

"Hardly a unique drug in these sorts of crimes."

"But enough unsatisfactory answers to keep the cases open."

Kane gestured with both hands. "I've been told that's it."

"By whom?"

"Military Intelligence is satisfied that the unholy trinity of Ryman, Evans, and Howard are currently burning in hell. They have no desire to have their prints over this case at all, so there will be some evidence that will remain classified. Fortunately, with no living defendants against their Murder Club, that's going to be easy to sweep under the rug. Drury is satisfied that her hero saved Ms Meyers. And Commissioner Edwards has told her Whitehall is keen to close the lid. Because of the military connection."

"Colin Ryman had Parkinson's disease, so he couldn't have done it all on his own."

"His diagnosis must've been wrong. They said stage four, but it mustn't have been. He was obviously still capable of murder."

"There was no need to kill him."

Kane waved his hand helplessly. "What would you have done in my position? You and Meyers right there, and him with his finger on a detonator. It was impossible to tell it was a fake. In America, they call it suicide by cop."

"He was telling me about my sister, for God's sake. Then you come trouncing in, guns blazing."

"I thought I was saving your life. Next time I assure you, I'll wait and give it a lot more thought."

Garrick drew in a sharp breath to argue, but Kane continued.

"And the FBI has confirmed that Colin Ryman was in America at the same time as John Howard. Both our surviving Murder Club members were at that ranch. The FBI is working on the assumption that they were having a good old knees-up with some of their other members."

"And Emilie just so happened to drive by?"

Kane leaned back in his chair and steepled his fingers. "That would be one hell of a coincidence. And I know how you feel about coincidences. That's the one trait we share." He wrestled with how he should continue. "What do you know about Sam McKinzie?"

Garrick's thoughts had been drifting, but at the mention of Sam's name, they slammed back to the present moment.

"Emilie's fiancé. The road trip was supposed to be their last adventure before they married and settled down. He was one of the victims at the ranch."

Kane chose his words carefully. "The current line of thinking suggests he may not be as much of a victim as we all first thought."

Garrick had never met Sam, although he attended the funeral and lamented his passing, but he'd honestly never factored the man in his thinking, other than just another poor victim. After all, his body had been recovered. Emelie was still missing.

"Are you suggesting he *took* Emilie there?"

"I'm not suggesting anything. I'm telling you what I read between the lines when we spoke to the FBI. If you thought I was keeping information from you, the FBI is doing a far better job against me. I'm trying to help you out, David."

"There's a first. Maybe it's too late for that."

Kane chuckled as he stirred his tea again before taking a sip.

"I'm on your side. Always have been. Maybe you hate me. Maybe you hate the Met. I don't know. Perhaps you'll thank me for this later."

He held up a small square of plastic. It was an SD memory card.

"I retrieved it from Ryman's SLR. It caught an interesting exchange before I arrived. You know as well as I that we're all held to the highest standards. I mean, these days we can't even push the proven guilty down a staircase. Even convicted criminals have rights." He gently waved the SD card. "And in some quarters what people see on this may be perceived as police brutality."

"I stabbed him in the hand to stop him reaching for the cleaver."

"Arguably a use of appropriate force. Punching him repeatedly in the face, however..." Garrick shifted uncomfortably in his chair. "You could always blame this." He tapped the side of his head, indicating Garrick's tumour. "But of course, then questions will come out as to why DC Lord concealed evidence."

The temperature in the room plummeted. Kane didn't make eye contact as he sipped his tea.

"Don't think this is anything more than me trying to help you. I want *nothing* to weaken our case against Colin Ryman. Especially not a detective who was hiding a potentially problematic tumour that was interfering in his duties."

He finally locked eyes with Garrick. His gaze was steady and lacking any of the warmth in his voice.

"Understand, David, I don't report to Drury. This is a Met investigation, not Kent Constabulary's. And that's just the way it is because we're also looking for corruption in your Force. We have a wider remit, one which you have helped along several times over."

Garrick couldn't believe that DCI Kane was essentially willing to let evidence slip in order to allow the bigger case to run its course. Although some of it was in Garrick's own interests, he felt very uncomfortable. He finally found his voice.

"What's your conclusion?"

"A simple one. Considering. Our Murder Club trio recruited around the world. They all had, and those out there still have, their perverse fantasies. The FBI will continue to pursue that. British involvement lies at the feet of our founding trio. They're all now gone. You were dragged into this because of your sister. I said we are wrapping everything up here, but that's not strictly true, as our focus is now on Sam McKinzie. Emelie's fiancé. Somewhere along the route, he and John Howard had contact. To a messed-up group like that, the lure of killing a brother and a sister, particularly with one being a DCI, must've been seen as a challenge. A powerful lure. Don't forget, these people treated killing as an art form. Their victims were always toyed with. There was no honour in stabbing some poor wretch in the back and running away. That lacks elegance and finesse."

"That's exactly what happened to poor Eric."

"He was killed by a middleman. Thugs paid to transport things. They're not killers. If you pay enough, you can get anybody to transport anything to anywhere."

"So all this bullshit I've been through has just been to wear me down?"

"I believe so. What a hoot, eh? A psychological experiment to see just how far they can push you. According to our psych reports, it fits with John Howard's philosophy."

Garrick nodded. "I hate to say it, but that fits. That's what made him a useful bloke to speak to. His psychological approach to cases."

"And he clearly had you in his sights, right after they killed Emilie."

Garrick still couldn't believe that her fiancé would have anything to do with such an insane collective. But then again, he knew nothing about the man.

"Then who killed Sam McKinzie?"

"They're predators. Maybe they turned on him? Who knows? I don't pretend to know all the ins and outs of what he had in mind. But making you think Emilie's ghost was reaching from beyond the grave, subtly breaking into your house to make you question your own sanity, even the gift of the car – all planned when John was alive."

"And Ryman was just finishing the mission."

"Once a soldier, always a soldier. The impulse to obey the chain of command is burnt into you from day one."

"You were a military man?"

Kane gave a jaded smile. "Which is why I recognise the behaviour. Ryman, a founding father of their little cult, facing an unstoppable decline in his own health, has the chance for one last piece of pre-planned mischief."

"And then Molly Meyers blunders through, suddenly threatening to expose the group and all their past crimes."

"And as the sole survivor, Colin Ryman will get the full force of blame. But he thinks he has the chance to become a legend in his own mind. Kill two birds with one stone. Kidnap Ms Meyers with the intention of killing her, which would bring you down with it. Throw in some new victims from the case that led to John Howard's death, cover it with some symbolic bullshit about carving them up, and we have a man on his last mission."

Garrick watched a small, satisfied smile creep across DCI Kane's face as he sipped his tea.

"You're forgetting three things," Garrick said. "One, I saw the state Ryman was in. I don't care if you think he was misdiagnosed. He was stammering, half his face was paralysed. He'd have trouble wrestling a child to the ground, never mind killing somebody. Two, we still haven't traced the woman who planted the malware on the computers."

Kane waved his hand dismissively. "She's a bit player. Ryman employed hundreds of freelancers. We'll find her, but I don't think she was at all aware of why she was doing it. And three?"

"Mmm?"

"You said there were three things."

Garrick stood up. He'd had enough of DCI Kane and couldn't stand to be in the room with him any longer.

"Three? I forget what that was. Obviously, it wasn't important."

Garrick congratulated Kane on closing the case and quickly left.

The third thing loomed in the foremost of his mind. And right behind that was the urgent desire to see Wendy. It had been far too long since he'd held her.

26

Cases never closed the moment the victim was arrested, or in this case, shot dead. Garrick was fond of telling anybody about this truism of police work, which seemed to be the fundamental theme of most TV dramas. As practical policing stopped, the titles didn't roll; a mountain of paperwork began. This transition was taking place as he walked into his incident room in Maidstone.

The tension in the air was palpable. Perhaps it was Garrick's imagination. Or maybe the unseasonably warm weather was creating an atmosphere so cloying that he could take a bite out of it. DC Harry Lord was at his desk, assembling the huge amount of forensic data the kidnapping had left behind.

"Any plot holes?" Garrick said, glancing through a neat stack of printouts arranged on the table next to him. Despite efficiency drives and environmental targets, printed paper was a detective's friend.

Harry glanced around and kept his voice low and uncharacteristically cautious. "DCI Kane's mob wants everything funnelled to them and Drury's authorised it."

"You mean as soon as we close things, they hoover up the accolades?"

"Kane's pushing to close everything quickly. And you ask for plot holes..." his gaze swept the room. "It feels like Ryman is a patsy." He didn't want to say more.

Garrick nodded. "Have you got his medical file to hand?"

Harry gestured to his computer. "It's in here somewhere. How urgent is it?"

Garrick recognised a man drowning under paperwork. "Don't bust a gut, but the end of the day'll be handy. Before Kane and co. decide it's off limits to the likes of us."

Harry nodded in understanding. "Oh, the Super wants to see you."

"Is she in her office?"

"On the golf links. She sounded in a good mood."

"Crap..."

"My thoughts exactly."

DC Sean Wilkes entered the room, looking wan and pale. His schoolboy good looks were distorted by heavy bags under his eyes. Garrick crossed to him as the DC used all his willpower to sit at his desk.

"Sean. How're you feeling?"

Sean and DC Fanta Liu had been dating for some months now. It wasn't something Garrick wanted to encourage, but he could hardly deny them the follies of youth.

"OK, sir," he mumbled without looking up.

"If I could, I'd send you home..."

"I can't leave the others wading through this. Besides, what would I do at home? It's not as if I can sleep."

"Any word from the hospital?"

That caused Sean to glance up at his boss. "Same. No worse; no better."

Garrick stopped himself from pointing out that stable was a good condition, and it dawned on him that Sean might be holding him responsible for what had happened to his girlfriend. He could hardly blame him, even if events had spiralled out of his control.

"She'll pull through. If there's one thing I know about our Fanta is she's stubborn enough to piss off every doctor in that hospital."

Sean stood and took a file from the table near Harry. "Let's hope so, sir." He left the room.

"The kid's cut up," Harry said when Sean was out of earshot. "Can't say I blame him. Don't take it personally. He's not got enough scars from policing yet, so he's not worked out that it's the scumbags we should be blaming."

Garrick gave a terse nod. Until now, he hadn't realised he needed to hear some words of comfort that the world wasn't going to shit around him. Or because of him. The guilt of being at the core of John Howard's twisted legacy was tying him in knots. His shoulders throbbed with tension, sending convulsions of pain up his neck. He'd never felt such a need to take a break from reality. His first port of call was to see Wendy. Tonight.

Garrick cleared his throat. "Speaking of scars... Chib?"

"That's not for me to comment on, sir. It's out of my pay grade."

"Where is she?"

"Ebbsfleet. DCI Kane summoned her."

Garrick cast his gaze across the evidence board. Lives taken for no reason. Killers fuelled by selfish gratification and perceived injustices. He reflected on what he might be doing if he wasn't a detective. Garrick didn't really have any skills that were practical in the real world. He'd been drawn to the profession by the lure of getting into the criminal mind and thinking five steps ahead of a villain as he hunted him down, bringing him to justice. That gloss had soon faded the deeper he stepped into the mind of a killer. He reflected that, if anybody else had asked him why he was a copper, then he'd come up with some tosh about serving justice for those who deserve it. The reality was that Garrick appreciated the companionship of a small team. He'd never really socialised with them and maintained an air of professional detachment, but hanging around with them all, cracking cases together, that gave him a sense of completeness. It must be what it feels like to be in a gang. Or perhaps he'd read too many Famous Five books as a kid.

Harry broke his thoughts. "For what it's worth, she never enjoyed working behind your back."

Garrick didn't turn around. He was focused on the file picture of Colin Ryman.

"How long have you known Chib was a plant?"

"Not long. Shortly before you came back from compassionate leave, one of Kane's lot asked us all questions about you. Then DS Okon appears, and Wilson wasn't returning anyone's calls. But it wasn't until Doctor Harman was killed and we were taken under Kane's wings did we know. She admitted it. Fanta had a go at her. Called her a traitor. Even Sean stuck up for you."

Garrick wiped a tear rolling down his cheek. It didn't belong there.

"And you?"

"Somebody's got to keep you in check. Sir."

Garrick turned and was delighted to see Harry's wry

smile had returned. It was a hint of normality. He looked at the time and was dismayed to see the glass on his black Guess diver's watch was cracked. How come he hadn't noticed until now? It was stopped at 20:38 – the time of the house explosion.

Checking the time on his phone, he started walking to the door. "I best see what fate Drury has in mind for me. Let me know when Chib gets back."

The thwack of Margery Drury's three-wood on the golf ball sounded reassuringly solid. She froze in position, with the club poised over her shoulder above and behind her as she tracked the ball down the fairway.

Garrick was not a sportsman and had already lost sight of it against the clear blue sky, but Drury's unblinking gaze followed it as it bounced on the edge of the green. Garrick felt he should say something complimentary, but he didn't want to sound sycophantic, so kept silent. She slipped the club back into her wheeled caddy and pulled it behind her as she ambled towards the green. Garrick obediently followed, as he had since the last hole where he'd debriefed her on the final moments of releasing Molly Meyers.

"She's responded well to fluids," Drury said at last. "Although she's almost deaf, but that's temporary. She's been talking, but you know reporters. Oliver thinks she's holding back on some things she can later use them as an exclusive."

"Why is Kane interviewing a witness in *my* case?"

"In both your cases, remember? Let's not get territorial about this. The Met has been taking the lead from the beginning."

Garrick was an old enough hand to know he was being muscled out of the glory, as was the Kent Constabulary.

"As for you," Drury continued, "I'm aware of your medical

condition, and I expect you to take time off to sort it out." She had a knack of making a brain tumour sound like a mild aliment. "Then I expect you back behind your desk."

Garrick had dreaded telling her about his condition. The side effects alone could be seen as a detriment to his work. Nobody wanted a lead investigator suffering from occasional bouts of hallucination. Her *laisser-faire* attitude was more than a surprise, and probably the best compliment he'd receive for a job well done under extremely stressful circumstances.

"I was thinking of a little time off to talk to the FBI about Emelie."

Drury shook her head. "That's not happening, David. And before you try to insist, I had a word with the right people Stateside. This isn't a bad sit-com in which a Brit teams up with the FBI and solves crimes. The Feds are handling things on their side. DCI Kane is working closely with them on this side, and you would just be in the way. That's how it is. You're in the same shoes as all those poor sods you've helped over the years in bringing down their bad guys. You get to sit and watch others tie things up."

"And that's it?"

"Kane's unit is pairing down. He's going back to London to oversee the final bits and bobs. And as for DS Okon..."

"I'd like to talk to her myself."

Drury nodded and didn't pursue the matter. They caught up with Drury's golfing partner on the green. Kent Police's Crime Commissioner, Scott Edwards.

"Lucky shot, Marj. You're about four yards from the hole. Knock it in and you'll be on par."

"Luck has nothing to do with it."

Edwards had congratulated Garrick on the Molly Meyers

case when he'd arrived, but otherwise had given them some space. As Drury selected her putter, Edwards stood next to Garrick.

"I'm sure Margery has explained the minefield we're in."

"Not exactly." Garrick glanced up at the sky. Black clouds were clustered above the links, and a cool wind was blowing the first browning leaves from the tree. It marked a clear delineation that change was coming.

"The BBC are running a feature on the case. I mean, from John Howard upwards. And we can't exactly muzzle them. Played the wrong way, it could make Kent law enforcement seem like a mob of bumbling amateurs."

"You mean because we solved it?"

"Because it was going on under our nose."

"Not just ours."

"No, but it can be painted that way. That is why DCI Kane and the Met are going to be very much front and centre and you're going to wind down the kidnapping case and pass it along in forty-eight hours."

"Am I?" He said it as a challenge.

The Commissioner raised an eyebrow and looked at Drury.

"Yes you are," she said, taking a putter from her caddy. The way she said it left no room for interpretation.

"And what about their Murder Club, and what happened with the military?"

Edwards waved his hand dismissively. "They're locked in records protected by the official secrets act. That's the one ace card we always had in the military when the shit hit the fan. But it doesn't protect people like you."

"Me?"

"If Molly chooses to talk about Emelie, then the spotlight

is going to fall very much on you, and you alone. There's only a certain limit to how much she and I can protect you."

They both looked at Drury as she tapped her ball straight into the hole.

The sentiment was genuine, but Garrick couldn't shake Harry Lord's words out of his mind: *a patsy*.

"I haven't closed Molly's case yet. An active case would help limit how much Molly could say." Even as he said it, he was reviled by the idea he was suddenly in cahoots with his superiors to deflect any blame from Kent.

"I was told it was."

"There are a few loose ends to tie up." Garrick was suddenly not in the mood to divulge any more information. Drury had overheard as she joined them.

"Ah, your mysterious third party." She explained to Edwards. "A woman was used to plant malware on computers. David here thinks she may be involved in the kidnapping. Kane, on the other hand, thinks she was just a hired hand."

"We need to eliminate her–" Garrick said.

"He even questioned Zoe Clarke." She frowned slightly when Garrick didn't recognise the name. "Your Aussie SOCO who seems to be your super-fan."

"Zoe? Why?"

"Because you got under Oliver's skin, and he started suspecting every woman with links to you."

Garrick was shocked. Shocked that Kane had listened, or half-listened, to his theory, and now everybody around him was being treated as a potential criminal. Perhaps they were right, and it was time for him to back away and let DCI Kane take the glory... and the blame.

Just before starting the next hole, Drury made it plain

that their *tête-à-tête* was over. Garrick was pleased. Aside from the fact it was just spitting rain, he wanted to see Wendy. He'd just unlocked the car when Colin Ryman's medical report arrived in his inbox. Harry had sent it along with a message telling him that Sean had returned to Fanta's hospital and Chib had arrived to pull a late night.

After mashing the accelerator several times and almost flooding the engine, his Land Rover started. His plan to chat with Chib, then head to Rochester to take Wendy out for a bite to eat, had suddenly taken a back seat.

There was somebody else he desperately needed to talk to first.

27

On the drive to the K+C Hospital, Garrick's phone was ablaze with a constant stream of messages. Now most of the information was in, blocks of it were being assembled and shifted between departments, and the ever-hungry legal team was just getting on top of things. The very nature and level of legal missives made it apparent, even without being told, that Scott Edwards was keeping an eye on things, and that made Garrick feel uncomfortable.

He sent several phone calls straight to voicemail, including one from Chib, who'd rang back almost immediately. He wanted to talk to her in person and couldn't summon up enough fake enthusiasm to get through an entire phone call without bringing up the elephant in the room. Tact was never one of his strong points.

The Kent and Canterbury Hospital was as busy as ever. Used by medical students, Garrick considered it was one of the better places to be if you were suffering from some unknown ailment, but trying to have some peaceful rest and recuperation wasn't an option when being hounded by eager medical students. In his professional career hospitals lingered in the top three regular locations that he spent his time, if you lumped 'crime scenes' together in the number two slot.

He hated them. Whether visiting victims or colleagues, he couldn't escape the clutches of the clinically sterile environment. It never made him think of recovery, health, or optimism. It made him think of the inevitable steps towards death. His parents had died within days of each other together from a rapidly deteriorating illness that had sent him in spasms of fear in case it might be inheritable. He'd left home as soon as he was able, leaving his sister behind – not that they ever got along, either.

He'd been at both their sides in Liverpool as they'd passed away in their sleep. His father had never gained consciousness, so Garrick never had the chance to clear the air with him. For most of his own life, Garrick had never suffered an illness that would drag him into the maw of a hospital. Until now. A string of messages from Doctor Rajasekar – another person he couldn't bring himself to talk to in person – told him that his surgery appointment was measured in days. Not weeks.

He cast that from his mind, as Wendy called. Now that was the one person he wanted to talk to. Her voice sounded light and cheerful across the car's Bluetooth connection. There was no trace of the ordeal she'd been through.

Searching for an upbeat conversation starter, he asked: "How're you feeling?"

"Terrible!" Garrick's heart sank. Then she laughed. "I'd forgotten what it was like living with my parents. At least I'm allowed back home now. At least that's what the officer said before he left. I didn't notice you had me under surveillance."

"All the time, of course," Garrick joked. Or at least he hoped it sounded like a joke. "Are you going back tonight?"

"No. I promised to help mum with the shopping tomorrow as a thanks, then I will. Besides, it's a good excuse to take the rest of the week off work. I'm not in a hurry to go back. To be honest, it's given me some time to think about my priorities."

"I was thinking we should go out for dinner tonight."

Wendy gave an audible gasp. "Us? Alone? After all this time? And unchaperoned?"

"It's a risk I'm willing to take."

Wendy chuckled. "Brilliant! I'll have a think about what Michelin Star restaurants are around Rochester then."

"I think I know the answer to that already. Anyway, I've got a few more things to do, then I'll pick you up."

He wanted to pop back to his hotel room to change. Not that it mattered, as he'd bought limited clothing with him and had used them all several times. He hadn't the opportunity to visit a laundry to clean any of it. While he'd been given the all-clear to return to his house, the memory of finding Amy Harmon's mutilated body was something he thought he'd never shake. It was no longer a home to him.

As he pulled into the hospital grounds, a thought struck him.

"The copper left?"

"At lunchtime. Why?"

I'm just being paranoid, Garrick told himself. There was no longer a reason Wendy needed protection.

"Just checking. It'll see you tonight."

"Great. And you'll get to meet my father," she added with ominous overtones.

The elevator doors opened, and he found Molly Meyer's

private room a short walk to the left. To his surprise, Molly was sitting in a chair at the side of the bed, with a thin blanket covering her legs and dressing gown. A clean white bandage covered the stump where her little finger used to be. She was feverishly typing on her laptop and didn't look up for several moments. When she did, and recognised Garrick, her face split into a wide grin and she tossed the laptop onto the bed and sprung from the chair. Her cheeks were sallow and mottled with red bruises, and her arms and shoulders looked a little too frail. But as she embraced him, he was almost crushed.

"David! I was wondering when you'd turn up." Her voice was loud but croaky. He noticed she wore a hearing aid. "Is this a formal interrogation?"

"I think you've had enough of that from my team."

"Sorry, you'll have to speak up! My hearing's knackered. The doctors say it'll heal." She shrugged helplessly and sat on the edge of the bed and gestured to the chair. Garrick sat. His knees cricked, and he couldn't stop a sigh from escaping. Despite suffering at the hands of a kidnapper, he realized Molly was still in much better shape than he was.

"The most important question is, how are you feeling?"

"They're talking about discharging me tomorrow."

"They need the beds, I suppose. Do you feel up for it?"

"Absolutely! These four walls are already driving me bonkers."

Garrick couldn't help but admire her buoyant spirit. If he couldn't see her physical condition, then there was no way anybody could tell what ordeal she'd just endured.

"And I'd say thank you for saving me," she said with uncharacteristic shyness. "But that sounds stupid."

Garrick chuckled. "You mean because I was only doing my job?"

"I mean, it's impossible to thank you."

"Well, a good start would be to leave me out of any stories you plan to do." He'd wanted to broach the subject a little more subtly, but it was out there now. "I'm not the type of bloke who likes the limelight. I'd prefer to be the Scarlet Pimpernel or Zorro."

Molly's green eyes peered at him from under her eyebrows, which were no longer plucked and camera-ready. Her lips pursed for a question, but she didn't speak.

"I'm glad to see that you're back on your feet. I've read the reports about what happened, but I'd like to hear it from you."

Molly lifted her feet onto the bed and settled back against the pillows and closed her eyes as she recounted her ordeal.

28

Molly's Beetle skidded across her driveway as she came to a stop. She scooped her Louis Vuitton bag from the footwell where it had tumbled from the seat during her fast drive from the office. During the journey, she'd checked in her mirrors for any signs that she was being followed, although the truth was that was something she'd only seen in the movies and did not know what to look for in the real world.

Her investigation into John Howard's killing spree had taken her in several unexpected directions. She'd originally thought it would turn into a tasty piece to run as a BBC special, as she knew that once the case was officially closed, John Howard would be catapulted into the top rank and file of Britain's most notorious serial killers. It was only when she stumbled on the report from Susan Foss did the sickening story of the Murder Club reveal itself.

And with it, the tie-in to David Garrick's sister.

Suddenly, it wasn't a story about a lone psychopath. It was one that had its roots in the British Military, and it stank of a cover-up. A BBC special was now the furthest thing from her mind. A Netflix one, perhaps, but this was suddenly in the realms of serious award-winning journalism.

Corporal Simon Evans was dead. A suicide which may well be murder.

Second Lieutenant John Howard was dead at the hands of his arresting officer.

And the only survivor, Corporal Colin Ryman, was suffering from stage four Parkinson's disease. She'd tried to interview him, but he'd become instantly hostile the moment she had mentioned the Murder Club. Molly had dozens of photographs on file from his military days, as well as promotional shots from Guardian Solutions. He'd been a dashing man in his youth and had aged wonderfully, but when she'd seen him in his frail and weak form, she'd felt sorry for him. Until she remembered the disgusting string of deaths that he could be responsible for. He wore a smugness at avoiding prosecution for so many decades that he no longer denied involvement, but gave a knowing smile, but no information. She felt a compulsion to bring down the trio's last surviving member.

Even with Susan Foss's help, she faced a labyrinth of dead-ends, faded evidence, and third-hand accusations. Reaching out to DCI Kane's investigation had been met with the usual garbage about ongoing investigations, and the Military wouldn't even engage with her.

But it was at that point she suspected the military was keeping her under surveillance. Her computer was acting oddly, although the virus checker she relied on claimed everything was okay. That's when she became convinced that she was being followed, and maybe even her phone tapped.

She swore that it was the same black Hyundai she'd seen several times.

However, despite a creeping sense of paranoia, she was moving in circles and getting nowhere – that was until the murder of Doctor Amy Harman. Discovering it had happened in David Garrick's home left no doubt in her mind that it was somehow connected to John Howard and the Murder Club. The sheer lack of information and obfuscation from the police confirmed that.

What had felt like a breakthrough quickly run foul due to lack of information. Susan Foss believed it was connected and reluctantly revealed her theory that somebody in the Military had suppressed the incident.

Like every other lead, this one led to a dead-end. Until she received a message from a whistle-blower claiming they had connections in the establishment. Molly's investigations had caused concern in some quarters, and it warned that she may be waking a kraken. Despite two more warnings, Molly made assurances she was willing to get the truth out, no matter what. The whistle-blower had finally agreed to meet, giving her only two hours' notice. She left the BBC office in a hurry, convinced that her every step was being watched, and convinced more than ever that it was the same military sources that the whistle-blower was about to reveal.

She was in the bungalow and waiting for her mobile to connect to the house Wi-Fi when she remembered the car's keyless ignition fob was still in the cupholder outside. Just as she was about to pop out to get it, a message came through on text. They were to meet at Davison's Mill, just around the corner from her house. It came with a warning not to drive and to be as discreet as possible in case she was being followed. The windmill was on her regular run, so what could be more circumspect than carrying out her usual exercise routine. A quick change into her running gear, and Molly sprinted out of the door.

She kept a brisk pace, her mind running through various scenarios. A gentle beep from her Apple Watch told her it had detected she was running, and her Strava running app activated to plot her path.

The mill was closed as the volunteer guide was ill, yet the door to the windmill itself was open. Molly was naturally fearless, and she knew that sometimes bordered on recklessness. But how else was a reporter supposed to find stories? She used to be a regular attendee at a self-defence class, so had no worries about looking after herself.

But she had no time for her training to kick into action. She felt a blow to the back of her head the moment she entered. She vaguely recalled dropping to her knees as a cloth was pressed over her mouth and throat. Then she woke up, bound to a chair and staring into the leering face of Colin Ryman.

During her story, Garrick had leaned forward to prop his elbows on his knees as he tried to picture what Molly had gone through.

"What did he say?"

"Very little. I was gagged, so I couldn't say anything. The rest of my time there is just a haze. I was kept sedated. I lost track of days and I didn't see him all the time. At one point, he was very anxious, as if something hadn't quite gone the way he wanted it to. He punched me then. Screamed at me and called me a whore."

"In your report, you said he didn't take advantage of you."

For the first time, Molly looked embarrassed. "He kissed me after he hit me. That became a routine. When he cut my finger off with some shearing scissors, I was awake. He did nothing to relieve the pain. But he took off my gag, just so he could hear me scream. But he didn't take advantage of me sexually. At least, not when I was conscious." The thought that she may have been raped while sedated deeply concerned her.

"How would you describe his condition?"

"Irritable. I could tell his Parkinson's was frustrating him."

"You would agree that his condition was at stage four?"

Molly shrugged. "I'm not medically qualified to judge that, but it looked bad enough."

Garrick nodded and leaned thoughtfully back in his chair.

"That's the issue I have. I would describe you as a petite woman. Your self-defence class aside, I'm not sure I'd have a problem pushing you around. Colin Ryman, however, a man much older than me and suffering from Parkinson's…"

"I was sedated a lot of the time."

"Granted. Let me put it this way. Doctor Harman was like you. In that, she was more than capable of breaking the neck of any would-be attacker. Father Cillian, I would say, falls into the same boat too. Yet, not only did Colin Ryman kill them. He moved the doctor," every time he said her name, his voice cracked; Molly had noticed but didn't comment, "into position, upstairs. And he dismembered Father Cillian's corpse. I would confess, I'd have trouble doing that myself."

Molly folded her hands across her stomach and gave Garrick a calculating look.

"Ah. The third-man."

"Not necessarily."

"Surely you're hinting that he had help? This was something I was hoping the other officers would mention when they interviewed me. They didn't even raise the subject."

"What I mean is, a third-man is very gender specific."

Molly said nothing as she turned her thoughtful gaze onto the wall.

Garrick pressed on. "Did he ever speak to anybody else? Did you ever hear other voices outside? You were in an out of consciousness, so think of any times you thought you'd imagined a voice."

"A woman's voice."

"Maybe."

"No... there was a woman's voice." She hesitated. "Nothing is very clear."

"None of this is on the record, Molly. No matter how unlikely you think it may be, tell me."

Molly closed her eyes and for a moment, Garrick thought she had fallen asleep. Then she spoke softly.

"I think he may have been on the phone a couple of times. I heard him outside the hangar, but I couldn't make out the words. But from his tone, he was stressed about something. Another time, I swore I heard a woman talking behind me. I couldn't move. I couldn't even make out words. But he was talking about the legacy."

"The legacy of what? His own?"

Molly opened her eyes and laughed. "I didn't sound like it was his. Look, David, this is from me as high as a kite and as groggy as a fish. It's not something I'd used in my own stories." She lapsed into silence when Garrick didn't react. "But you think I wasn't hallucinating?"

"I'd appreciate your take on Susan Foss's opinion that there was somebody in the military covering things up."

"I think that's the most believable aspect of this whole

thing. That was going to be the core of my story. It wouldn't be the first time the military, any military, has covered up the behaviour of soldiers who conducted war crimes. But that's very different from somebody in the military being connected to the Murder Club. That's the point somebody like you tells somebody like me not to go around making baseless accusations."

Garrick chuckled. "You missed your calling as a police detective."

"No. I actively chose not to pursue it."

"That Hyundai you mentioned. It was a black saloon?" Molly nodded. "It followed me, too. It belongs to a woman from Military Intelligence who was working with DCI Kane's team." That got Molly's attention. "She was the one who put me onto Susan Foss. And my idea about this mysterious woman comes from two places. The first is a woman who was seen planting malware on your computer." From her reaction, that was the first time Molly was aware of that intrusion into her privacy. "My second pointer is that Kane's team took my idea so seriously that they even interviewed the woman leading the SOCO investigation." He thought it wise to leave Zoe's name out of it. The conversation may be off the record, but Molly was storing away every factoid to use and exploit at a later date.

Molly shifted position on the bed. The small moves made her wince in pain. "To play devil's advocate. If the intelligence services were following you and me, then I wouldn't put it past them to have planted the same malware on your machine. It smacks of a cover-up, not involvement."

The idea that Garrick's own computer had been hijacked had never occurred to him.

"It was the same person who placed the same malware on Dr Harman's machine before she was killed."

"Ideal for anybody wanting to keep tabs on *you*, not necessarily her."

That made sense to a degree. His records had been specifically targeted, but they still had found their way into Ryman's hands. He kept that piece of information to himself. He was trying to figure out why Molly was so unconvinced by the idea of a fourth member of the notorious club. Had she drawn her own conclusions and anything threatening that would mean unpicking her Pulitzer Prize-winning story?

He couldn't blame her. She'd unwillingly taken part at the heart of events and suffered who-knows-what psychological damage that may not even surface for years to come.

He spent another thirty minutes in idle conversation. Not once did she reference his sister, or any involvement she may be planning to drag his name through the media, and he thought it wise not to bring it up again. There will be plenty of time to see what she had in mind.

29

The drive back to the precinct was the most anxious Garrick had felt for a while, and that was saying something. It had started with a message from DC Lord informing him that Fanta Liu's condition had deteriorated. There was an irritating lack of detail, but that didn't change the nature of the bad news.

He wasn't worried about facing Chib. He'd come to terms with events, and it came down to whether either of them saw a future for her on the team. It was midway along the M20, heading back to Maidstone, that Garrick was hit by what he considered was a panic attack. He'd never had one before, so it was a new and unwelcome sensation. He'd pull over on the hard shoulder if they hadn't stupidly removed them from the motorway network in a failed attempt to improve traffic flow.

Playing the conversation with Molly through his head was making him increasingly agitated. In his mind, it had solidified the idea that Colin Ryman wasn't acting alone. The thought that the woman they had been hunting may be part of the Military investigation made unwelcome sense. He needed to get his own machines checked for malware. But if that was the case, it still didn't explain who was helping Colin Ryman. Kane's mysterious Ms Jackson was the one who had reopened the Murder Club case in the first place.

Molly thought she heard a woman's voice, but then immediately rejected the notion. Had Garrick unintentionally fed her that idea? What if she'd heard a man's voice instead, and he'd accidentally coloured her recollection? Leading witness statements was a well-known hazard of the job, and Garrick had hardly been careful with his choice of words.

He mentally wound back the gears. Ryman and Howard were involved with his sister's death. Even her fiancé was a person of interest. Everybody except Colin Ryman was dead when Amy Harman and Father Cillian were murdered, and Molly was kidnapped. There was no question that she would've been killed, and her severed head would have joined Ryman's other trophies. Her investigation into the Murder Club had touched somebody's nerve. Garrick suspected her death would have been engineered to make it look as if he'd done it. What a perfect way to conclude investigations into the Murder Club and bring Garrick down with it.

The revelation rang like a beacon of obviousness. By stumbling across the story, Molly's death would've provided the perfect, darkest conclusion for the whole affair.

At this stage, he could only assume that Colin Ryman had been concluding an insane act to bring Garrick to his knees that had originated with John Howard. Howard was central to everything. He was the only connective tissue between the Murder Club and Garrick.

And Ryman and his phantom colleague were the last of

the old guard, playing their sickening games. Somebody with military connections and the age to be serving the same time as John Howard and co.

Or was Garrick making an assumption?

He wasn't applying the usual critical process he usually did in every case. This had become too deeply personal: murdering his family, those around him, toying with him to breaking point, and perhaps hoping to see a distinguished police detective take the fall. Is that what DCI Kane had concluded? Is that why Drury and Commissioner Edwards were eager for him to take a step back from the investigation?

Molly had used the word *legacy*. That had suggested the end of an era.

But the Met and FBI investigation had uncovered a string of people around the world. Kane had confirmed this. The Murder Club had expanded its membership, and Garrick could see no reason that wouldn't cover younger members. A continuing legacy. People who were willing to push the boundaries of personal risk to fulfil a hobby that he couldn't comprehend.

And suddenly a new slate of suspects appeared before him.

"Shit..." he muttered. How could he have been so blind when they had stood so prominently before him... aside from lacking *any* form of evidence? What he suddenly needed was time. And that was being snatched from him.

While he had been distracted, the entire investigation had been taken away from him. It had been shut down from above and shunted out of reach from the side.

Suddenly, Garrick was seeing enemies all around him.

Or was it the cocktail of drugs he'd been taking to quell the monster inside his skull?

Detective Sergeant Chibarameze Okon didn't have to be an accomplished police officer to deduce that she'd be having a come-to-Jesus moment with Garrick. Her hangdog expression when he entered the incident room changed to puzzlement when Garrick briskly marched past her to his desk and began to log-in on his computer.

"You the last one here, Chib?"

"Sean's at the hospital. Harry left about fifteen minutes ago."

"Then go home and rest."

"We still have a lot of information that needs processing. The Super told us about the deadline–"

"Yeah, well, she's also nagging me about overtime." Garrick paused midway through, entering his password. If his machine was infected with malware, then he didn't want to give any hint about his new thought processes. He glanced across at Chib's computer, which was logged onto HOLMES. Without a word, he crossed over and sat at her desk. "My computer's playing up," he mumbled.

"Sir, don't you think we should discuss–?"

Garrick held up his hand to stop her. "I'm tired and in a bad mood, and God knows I'm not the most rational at times, so let's do ourselves both a favour and pick it up tomorrow. The case is to be closed in less than forty-eight hours. I've got my marching orders."

Chib's fists clenched with indecision, but she finally turned away and lifted her coat from the hook near the door.

"Goodnight, sir."

"Night, Chib." Garrick opened Colin Ryman's medical report that Harry had sent him and was skimming it as she left.

Ryman has some influential friends somewhere who

prescribed him *Tasigna*, an experimental drug designed to help control motor and cognitive degeneration. A treatment that was out of the price range for most patients. It must have cost him a substantial portion of his accumulated business wealth. Reading the report further killed the idea that the drug would have restored Ryman back to his previous strength. The doctor had concluded that it had offered no tangible benefits and a side effect had given him an acute heart arrythmia that had further crippled him.

"He couldn't have done it," Garrick murmured to himself.

He searched through the case files for any references to Kane's investigation or mention of the Military Intelligence liaison. There was nothing obvious, which was infuriating. He searched for any files on Ms Jackson. Without a full name or specific department, it was slow going and drew nothing. Military involvement, tailing both him and Molly Meyers – it was circumstantial at best, but it was something.

He glanced around to double check he was alone. The next name on his list would prove controversial. His fingers rested on the keyboard, and yet he hesitated from typing. *If* his computer was infected with malware, then it was easy to suppose the others were, too. The moment he committed a name to search, there was no going back.

The keyboard made a gentle plastic clicking sound as he lightly tapped it. He wrestled his indecision – before typing: Oliver Kane.

DCI Kane's service record was the first thing to appear. Garrick scrolled through it, noting the various accomplishments against Albanian people traffickers, and breaking huge drug rings in the London East End. Before that, he was in the military police. Beyond that statement, his record didn't divulge what he'd done there.

Two lines of enquiry blocked by a government wall.

There was one other name he wanted to run through the system. Pausing to listen for the cascade of boots running down the corridor from Kane's omnipresent team, he entered Susan Foss's name.

After a brief search, it came up with her file. And her criminal record.

Susan Foss was charged in 1985 for offences the previous year, which reconciled with her complaint about not being brought back for further consultancy work for the military. She was done for thirteen counts of selling psychotropic drugs to ex-soldiers. She 'd claimed the drugs were thera-peutic and helped deal with PTSD, but as the substances were untested and unregulated, she was sentenced for selling narcotics. Another charge came in '96 when she was caught with thirty kilos of cannabis that she insisted was purely for medicinal use. It was the birth of the internet, and she'd set up an online consultancy trying to help ex-offenders. The judge had been lenient with his sentencing, stating that while her actions were illegal, her motives had come from a misguided approach to help people.

Garrick leaned back in his chair and tried to give a mental overview of the evidence before him. Like a jigsaw, he had the pieces. But unlike a jigsaw, he had no master picture in which to slot them. There were three elements that didn't fit together, and only one that matched with John Howard and his accomplices. He needed to trace the movements of his three suspects to see if they had alibis. As he knew the times of both Amy Harman's murder and Molly Meyer's abduction, he would start there. But with time against him, there was no way he could do this alone. With Fanta down and Chib on the naughty step, that left just Harry and Sean. And in the mental state Sean was in, that just left Harry. But at least that was somebody he could trust.

30

G arrick had planned to head straight for his hotel to change before he picked Wendy up at her parents' home in Rochester. However, she texted him to say she'd made reservations at *Hengist,* a swanky restaurant in Aylesford. It was much closer to him, and he assumed that she probably wasn't ready for him to meet her parents yet. He was certainly relieved not to have to.

He Googled the restaurant. The lovely white 16th century building looked quintessentially English, and the price list was suitably eye-watering. He was normally prudent with money, which is why his car was falling apart, and he remembered his first terrible dinner with Wendy. It had been cheap, and he'd been convinced that he would never see her again – and yet she had found something endearing about him in the narrow window of personal mortification and had asked him on a second date. He'd never understood why she hadn't walked away, and he was far too worried that if prompted, she may tell him.

With more time on his hands than he anticipated and

nothing more to do in the incident room other than compile paperwork, he left. He was on autopilot, heading away from his hotel and towards Fanta's hospital. He'd wanted to know more about her condition than Harry's brief message had divulged, but felt he needed to find out for himself rather than be told second-hand.

Garrick hesitated at the door when he saw that Sean Wilkes was in the seat by her bed, holding her hand. Fanta hadn't changed position, but it looked as if more monitoring equipment surrounded her. Just as he was about to retreat from the open doorway, Sean looked up and spotted him. Garrick sheepishly entered.

"I didn't want to disturb you," he said quietly.

"You're not, sir."

Garrick stepped into the room. It was uncomfortably warm, so he took off his Barbour. "We're not on duty, so David will do."

Sean didn't respond to the tiny olive branch Garrick had offered. His attention was back on Fanta.

"Her parents left an hour ago. I thought somebody needed to be here, just in case."

"She'd appreciate that. I've heard that people in states like this can still hear what's going on around them."

Garrick hated the idea of being trapped in his own head, with no way to communicate or reach out to the world and being forced only to listen. Listen to those mournful sobs from your loved ones. Listen to the interminable noises from the ventilator breathing for you; the steady pulse of the heart monitor as the only proof you are truly alive. It must be a living hell. His thought briefly touched back to Molly's ordeal and the vague awareness of what was happening around her. How close was that to Fanta's condition now?

He cleared his throat. "I was told she'd deteriorated. What happened?"

Sean's free hand quickly moved to brush his nose.

"Her blood pressure dropped, and heart rate slowed. They don't know why. She's suffered some second-degree burns, three broken ribs and bruising. Coupled with smoke inhalation and a blow to the head..." He knew that sounded more than enough. "But other than a concussion, they say there's no visible brain damage..." He choked on his words. "Sorry, sir."

"If anybody knows about brain damage, you're looking at a walking textbook here. They don't even know what's wrong with me. And, let's face it, nobody really considers me a healthy specimen, and I'm still functional." Barely, he mentally added.

"It's just not fair."

"No, it's not, Sean. Life isn't, and our job certainly isn't."

Sean's expression hardened as he looked at Garrick. "He's not even going to stand trial for what he did."

Garrick was impressed. Most mortals, himself included, would have been satisfied that Colin Ryman was gunned down in a hail of bullets. But not Sean Wilkes. He was the quiet detective constable on the team, the opposite of DC Liu, and yet he was clearly married to the idea that a criminal must be judged by the law.

"Like I said, life isn't fair. And we both know it should be me lying there." Sean said nothing, not that he expected him to. "She was just quicker than me. Heard the voice and ran straight up without thinking. As bold as brass as my mum would've said."

Eager to experience fieldwork, keen to make her mark on a case, there was no holding DC Liu back.

"I remember little about what happened. Just flashes of images. Calling her name. Picking her up. I don't know who called the ambulance or how I ended up in hospital. I'd asked her to come with me because I was following a hunch and I needed somebody I could trust."

"Everybody trusted her."

"They still do, Sean. And I feel as guilty as hell for allowing this to happen."

For a long moment, Sean didn't speak. Then he tilted his head to study his boss.

"It isn't your fault. And none of us ever thought it was. Not even her parents. She always said she was lucky having you as her boss. She'd lose her shit at me for telling you that."

"There's a first for everything."

"When the call came in, it mentioned Fanta and you. Me and Harry were in the station. Chib was faffing around with Kane."

Garrick couldn't work out who the disapproval in his voice was aimed at.

Sean continued as he gently stroked Fanta's hand. "We headed straight there. The ambulance had picked you up before we could make it, so we diverted to here. I glimpsed her as they wheeled her in. She was covered in blood." He choked up for a moment before continuing. "And you looked like a madman. Delirious. Shouting at the doctors not to touch you. You were more concerned about her than your-self." He managed a small smile. "And you looked like utter crap, too."

Garrick chuckled. That sounded about right.

"You kept talking about hearing her voice and how it had been a trap. Well, I say talking. You sounded as if you were having a fit. They had to sedate you just to calm you down."

There was a displaced sense of familiarity about the events Sean described, but nothing came to mind, as if they had been surgically removed from his mental library.

"The Super went insane when she heard what had happened," Sean said thoughtfully. "I was in the incident room the next morning and heard a mighty row between her and the Commissioner."

"What about?"

"I didn't want to loiter around to get in their way. I heard your name more than once."

"Perhaps that explains why they're trying to get me off the case so quickly." Garrick was thoughtful. He waved a finger to guide Sean back into the conversation. "You said 'her voice.'"

"Whose?"

"You said I was ranting. And I said, 'I kept talking about hearing her voice'. You mean Fanta's?" With only a fragmented memory of pulling a plasterboard wall off her, Garrick did not know how he'd found her amongst the debris. Had she been crying out for help?

"I don't think so. I assumed it was from the baby monitor."

That had been a man's voice, hadn't it? Garrick tried to recall the moment. It was Colin Ryman's voice... surely it was. A man's...

But he couldn't swear on that. The words had burned into his memory: *you shouldn't be here.* How he remembered that, and not the frantic search for Fanta, nor the sex of the voice, was beyond him. Just those words stood out like a beacon.

And no stammer.

Ryman stammered on his esses. The person on the other end of the baby monitor hadn't.

It wasn't him.

Now, as the voice replayed in his mind, it was distinctly feminine. A luring whisper enticing them to walk into a trap. Low enough to disguise any accent or estimate an age. But feminine, nonetheless.

That focused his search on a cast of two, and he needed more help than Harry Lord could provide on his own.

"Sean, I need you to check on some people when you go back to the station. It's something a bit off-piste."

Sean gave him a quizzical look. "Is this another one of your hunches?"

Garrick couldn't tell if that was a loaded comment or not. He nodded.

"Good," said Sean, squeezing Fanta's hand a little harder. "I won't sleep. I may as well do something useful."

Garrick outlined his second kidnapper theory. He deliberately omitted DCI Kane as a suspect because it may lead the lad down a path that could cause his career irreversible harm, and because he had lost faith in that theory, anyway.

"Susan Foss has had a long association with all three Murder Club founders. Maybe she was seduced by what they did, or maybe she was the one covering it up originally."

Foss had told him that she'd reached out to Molly when she'd heard about the detective's involvement with John Howard. He thought that had sounded reasonable. But since floating the idea that Molly had been used to further get at him, it suddenly sounded like the perfect excuse to snag her as bait. The more he thought about it, the more Susan Foss looked like a good fit.

He capped off the impromptu briefing by telling Sean about his dismay that Drury and Commissioner Edwards were hellbent on closing the kidnapping case.

"Time is against us on this. We have to hand everything over and close the case while it goes to court."

"It smells fishy. Susan Foss is going to be easier to trace, and I wonder where she was before the Falklands. I met that military liaison a few of times. She interviewed us all about your involvement with Howard."

"Just snoop around and let me know what you find out." Garrick felt as if a weight had eased from his chest just by including Sean in his circle of trust. "I'll leave you two alone. I just wanted to see her for myself."

Sean nodded his understanding. Garrick left the hospital with a surprising sense that he'd accomplished something in the presence of DC Liu – the recovery of an erased memory that might help crack an investigation everybody was telling him was already solved.

31

G arrick had just enough time to swing past his hotel room to shower, run a razor over his stubble, clean his teeth, and spray the remaining half can of deodorant over his body before he changed clothes. He wore a shirt and black suit jacket as he wanted to make some sort of effort, and he was out of practise at doing that. Squirting a marble sized globule of hair gel on his fingers, he rubbed it through his hair and attempted to style it. Satisfied that he needed a haircut, he dashed to meet Wendy, snagging his beloved Barbour jacket from the bed on his way out.

Even though he was on time, Garrick couldn't shake the ominous sense that something was wrong as he found a parking space several streets down from the Hengist restaurant. Sitting on Aylesford's old High Street, the beautiful old building had the ignominy of sitting across the street from a stark 1960s pile of bricks that had been shaped into three-storey apartments, shattering the effect of a quaint British town.

It was 8 pm, and it was dark. After speaking with Sean,

his imagination was firing on all cylinders. Why hadn't Wendy let him pick her up? They could've spent more time together on the drive. Why had Drury withdraw the police presence at the end of her road? Why hadn't she called instead of texting?

He'd tied himself up in so many knots as he entered the restaurant that the wondrous assault on his nostrils turned his stomach. The waiter took his name, his coat, and led him to a table where Wendy was waiting for him with a beaming smile.

Suddenly, the psychosis and tension vanished. The exotic aromas around him became enticing, and his stomach rumbled in response. She stood and embraced him. He could smell the subtle musky aroma of her perfume, which made all his worries take a backseat. That he'd expected something nasty happening to her was a clear sign all was not well with his own state of mind.

She gave him a soft kiss on the lips, and they sat.

"You look amazing." And she did. A pleated knee-length navy-blue dress suited her shapely figure. She had complained to him several times that she was a size 16 and desperate to drop to her previous weight, but it had meant nothing to Garrick. It was just a number, and he adored what it represented. Her long blonde hair was slightly wavy and hung over her shoulders.

"I didn't have time to straighten my hair," she said, self-consciously playing with it.

Garrick didn't know she straightened it in the first place. There was a long list of things he didn't know about her, even after several months of dating. He vowed to rectify that.

"And you look…" she paused as her large blue eyes looked him up and down, "as if you're still living in that hotel."

"That bad, huh?"

"Your clothes are creased."

"Like the rest of me."

"But the rest of you is very nice."

The first few minutes were spent trading flirts, ordering drinks, and scanning the menu. After they ordered the food – Garrick avoiding the burger and selected the Red Snapper because he'd never had it before, and Wendy ordering a trio of lamb, which they both had a hard time visualising – they took their drinks and leaned a little closer across the table.

The low lighting and proximity to Wendy felt romantic, but he was cursed as ever by the feeling of intense fatigue he always experienced when seeing her after an arduous day.

"I wanted to save you from my parents," she confided.

"They hate me already? Normally, it takes people weeks to feel that."

"No. I told them what had happened, and suddenly you're a hero. They still remember your amazing TV appearance the other month."

"Oh yes, falling from a conservatory roof. Brilliant." It had been a little more than that, and shown across national television too, but it was still an embarrassing moment, especially for the camera-shy Garrick.

After a little more banter, their starters arrived. Garrick did not know why he had ordered the grilled peach salad. Perhaps it sounded healthy, and at the back of his mind, he was mindful that he needed to get fit. Wendy launched into her seared scallops with gusto.

"I've always said my life needed big events to spice it up," she said between happy mouthfuls. "That's why I joined *Heartfelt*. Since we met, you've been on national telly, portrayed as a hero, rescued kidnap victims, and been almost blown up! And I've been evacuated because of a possible car bomb! These things don't happen to normal people."

Garrick winced at the pure joy she used in her descriptions. Poor Fanta Liu was fighting for her life, so he couldn't see any positives in such events. He had to remember Wendy was only seeing the jazzy media view of events. She didn't need to experience the truth.

Wendy had almost finished her starter as she continued. Garrick found he was slowly picking at his.

"I told you I was frustrated with my job." Wendy was a classroom assistant and felt the teacher she was supporting was borderline incompetent. She had meandered back and forth as she considered taking a teaching qualification, but had concluded she was too old for that. Garrick disagreed. "So, I've decided to broaden my horizons. I'm going to look for a job outside the school system."

"I thought your mum worked in a school. That it was a family calling." The one thing Garrick knew about Wendy was that she was conservative when it came to taking chances.

Wendy giggled. "Not really. It just sounds better. Or at least, it convinces me to stay and not rock the boat. I saw some admin jobs for the council and even one for the police."

"Whoa! Easy. If you do that, then you'll soon be taking my job," Garrick said, raising his eyebrows in mock concern.

"That's the plan."

Starters were finished and Wendy ordered another small wine as she lamented about the horrors of moving back with her parents, no matter how temporary he had been. Garrick was finding himself relaxing and feeling at ease, so by the time the main courses arrived, he was starving. The food was a masterpiece of presentation but, in his mind, lacked substance.

"I ordered food, not a piece of art," he said, ignoring the fact that his own tastes in art were apparently questionable. Despite his complaints, the Red Snapper was a taste sensation. For a man used to ready meals and starchy snacks, it was a revolution. He noticed Wendy had become thoughtful.

"Having doubts on which bits of the lamb your triple selection has come from?" He was about to blurt out a testicle joke, but stopped himself in time. He was trying to be sophisticated this evening.

"I got your text."

"Good." He was focused a little too much on his fish before he added. "Which one?"

"About how you feel."

Garrick froze. Shit. The text he'd sent shortly before confronting Colin Ryman. There had been no signal, so it had lurked on his phone until the network had reconnected. Written in the heat of the moment and sent under the cover of distraction.

"I... I was about to face Molly's kidnapper, unarmed, and with no idea when backup was coming. It's weird, but it's times like that when you suddenly focus on the future. The moment it's all potentially about to be taken away from you is the moment you realise you need more time. There is never enough."

He knew he was dodging the issue and probably digging himself deeper into trouble.

She didn't meet his gaze. "I wondered if you meant it."

He reached over and held her hand. "Of course I meant it! I might have thought I was about to die, but that doesn't make it any less real. If I'd had more time, I would've bequeathed my fossil collection to you, too. That's how serious I was."

Her hair partially covered her face as she looked at him. Garrick thought she looked beautiful. It confirmed his impulsive feelings were genuine ones.

"Are they worth much?"

"Other than my house, they're probably the most valuable things I own," he said truthfully.

"I feel the same," she said awkwardly. Even in the dim light, he could see her blush. She giggled. She took a deep breath and downed the rest of her wine before continuing. "I believe you have a hotel room." She chinked her empty glass against his half-pint and delivered a smouldering look that got his heart racing.

Like two fatuous teenagers trying to stay pure before they marry, Garrick and Wendy had failed to sleep together. Either, like now, Garrick had been a psychical wreck, or the time hadn't felt right, so it had never happened. The last time they'd had a romantic night in her house, he'd received news of a death that had punctured the moment.

And now, exhausted and mentally drained, she'd invited herself to his hotel room. They both had their own homes, which were out-of-bounds right now. But the illicit lure of a hotel room added spice to the occasion. Going back to his room wasn't something that had crossed his mind, especially because it looked as if a bomb had gone off in there and smelled as if a small mammal had died. The cleaning service hadn't ventured inside for almost a week.

Since when had getting laid become so damned difficult?

Dessert was rapidly skipped, and it took an age to attract the waiter's attention and pay for the bill. Wendy insisted they go Dutch, but Garrick handed over his card without looking at the eye-watering total.

They quickly headed out into the cool night air. It was drizzling as they trotted to Wendy's car. Making sure she'd remembered which hotel he was staying at, he waited until she started her engine before hurrying back to find his own vehicle. There was a spring in his step, and he didn't care that the rain was getting heavier. His phone buzzed. It was Chib. It was 10:34, so he sent the call to voicemail.

He found his Land Rover and prayed that it would start the first time for once. He pulled the door open as he slipped his phone into his Barbour's inside pocket.

Then something struck him on the back of the head, and he felt himself fall into a long black infinite tunnel as his mouth was covered and he detected the sweet smell of chloroform.

32

S omething slammed against Garrick's temple. It was forceful, but whatever had struck him had the give and hollowness of plastic. It was the jolt that woke him up in a world of agony.

He fought a wave of panic as he tried to lash out with his arms and legs. His feet were bound, as were his hands behind him. As he struggled, he could feel plastic zip ties digging into his wrists, so he stopped moving in case his actions tightened them. Something covered his mouth. He experimented by poking his tongue between his lips and felt the sticky side of the gaffer tape gagging him. It was dark and stuffy, but he could tell from the cloth brushing against his open eyelids that he had some sort of sack over his head. He could feel it ruffle his ears.

Great, he thought sardonically. *I've been kidnapped.*

His irony-metre was broken. Instead, he forced himself to relax and listen for any audio clues.

He was in the boot of a car. The low growl of the engine told him it was powerful and expensive compared to his own jalopy. It was spacious too – a van or a 4x4. The sound of the tyres on the road was smooth and even, suggesting a main road. There was a slight swishing noise to the road surface that meant it was wet. The occasional squeak from a window wiper confirmed it was raining.

He relaxed further, picking out the faint sounds of some soul music. The song finished to announce he was listening to Trevor Nelson on BBC Radio 2. He was familiar with the schedule, so that told him it wasn't quite midnight yet.

His thoughts strayed to Wendy. There was nothing he could do about her. He'd seen her safely to her car and heard her drive away, which suggested he'd been the target. His coat was still damp from the rain, so he doubted he'd been unconscious for more than thirty minutes. Moving from side-to-side, he didn't feel the sway of his wallet and phone in his pockets. The simple movement triggered a pain at the base of his skull where he'd been struck. It felt as if a metal spike was still being hammered into the bone, and it triggered his migraine. Even with his eyes shut, stinging flashes of light pulsed against his retina.

The car slowed and made a left turn. From the sharpness of the angle, he surmised they had turned onto a narrower B-road. His assumption was further reenforced by the steady sway to the left and right, and occasionally up and down, as his abductor navigated a winding road. Several times, the wheels thumped over potholes, causing him to bump his head against the floor.

Garrick rolled onto his knees and slowly pushed his arms upward, fingers extended. They touched the soft fabric inlay of the parcel shelf covering the boot, and further confirming his suspicions that he was in a 4x4. He could probably easily push through it and into the main vehicle. But without knowing who or what lay in wait for him, it would be a short-lived escape plan.

He considered the options of positioning himself to kick his assailant once the boot was opened, but cast that idea aside, as it would lead him nowhere. For the present moment, David Garrick had no other option that to wait and see what fate had in store for him.

In the darkness it would've been impossible to keep track of time, but thankfully the low sounds from the radio gave him a rough guide if he assumed each song was approximately three-minutes long. It was twenty minutes before the car slowed down and took a sharp right. The road gave way to gravel, then the distinctive clank of a cattle grid.

Then they stopped, and the engine died. Rain pattered on the rear window.

The gentle wheeze of the driver's door opening, followed by a single soft thud of it closing, suggested that there was a single occupant. He tracked the footsteps around the vehicle to the back of the boot. Then another hiss of pneumatics as the boot opened. Garrick played dead. He could hear his kidnapper's breathing. It was a little too fast, perhaps because of the thrill of his actions. No words were spoken as he tried to work out if Garrick was awake or not.

Then a low male voice. "Wakey-wakey, David. Stretch your legs out."

Garrick swivelled around until he felt his legs extend beyond the vehicle's boot. A firm hand gripped his ankle and heard the plastic tie binding them suddenly snip free.

"You can stand now."

Garrick did so. Out of the vehicle, he could feel the steady fall of rain. Each movement throbbed painfully in his head.

As his feet lightly touched the ground, flashes popped across his closed eyes.

"I'm going to remove your hood. You can try to make a run for it, but I assure you, you won't get far in your condition."

Garrick didn't respond. Then he felt something gently press against his neck, followed by a metallic snip. There must have been another zip tie around his throat, holding the hood in place. It was whipped off in one movement. Garrick swayed unsteadily as he took in the surrounding farmyard. Being kept blindfold aided his night vision, but everything swayed around him, and it was difficult to focus. There was a nagging familiarity about the buildings, which he just couldn't place.

He turned his attention to the figure standing two yards away. It was a man, dressed in a one-piece boiler suit and threateningly clutching a large pair of shearing scissors. His face was covered with a rubber mask depicting a crying baby.

"Oh my God, I've been kidnapped by the Phantom of the Opera," Garrick said contemptuously. He was finding it difficult to focus, but had decided that he would betray no fear until the last. And that appeared to piss his assailant off.

"Trying to be the hero, as usual?"

"No. Just refusing to be a victim."

Garrick wanted to keep him talking as he tried to place the accent. The kidnapper was speaking deliberately low, and he swore the accent sounded fake. Why do that unless his identity was already known to the detective? The fact it wasn't a woman had thrown him a little off kilter, but a quick mental calculation suggested the masked man before him was the same size and build as Oliver Kane. Then again, that was an average statistic at best.

Garrick took in deep lungfuls of damp air to clear his head. He glanced at the car and recognised it as a new white Range Rover Vogue. The very one he'd found in his driveway. It had been consigned to the police vehicle pound, which meant somebody had the authority to release it.

"Nice car."

The figure shrugged. "Wasted on you."

"I'd prefer to sit in the front, but on the whole I'd say it's got pretty good boot space."

The scissors bobbed irritably. His kidnapper wasn't a fan of his humour.

Garrick took in the farmyard. He was at the end of a three-sided courtyard. A large, empty, red-bricked farmhouse took up one side. Four stables, sealed with black shutters, ran perpendicular, while the third side was a huge scaffold-covered barn. The property carried with it an abandoned feel.

He realised where they were. Stan Fielding's farm. The man who'd been implicated in the trafficking of young women and the murder of a gypsy patriarch. The case had just gone to court, and he suddenly wondered if Fielding had been let off on some technicality. Was he the masked man in front of him?

The man indicated the barn. "If you'd be so kind."

"Time to die?"

"Time to suffer."

Garrick swayed unsteadily. He reckoned he'd make about twenty yards before his sense of balance betrayed him. Prone on the floor, with his hands tied behind his back, there was little chance of defending himself. With little other choice, he led the way to his slaughter.

Inside, the barn roof was held up with long steel scaffolding poles. Horizontal braces were positioned to support the walls during the renovation. Since Stan Fielding's arrest, all work had ground to a halt. Enormous plastic sheets had been pinned across exposed areas of roof and wall to prevent the rain from getting in. Instead, it beat an increasingly heavier tattoo against them.

A large wooden table had been erected in the middle of the space. Made from thick wooden railway sleepers balanced on concrete blocks, Garrick recognised it as the same set-up he'd seen in photographs DCI Kane had showed him. A heavy killing table where John Howard – and presumably his collective of malcontents – hacked apart their victims. Two spotlights, like those Colin Ryman had used, were positioned around it and connected to a small generator. At the flick of a switch, the kidnapper turned the machine on. It gave a low grumble, and the lights illuminated the table.

Garrick turned to his captor and forced a laugh.

"You don't think that I'm just going to lie down and let you play Operation on me?" He shook his head. "I'll go down kicking and biting until I pluck your eyeballs out." He shrugged. "And if I fail, never mind. I would've hurt you even a little."

The masked man cocked his head and spun the scissors around his finger like a gunslinger.

"You're an infuriating man, David."

"I aim to displease."

"This is not about you. This is *for* you!" He sounded hurt that Garrick could think it would be any other way.

"In that case, thanks for everything, but I decline the gift. I'll take the car and drive myself home."

He motioned for the door, but the man took a step to block his path.

"As I said. Infuriating. If it were my decision, I wouldn't have gone this far, but John thought it would be a *coup de gras*."

"Ah, for your little club. Were membership numbers flagging?"

"I blame his obsession with your sister." He waited for a reaction, but Garrick had mentally prepared himself for the obvious torment. "Such a beautiful girl." Garrick's continued lack of response clearly provoked the man. He sighed and stepped closer, using the shearing scissors to gesture to the table. "That obsession inevitably led to you becoming the poster boy of our movement. Proof that we can get anywhere. Reach anybody."

Garrick shook his head in bewilderment. Annoying his captor was the only strategy he had to stall for time.

"You will watch Molly Meyers being slowly carved up right there." He moved closer, stabbing the scissor towards the table, but uncomfortably close to Garrick's face. "And the story will unfold about the corrupt police detective who had killed those under his care. Those who he was sworn to protect."

"And nobody will believe any of it."

"I assure you they will." The retort was sharp and clipped, as if Garrick had offended his pride. He gestured outside. "Molly Meyers, abducted *again* in your car. The one *you* released from the pound. In your second obsessive attempt, you brought her here, at the scene of one of your previous deviant cases, to be killed just as you killed the others. Just how you slaughtered Amy Harman as she struggled and screamed in your hallway. Oh, what a fighter she was."

"Flimsy evidence. I have so many files that point the fingers at your little organisation."

"And one you are now indelibly part of. Your DNA is all over Amy Harmon. It will be all over poor little Molly."

"And it would've been all over Father Cillian if we hadn't pulled what was left of him out of your chest freezer?"

That was cause for hesitation. "That is where this should have all ended, and we could have gone back to living our lives. Colin really screwed things up."

"That's a shame. He seemed so competent. Just unable to actually perform any of the killings."

The man shrugged. "You don't understand the power of taking a life that you have become emotionally entangled with. It's like no drug. It's intoxicating. Although, only when it's your own choice. Killing for others is so pedestrian. Had he been here, dear John would have got a kick out of you. He was so emotionally invested in your life. That's what made it so special for him."

"And poor you is left to carry out orders."

"Once things are in motion, loose ends need to be tidied, so it doesn't come back to us. Just to you. Crippled by Emelie's death, obsessed by the lovely Dr Harmon and Molly Meyers, driven by compulsions caused by a brain tumour. It's almost too perfect. Then Molly Meyers accumulated all the evidence that can so easily be manipulated to be directed at you. So you must silence her. Brave DCI Kane stopped you last time, and being the corrupt cop you are, you convinced them it was nothing to do with you. So you later had no choice but to take Molly again to silence her. Of course, it goes terribly wrong, and you end up dying, too." He pointed through the open door at the Range Rover. "In your car, of course. The one you bought from the same bitcoin wallet they'll find in your home, stolen from the money extracted from your victims. That is a strong paper trail."

"And they'll close the case? Like that?" He snapped his fingers, his hands still bound behind him.

"We've done elements of it before, to varying degrees. But this brings everything together. It elevates our position. It shows everybody who is watching that we can cause chaos at the very top, and then conceal it so we remain ghosts. That's when we find ourselves in a very powerful position."

"I'm flattered you think I'm so high up in such circles. You should talk to my boss about that pay rise I never got."

"David. Your light-hearted repartee just makes me want to kill you faster. Don't spoil the moment. And do not think you're stalling for time and that the cavalry is coming because it isn't. I have eyes and ears everywhere. I knew your every move before you did."

"Not *every* move or this would have ended at the airfield."

The man waved the scissors. "Enough! I have to fetch Molly now to reunite you both."

"She's under police protection. You won't get close."

"Protection can be ordered away at a moment's notice. Didn't your darling Wendy tell you that?"

Until now, Garrick had proudly kept his feelings and temper in check, but the mention of Wendy's name made him angry. His face flushed, but he bit back any harsh retort.

His kidnapper chuckled. "See David? You're not very good at covering things up. I can do anything I want." He cocked his head. "But you never worked that out, did you? You still don't know who I am."

For the second time in his career, Garrick wanted to kill

the man. How Sean Wilkes had nobly wanted justice to fall on Colin Ryman, Garrick couldn't fathom. His DC was a far better man than he was. The snarl crossing his face told the masked man everything he needed to know.

"And John Howard thought you were a much better detective than this. How wrong he was."

The man stepped closer.

"You are not leaving this place alive, David. So I see no reason to keep you in suspense. Not least because the truth will hurt you more. The *whole* truth."

He stopped just two feet away and slowly reached for his mask. With agonising slowness, he pulled it away to reveal a familiar face.

33

W hile other parts of the police station were just as busy in the night because the Serious Crime Unit shared the building with the regular uniformed police service, the incident room itself could sometimes be an oasis of calm.

Harry Lord had left many neat piles of printed files on almost every desk, waiting for the next poor sap to come in and take over the shift. With a day left to officially pass the case on, there was still much to do. The poor sap who walked through the door was Sean Wilkes, but he had no intention of tackling the paperwork. He had bigger game in his sights.

As he suspected, finding information on Susan Foss was straightforward enough. Garrick had already culled the most accessible records, and now Sean had to see if there was a pattern to her movements so he could find out where she was the night of Dr Harman's death. The first thing he did was to put in a request with her bank for financial details that could target her location, such as a petrol station or a cash withdrawal from an ATM. With restrictive data protection laws, it would be a drawn-out process. A quick check with the DVLA and he had her licence plate. He fed that into the various Automatic Number Plate Recognition systems to see if she had been flagged up anywhere else. They were the simple steps. The next required actual police work. She was retired, so didn't have anywhere she needed to go. He would have to speak to her neighbours to see if they remember seeing her. Nothing would be quick or straightforward, but he was determined to follow Garrick's request to the letter.

He was about to close her file and move on to the more impossible task of finding more about Ms Jackson from Military Intelligence, if that was really her name, when something caught his eye. At that moment, Chib hurried into the office.

"Sean, what're you doing here?"

"The Guv asked me to do some searching for him. Turns out I didn't have much to do at home." He wanted to ask her the same question, but accepted there was a chain of command to follow, which required a modicum of respect. He knew if Fanta were here that she wouldn't respect it at all.

Chib's face was furrowed with concern. "Have you heard from DCI Kane?"

"Why would I?"

"I haven't been able to raise him for the last two hours."

"Maybe he's gone home like a normal person. I thought you had."

"I had. And Kane doesn't qualify as a normal person. There's never been a time he hasn't responded." She caught the file Sean had on screen. "Foss? What does he want to know about her?"

"Where she was when Dr Harman was killed."

"He doesn't think that she–?"

"Then I saw this." Sean tapped the screen. "She was divorced and remarried."

"Hardly a crime. I can tell you for a fact that Susan Foss is not implicated in any of this, other than reaching out to Molly Meyers in order to bring about some justice. Kane's team ruled her out months ago."

"Foss is her maiden name. The one she kept professionally. Her current husband is Laurent. A Belgian."

"Sean, I'm a little pressed for time."

He clicked the mouse, expanding the text on Susan Foss's marital status. "This is who she was married to until '94."

Chib read the surname. "Wow. It can't be the same person."

Sean clicked the mouse again to access the spouse's data. "One and the same. He was a captain for the Royal Marines during the Falklands War."

"How did that go by unnoticed?"

Sean couldn't resist a little gloat. "I guess Kane's lot are not as good as us."

"We have to tell the Guv. Where is he?"

DCI David Garrick felt as if he'd been punched in the stomach. So much suddenly made sense, but it collided head-on with many more questions.

His captor tossed the mask onto the table and used the sleeve of his boiler suit to dab the sweat from his brow. Despite the rain, it was still a warm night, and his grey hair was pressed against his scalp.

Scott Edwards, Kent's Police Crime Commissioner, held out both hands in a theatrical *here I am* gesture.

"That's why you were in such a hurry for me to close the case."

"Oh, you're sharp. I need to keep my eye on you. Did you

know the crime commissioner is such an easy job to nab? Hardly anybody looks at the candidates on the voting slip. They don't care. They just tick the first name. The suckers vote you into office, then suddenly you're hobnobbing with *your* boss. Suddenly, you have respect and influence. It was all part of John's great game. I'd adored him since the day we met, although back then people had such narrower views."

"You were lovers." The words spilled from Garrick's mouth before he could stop them.

"When my wife found out, we had an amicable parting of the ways. After all, we were too deeply entrenched with secrets that could destroy us both. That all helps preserve a veil of secrecy over events."

"She was one of you?"

"The bloody stuff never interested her. She was fascinated by what happened up here." He tapped his head.

Scott twirled the scissors in his hand. "You can see why killing you would be such a deeply personal resolution for me. But I can't. Instead, I'll have to snip away Molly's flesh as you watch," he repeatedly snapped the scissors close to Garrick's face. "Down to the muscle. And it will be all your fault."

"After John's death, you still can't bring yourself to kill me."

"I told you the pleasure in death has to be personal. There are those with more personal claims to your soul, Detective Garrick."

"There's nobody left. Your little troop saw to that." He thought back to DCI Kane's accusations. This may be his only opportunity to garner the truth. "You lured Emelie's fiancé into your sordid little cult. Was he tiring of her? Did he realise she was far too good for him? Were you there too? With lover boy and Ryman?"

He'd clearly touched a nerve. The scissors in Scott's hand rotated into a stabbing position.

"I wasn't there. Which was just as well as everything went wrong that evening. Think of it as an initiation ceremony. A chance to prove you have what it takes. John, Colin, and I were keen to hand things over to a new generation."

"Of course. How terrible it would be without keeping tradition alive... so to speak."

"However, some of the selected victims turned events into a revolt. A few more people were killed that day than needed to be. It was rather senseless."

"Rather than roll over and die, they fought back."

"John had to run for his life. They nearly got him. And your sister... she cut off two of her own fingers because her beloved fiancé almost got her."

Garrick frowned. "Almost?"

"It was John who saved her life."

Once more, Garrick's perception of reality shifted perspective. He'd been fighting to keep from swaying; determined not to show any weakness – but now his mind was crashing in on itself as the events of Emilie's life that night began to untangle.

"I don't..." he began.

"Sam McKinzie was *Emelie's* offering. She didn't want to marry that worthless shit."

"Bullshit."

Scott smiled pleasantly and tilted his head. "It's not my job to persuade you. It's hers. She and John had been friendly for maybe two years when he started seeing potential in you. A hostile sibling relationship was just the dynamic to make things juicy. But it was not to be. She was not born a victim, and she was very persuasive."

"Emilie is not a killer."

"You do not know what that girl is capable of. Quite the imagination, too. I mean, without her, you and I would be working with one another in blissful ignorance." He ran a finger slowly down Garrick's cheek, like a lover. "Davey, Davey, Davey. It really seems as if you have been playing the wrong game after all. This is not something conjured up by a dead man. This is a task orchestrated by a dead woman. Or maybe she is not as dead as you think."

Scott was so close now, almost intimately within kissing distance. Garrick couldn't hold back. The rage and hatred he felt inside was now overwhelming.

He butted Scott Edward's in the nose with as much force as he could muster - and followed it up with all his body weight. He heard a loud snap and blood flicked into his eye. The impact amplified the pain in his head, and Garrick dropped to his knees.

He tried to stand, but his head told him he was in the middle of a hurricane, and he toppled to one side. His vision quivered so violently that he could barely make out Scott Edwards writhing in pain on the floor. In the dim light, the blood around his face appeared overly saturated to Garrick's eyes.

He tried to stand again, but with his hands zip tied behind his back, he just couldn't catch his balance. A spear of clarity pushed through his swamped mind. Zip ties were the go-to product used for restraining people. The thick plastic and one-way locking mechanism were simple and foolproof. Few people knew that they were intrinsically weak. The lock relied on a single thin, easily breakable plastic spike.

Garrick steadied himself and extended his arms back as far as they could go. Breaking the lock was just a matter of putting the most stress on it. He'd seen enough videos on YouTube to know how it was done. He slammed his hands down against his butt as hard as he could, at the same time flexing his elbows outward with force.

The plastic bit into his wrist as it tightened. He grunted in pain.

Scott Edwards rolled onto his hands and knees as he scrambled on all-fours, searching for the shearing scissors he dropped. Garrick could hear a tirade of cursing, but couldn't make sense of the words. He raised his hands again, as high as he could behind his back – then thrust them forward with all the strength he could muster while snapping his elbows sharply out.

The zip tie lock snapped.

Placing his hands on the ground before him, like an Olympic sprinter, Garrick launched himself at Scott just as he was standing. With his vision swimming, it was pure luck that Garrick crashed straight into him. He'd moved with such speed that Scott backpedalled as Garrick thrust forward.

He felt a sharp twinge in the side of his stomach as Scott stabbed the shearing scissors in his side. Garrick couldn't have stopped if he wanted to. They smashed against a metal scaffolding pole with such force it slipped aside and clanged against the wall.

The other poles it was supporting were suddenly pulled away. A plastic sheet across the roof, sagging with water, tore away – the pool of liquid splashing down on them as they struck a second spare. That jounced from the block it was standing on – and toppled across the barn – bringing down more of the horizontal bars in a real-life Jenga tower.

The hollow poles clattered against one another, emitting mournful death knells. One horizontal spar struck Garrick across the chest, sending him to the floor. He recovered and looked up in time to see Scott Edwards loom above him, the pointed scissors ready to strike. His face was contorted with hatred, made worse by his bloody nose that lay to the side like a smashed rose petal, pumping blood that flowed across his open mouth. Two teeth had been knocked out, adding to the image of insanity.

He tilted his head back and gave a feral scream as he thrust the weapon towards Garrick's head, just as a metal scaffold pole falling from the highest point in the barn - and flipping as it bounced from other spars - pierced into his open mouth. It tore down his throat and shredded his trachea, stomach, and pierced his intestines like a javelin. The jagged end burst from his arse and slammed into the ground, holding Scott Edwards in place like a kebab – a full four feet of scaffolding still poking from his mouth. Rain entered from the hole in the roof, landing perfectly on the small patch of ground Scott was skewered on.

The impalement didn't instantly kill him. His body twitched as his nervous system randomly fired. It took seconds before he relinquished his grip on the scissors. Blood oozed from his mouth, causing him to gurgle instead of shrieking in agony.

Fortunately for Garrick, his head was juddering like a pneumatic drill, and he could barely focus on the horrific sight before him. Not trusting his balance, he scrambled on all-fours to the exit. Outside, the wet cobbles felt reassuring, as did the cool rain on his face.

He could barely see, but still he forced himself to stand and relied on instinct to guide him towards the Range Rover.

Each step triggered an excruciating pain in his side. He blindly felt for the stab wound. His shirt was slick with blood, but he couldn't bring himself to see how bad the incision was.

He ran into the bonnet of the Range Rover. His blood-soaked hands squeaked across the wet body as he tried to prevent himself from falling. Then a strong grip around his waist caught him and gently laid him flat on the cobbles. Rain stung his eyes, but he could just make out Chib's face as she filled his vision.

"I've got you, sir..."

34

For once in his life, David Garrick had hoped he'd fade into unconsciousness, which he did with great regularity. Sadly, he remained conscious during every excruciating minute. From Chib and Sean's impromptu first aid, the paramedics tearing at his clothing in the ambulance, and the wild gurney ride through the hospital corridors.

Only when a stern-faced doctor looked at the wound on his side was he administered something that knocked him completely out.

For three days, he was kept in a private ward with a uniformed officer on the door and denied any visits. His wallet and phone were still missing since his kidnapping, so he couldn't even call Wendy. Most of the time he'd been kept sedated and fed a cocktail of drugs through an IV drip that stopped the pain thundering through his skull. His vision had been sensitive to light. Even an ordinary bulb seemed searingly bright, but now it had settled down. The stab wound had perforated his intestine.

The morning of the fourth day, he was just feeling a little more like himself. That was the day Margery Drury visited him. She was subdued and looked as if she hadn't slept for days. After a perfunctory query into how he felt, she turned the conversation straight to business.

"I'm on leave, so technically I'll get a slap on the wrist for being here." She sat in the chair next to him and opened a Snickers bar that had softened in her pocket. Garrick's stomach wambled as he watched her eat it. "My time with the Commissioner is being scrutinised," she exclaimed indignantly. "How was I to know what he was?"

Garrick opened his mouth the deliver his thoughts on that, but Drury ploughed on.

"Just so you know, he was laying pressure on me to close your investigation, claiming Whitehall wanted it to disappear. It made sense to let Kane deal with finishing things off..." She bit her lip and, for a fleeting moment, looked vulnerable. "Remember when I said that I had you back? That's what friends do?" Garrick nodded. That appeared to relieve her. "Shit, this mess is going to be a blotch on my career."

"No one could know, Ma'am," Garrick finally said, although he didn't know why he was defending his Super. She was more concerned about her reputation than the lives lost.

"With Scott dead and unable to be interrogated, they're going to dig deep into everybody. Why couldn't you have kept him alive for once?"

It was rhetorical, of course, but it irritated Garrick. "I'll try better next time. Maybe I'll just shove the suspect down the stairs and see what happens." He didn't have the patience to listen to Drury's self-indulgence. "I want to know why I can't see anybody." He nodded towards the open door where a uniformed officer in thick black spectacles was keeping guard. "Why is Joe 90 over there watching me?"

"Kane is waiting to question you and thinks you could be a high-profile target."

"From whom?"

Drury shrugged. Garrick had time to consider how much of Scott Edward's confession he should divulge. The implication that his sister was not only behind events, but alive, was just too unbelievable. It was the sort of mind games John Howard and his ilk enjoyed playing on their victims.

"How's Fanta and Chib?"

Drury stood up and decided that their catch up was over.

"As I said, I shouldn't be here. I'm sure Kane is on his way and can tell you everything." She paused and nodded at the doorway. "I hope to see you at the office soon. For both our sakes."

Feeling more frustrated, the next three hours dragged on before DCI Kane finally paid him a visit. He closed the door behind him and placed his phone on the table, which still had the remains of Garrick's tasteless lunch.

"I'm recording everything. Afternoon, David. How are you feeling?"

"Do you really want to know? As pissed as hell and feeling like a prisoner. I want to see my team, I want to see my girlfriend, I want—"

"After this, it won't be a problem. I can't have you speaking to anybody else at this moment. I know Drury came earlier when I'd specifically told her not to."

"Well, that's just inviting trouble."

"Tell me everything that happened from the moment you left the restaurant."

Packing away his frustrations, Garrick kept a professional composure and recounted everything. He made a few deliberate hesitations and left some details out for the sake of the recording. Right now, he still didn't know what to think about Emelie, so he omitted all references to her. He'd sown enough seeds to claim faulty recollection if it came up again. Kane listened without interruption, both index fingers steepled across his lips as he slunk low in the chair.

When he finished, Garrick tacked on his own questions. "Before anything else, I want to know how Fanta, Chib, Wendy, and Molly are. Nobody is telling me anything!"

"Wendy was distraught when you didn't turn up at your hotel. She called your mobile and headed back to see if you'd broken down or crashed. Then, she called the police. Harry has been updating her on your condition. The good news is she doesn't think you stood her up." Kane flashed a rare smile. "Molly is out of hospital and preparing a special report for the BBC. We're trying to help, at least in damage limitation. Chib, well, I apologise for that. I put her on your team. Drury really didn't have a say in it."

Kane stood and stretched. As he talked, he paced the room, flexing his shoulders and neck to relieve the tension.

"You know that I was running a Met investigation into this Murder Club. Again, if you hadn't identified John Howard, they may still be operating. The main cornerstone of my investigation was how high did it go. Who had the power to suppress reports? Because of John Howard's location, and those strings of murders, the spotlight obviously fell onto Kent. I needed somebody on the inside I could trust, and DS Okon fitted the bill. You see, we couldn't risk using anybody in the Kent Force. Even Drury was on our suspect list."

"And Scott Edwards?"

"His past military career flagged him up, obviously. But he wasn't in a position to cover things up, so he was discounted. Nobody saw the connection with his ex-wife. She hadn't taken his name, and she was the one apparently seeking justice."

"That was just a lure to get closer to Molly. To silence her and use her death against me."

"All because John Howard wanted to crown his achievement by bringing down a distinguished cop so he could melt away into the shadows." He studied Garrick for several moments.

Garrick had to admit that Emelie's involvement had a ring of authenticity to it. It plugged the gap of incredulity that connected Howard's motives to Garrick.

"I'd like to know why, too," Garrick replied with a sigh.

"With the last witness dead, we're out of credible witness statements. Foss has been arrested, but I suspect her involvement was from afar." Again, his gaze lingered thoughtfully on Garrick. "We've gathered some evidence confirming John and Scott were in a relationship. They were very circumspect about it. And it makes it clearer to see why Scott wanted to go after you, more than John did."

Again, he looked thoughtful. Garrick closed his eyes and hoped his internal paranoia was reading too much into Kane's expression.

"So, DS Okon," Kane continued, "is no longer required on your team and she can come back to the Met."

"If that's what she wants to do..."

"She doesn't. And she's been quite vocal about that. One could say insubordinate."

Garrick opened his eyes and laughed. "That fills me with so much joy to hear she's being a shit to you."

Kane grinned. "As far as I'm concerned, you can keep her."

"I bloody well will."

"Good. I'll tell her the bad news then."

And just like that, Garrick scrubbed Chib off his hit list. He hadn't wanted an awkward conversation with her. He trusted her implicitly. Besides, without her dragging him out of peril, he might really do himself a mischief next time.

"And DC Liu?"

Kane sat back down in his seat. "Unchanged, I'm afraid. As far as we can tell, Ryman's house was booby trapped at a later stage." Garrick's frown prompted him onwards. "Neighbours reported a ruckus the day after Molly was taken. You said you guys found signs of a scuffle in the kitchen?"

Garrick nodded. "I thought he may have originally bought Molly there."

"We know she was taken straight to the airfield, and Ryman spent a lot of time coming and going. Now we know he had Scott, who was doing all the heavy lifting. The theory is that they had a falling out. My guess is that Ryman wanted out, but he was dragged back in. Perhaps he felt the Parkinson's was punishment enough? I don't think Scott trusted him. Anyway, the neighbours recalled a delivery van the next day, dropping off a gas cylinder. I don't think the explosion was meant for you and DC Liu. It was meant for Ryman if he bailed out again."

Just like Ryman and Howard had tossed their colleague off a bridge in Newcastle, the vultures had no qualms about preying on their own.

"And the FBI?"

"Ongoing. There are obviously more members of this Murder Club out there, but we think that's at an international level. You have almost single-handedly killed all the ones in the UK."

Garrick raised his eyebrows as he detected a reprimand. Kane held up a reassuring hand.

"Scott Edwards was clearly an accident. Nobody could accuse you of offing the suspect by driving a scaffolding spar through his arse. And if you did, I dare-say somebody would be trying to pin a medal to your pyjamas. But you know the drill. Due process and all that crap. We have a week left in Ebbsfleet, then we're folding the office and moving back to London."

"I'd like to say you'll be missed. But you won't be."

"I can live with that. Luckily, it seems you can, too."

Kane stood and retrieved his phone. He stopped the recording.

"There's going to be a lot of questions being asked after this. A lot of mistrust floating about."

"I know my place in the food chain. I'll keep my head down and try to stop a few bicycle thieves or something."

"Good. That'll be best."

Another two days rolled by in which he was subject to so many blood tests that he had several red welts on his forearms that refused to fade. He'd undergone x-rays and an MRI scan, which was more pleasant than being visited twice by members of Kane's team who kept asking him the same questions. Finally, Chib and Harry appeared with a balloon that read: *Happy 4th Birthday!* And a single chocolate doughnut.

"There weren't many folks left for a whip round," Harry pointed out.

Garrick placed the doughnut on his bedside cabinet as a treat to make up for the dinner that would be foisted upon him. After several minutes of upbeat joshing, Garrick rounded on the question that had been intriguing him.

"Okay, Chib, level with me." He took a little sadistic pleasure in seeing her tense. "How the hell did you find me? Not in the nick of time, of course, but…"

She couldn't repress a relieved huff. "Wilkes worked out that Commissioner Edwards was involved. I tried to call you, but you were on a date with Wendy. So that's when I had to resort to dirty tricks."

Garrick's eyes narrowed with suspicion.

"I won't like this, will I?"

Chib shook her head.

"When you visited DCI Kane in his office, they sewed a GPS tracker into your coat."

"What?" Garrick jolted forward in his bed and winced from the pain in his still fresh surgery scar. He fell back against his pillow.

"I only found out about it later. And that was an accident. Thank his friends in Military Intelligence. It was clear that the Club would eventually come after you since they're the ones who requested you take Molly's case. Kane couldn't risk you suddenly vanishing as a victim."

"How sweet of him," he growled. "Using me as bait."

"It saved your life," Harry pointed out, his eyes flicking greedily to the doughnut.

"Thanks for pointing that out. And eyes off my property."

They finished with the worrying news that Fanta was still in a coma and the doctors were uncertain about her stability. It seemed as if the machines were now solely keeping her alive. Harry assured him that he was keeping Wendy informed on what was happening, and that he'd been convincing her she was far too good for Garrick, a claim that

Garrick couldn't deny. She'd moved back to her own home, and Harry had to clear out Garrick's hotel room, as his tenure had ended. He advised that his boss should burn all his clothes rather than waste resources washing them.

Another day passed with another MRI and so much blood taken that he worried if he had enough left. But today held the promise of being discharged. It was towards the end of the day that a grim-faced Asian doctor marched in and declared that he and Doctor Rajasekar had decided that they needed to operate on his tumour immediately. It had grown substantially, and only the drugs fed through his IV were numbing him.

Garrick had wondered about the drugs' side effects. He'd started to have vivid dreams in which Emelie had been present. And more than a couple of times, he had to do a double take as he was wheeled through the hospital because he thought he'd seen her lurking in the corridors.

His pleas to see Wendy first were ignored, as he was starved overnight and prepped for surgery the next day.

Lying on his back, watching the strip lights slide by as he was wheeled to the surgery room, was one of the most terrifying experiences of his life. He felt hyper-emotional and had been on the verge of tears all morning. The doctor had been through the risks – from brain damage to death and ended with an upbeat: *"but it will probably be fine."*

They crossed paths with Harry Lord, who'd made an impromptu visit shouting news about Fanta. Garrick was feeling peculiar because of the pre-surgery meds that had been administered. Harry's words sounded slurred and unintelligible. Harry was shooed away by an impatient orderly as they entered the operating theatre.

Music was playing from a phone somewhere in the room.

In his hazy state, Garrick was confounded by what Harry was trying to tell him. How was Fanta? Had she woken up or had her condition deteriorated further? Either way, it had been enough for Harry to deliver the news in person.

The anaesthesiologist placed a mask over his mouth, and he could hear the indistinct chatter of the surgery team around him, punctuated by the occasional laugh. He wanted to shove the mask away and demand to know how Fanta was, but he lacked the strength.

The face of the pretty anaesthesiologist loomed over him. She was inverted, and as she studied him, she pulled back her mask and smiled. A small voice at the back of his head thought that was damned peculiar.

And as he drifted into unconsciousness, another faint voice screamed at him to stay awake. The face was more than familiar.

It was Emelie.

ALSO BY M.G. COLE

WELCOME TO MY CRIME SPREE

info@mgcole.com

or say hello on Twitter: @mgcolebooks

CONTINUE WITH

DCI Garrick 5 - CLEANSING FIRES

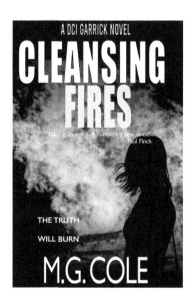

SLAUGHTER OF INNOCENTS

DCI Garrick 1

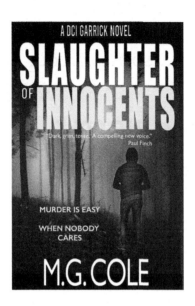

MURDER IS SKIN DEEP

DCI Garrick 2

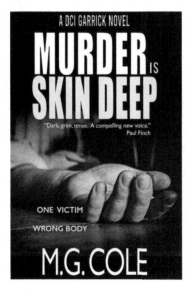

THE DEAD WILL TALK

DCI Garrick 3

THE DEAD DON'T PAY

DCI Garrick 6 - PREORDER NOW!

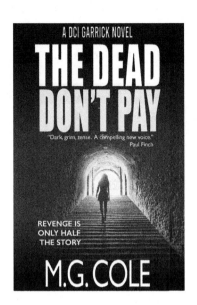

A DCI GARRICK NOVEL

THE DEAD
DON'T PAY

"Dark, grim, tense. A compelling new voice."
Paul Finch

REVENGE IS
ONLY HALF
THE STORY

M.G. COLE

Printed in Great Britain
by Amazon

39189777R00169